A Rumor of Drums

A Rumor of Drums

BY

HERBERT BEST

DAVID McKAY COMPANY, Inc.

NEW YORK

A Rumor of Drums

COPYRIGHT © 1962 BY HERBERT BEST

LIBRARY OF CONGRESS CATALOG CARD NUMBER: 63-19343
MANUFACTURED IN THE UNITED STATES OF AMERICA

TO

KENNETH & MARGARET

Chapter One

BATHED, relaxed, the pattern of living in the rest-house already straightening out, Ian Keith strolled slowly up Pankshin hill, Garuba Kano carrying an unneeded hurricane lantern a few paces ahead. It was a typical Northern Nigerian night of grey velvet, faintly luminous, with black holes for shadows and burnished silver mirrors where the moonlight fell. A leopard choked and gargled, to warn other leopards to keep off the beat he had selected for his hunting. Oily wood smoke and a low murmur of contented voices, like the hum of a beehive on a drowsy English Sunday, came from the barracks.

No point in hurrying. It would be chilly before morning, but the day's heat still lingered among the rocks. Keith's white office suit, crumpled and yellowed by storage in a tin uniform case since last tour, would look no better if he worked up a muck sweat.

Military honours are not paid after sunset, but the quarter-guard managed a creditable 'Who go deh?' to which Keith answered 'Friend!' He was past before the soldier produced the more difficult 'Pass, fren! All well!'

Garuba, a horse-boy and therefore a much-travelled sophisticate, muttered a word in good-humoured reply. There are two almost universal insults, one imputing illegitimacy, the other a low word for part of a woman and seemingly pointless without context. Garuba's '*dandurinwa*!' happily combined both, making it exceedingly popular as a deadly challenge, an ejaculation of admiration or surprise, a jovial form of address between intimates, or a murmur of contentment. Hausa is a versatile speech.

It was easy to guess why Garuba Kano felt pleased, also why he had elected to carry the hurricane lantern, instead of letting the house-boy's assistant do it. When *Tura-wa* dine together they often play cards; so waiting lamp-bearers, and any other servants who may have stepped across to sample remains of the strange drink and foods, set up their own gambling joint in the compound. It might have taken Garuba a week to make the right social contacts, but the lantern was his chance to get right into the game on his first night in Pankshin.

A horse-boy is not as other servants. He is usually in rags, having gambled away his money and clothes and pawned brush and curry-comb. Yet he has the panache of a dashing cavalier, and there is a saying *Maidoki, maimache*—'Man with horse is man with woman'. A happy-go-lucky type, Garuba, without a seeming care in the world.

Therein unlike his master. White men have a knack of creating difficulties where none existed before. Pettibone, the divisional officer, should have been damned grateful for an assistant. He certainly hadn't given that impression. Keith had considered cutting the dinner to which he had been so peremptorily invited, but had decided that in the end he would lose nothing by going.

Pettibone as host might be different from Pettibone as an official. With a few drinks inside him he might relax and become more human, or he might let slip some clue to his extraordinary behaviour. In any case it would be interesting to meet the other white men.

Keith was late, and the gunners were already installed in long chairs with drinks beside them. One of them wore tweeds, the other flannel trousers and a comfortable old shooting-jacket, leather patched at shoulders, elbows and cuffs. Pettibone, in white shell-jacket, heavily starched linen trousers, dark green cummerbund, and dress wellingtons instead of the usual canvas mosquito boots, looked the most military of the party. Except for his long hair.

He rose gracefully, or reluctantly—Keith didn't know which effect was intended—and made introductions.

Garrard, a red-faced bonhomous major, was the one in tweeds who smoked a cheroot. The other was his subaltern, Constable, as ascetic looking as the government schoolmaster at Bauchi.

A few casual enquiries from the soldiers, 'Have a good trip out?' 'I hear she rolls her scuppers under', 'Was so-and-so on board?' and Pettibone returned to the discussion which Keith's

2

entrance had interrupted: whether to patch some worn spots on the mud tennis court and try to keep it going during the rainy season, or take in the matting stop-nets and abandon the court to become a public playground for the local leopards and their kittens.

As a newcomer, who didn't know the conditions, Keith offered no opinion. He accepted a drink from a white-robed, red-fezzed house-boy, and let his eyes rove around the dining-room. Mud-floored, mud-walled, with mud arches supporting a roughly plastered ceiling, it was impressive in a primitive way. Beyond the group of half a dozen heavy hardwood armchairs, their severity tempered by leather cushions, stood a massive table, laid for four, which could place at least ten more guests. Beyond that a wide stone fireplace, since evenings could be chilly up here on the plateau. Trophies of shields, spears, arrows, battle-axes and a few pairs of horns adorned the walls, giving the effect of a medieval banqueting hall.

'Was "Sunshine Susie"' still running in London?' Garrard brought Keith back into the conversation.

Keith had seen the comedy twice. Yes, he remembered the girl Garrard described. She played the pipes of Pan in a chorus of shepherdesses, was a pretty young thing, and danced well.

'Pity I hadn't met you then. Could have given you an introduction to her.' Garrard blew a studiously casual smoke ring. 'Matter of fact, she's a distant cousin of mine.'

'"His sisters and his cousins, whom he reckons up by dozens; and his aunts"', Constable quoted with an air of resigned melancholy. 'And they all seem to be in show business. Garrard has all the luck. If I had any cousins they'd turn out to be gorilla-faced buck navvies! How about yours, Keith?'

'Only some hitherto sticky infants, and one suffragan bishop. I don't think they'd be any use to you as dine-and-dance partners when you go on leave.' Keith played to the lead, but let Pettibone swing the talk again, this time to some patching needed on Garrard's bungalow before the rains came.

Garrard and Constable had made an obvious effort to be polite. Too obvious an effort. Why did two perfectly normal soldiers dislike someone they had never met before?

3

Thinking things over after he had paid off his carriers that afternoon and gone shooting for the pot, he had narrowed down the cause of Pettibone's strange attitude to two alternatives. When in charge of the provincial office at the end of his last tour Keith had stood between the Resident and the divisional officers as a young adjutant stands between a colonel and his company commanders. Pettibone could easily imagine that in some routine correspondence Keith had treated him with disrespect.

Or Pettibone might resent Keith impersonally, as a symbol of official policy, to which he objected. In the west of the Pankshin Division lay the Closed Area of Kulere. It was believed to contain much alluvial tin and perhaps other minerals, and the government in England were pressing to have the area pacified and opened to miners. Pettibone might object to having his hand forced. With an assistant to do his office work for him, he would no longer have an excuse for delay.

The head house-boy announced dinner, and the party moved to the table. Seated below Constable, Keith got involved in the old shotgun versus rifle argument, while Garrard and Pettibone differed as to whether an established and endowed Church was better or worse than one free of political influence. In Africa, where people live alone most of the time, they tend to develop pet theories, about poetic cadence, astrology, dry-fly fishing, or whether Esperanto should be used in diplomacy. Keith wanted to listen.

But Constable was out to convert the heathen—that being Keith —to a belief in the one and only true God, which was a fourteen bore with choke and modified choke.

Keith protested that very few people could get the best out of both shotgun and rifle, as one seemed to spoil you for the other. Since this meant that you had to choose one or the other, obviously the rifle was the thing. A shotgun limited you to birds, but a rifle could be used on both birds and 'beef'.

'My dear imbecile, how can you compare your clumsy, calculated murdering with a rifle to the sheer poetry of a fourteen?' Constable got nicely into his stride, his thin face flushing with eagerness. 'The smooth flow of bird and invisible shot-pattern

4

coming together, and breakfast or lunch materializing out of the skies like manna falling at your feet. . . .'

'When I try it, all that falls at my feet is an empty cartridge.' Keith chuckled and finished his soup. 'All you're proving is that you ought to be in the "archies" and not the "mule-skinners".'

'Sir! You insult my profession!' with a fine show of mock indignation.

'What's that?' Pettibone broke in. 'What's that?'

Garrard mopped a speck of soup from his chin. 'A mere civilian has the temerity to suggest that my unrivalled second-in-command should be in anti-aircraft, not mountain-battery.'

Pettibone looked puzzled. He signed to one of his servants to refill the wine glasses, and turned his attention to his junior. For the first time since he had introduced him.

'Speaking of shooting, I think I heard a shot down in the plain just before sunset.'

Keith considered his host for perhaps half a minute. He was prepared to take what was dished out officially. But outside work, no! In this small station it would make social life impossible.

'Since you said your treasury was closed for the day, I used the last of my cash to pay off my carriers.' He made the point clear. 'That left nothing for my household to buy their food. So I shot them some meat.'

'Personally, I wouldn't think of shooting any beast during its breeding season.'

'I doubt if the kob knew what season it was, being a young male in a bachelor herd.' Keith allowed himself an irritating smile. 'And curiously enough he was not in foal.'

'I'm afraid we don't approve, do we?' Pettibone appealed to the gunners for support. 'Station custom, you know, Keith. Station custom not shooting near the hill.'

Having put his junior in his place, Pettibone turned his august attention back to O.C. Troops. Keith was prepared to listen and say nothing, but Constable wanted to know details of range, aiming point and weapon. Since Keith had used a Mauser with American ·30–06 ammunition, talk led to the English Lee-Enfield compared with the Mauser and Springfield, and thence to the Ross, Lebel and Mannlicher.

'How come you know so much about army rifles?' Constable was puzzled.

'From the Old Army. Sailed with them on August 13th 1914.'

The table was suddenly silent. So whatever Pettibone had said before Keith's arrival he hadn't mentioned his war service.

'"And gentlemen in England now abed shall think themselves accursed they were not here—on Crispin's Day!"' Garrard came back into the talk with cheerful emphasis. 'So Keith was being nasty to the Hun at Mons when Constable was still flipping paper darts about a schoolroom!'

The acclaim was embarrassing. Keith tried to lighten it. 'I bear my years remarkably well. Everyone says so. Nobody takes me for over sixty.'

But the hunt was on. Garrard wanted to know everything. Survivors of those early days were few, and if of the regular army, now unapproachably senior. So Keith must give. Why was General French Stellenbosched? Had Keith seen the Angels of Mons? Had there nearly been a rout at Maroilles, on the retreat? And what had turned the retreat into a counter-attack, almost at the gates of Paris?

Keith parried. No, no angels. There had been a bit of a mess at Maroilles, but the Guards had held Landrecies and things had time to sort out. Perhaps the Germans had over-extended their horse-transport. Keith was a corporal at the time, and the generals hadn't confided in him.

As they removed with coffee and liqueurs to the arm-chairs, a magnificent white Persian cat strolled in, and set the final seal of approval on the recent outcast by establishing herself on Keith's knees.

It may have been the cat's defection from her master that drove Pettibone to his indiscretion. As his guests lighted cheroot, cigarette and pipe and fixed their cushions, he stood up again. Cup in hand, teetering from heel to toe, he waited. Like an actor, Keith felt, who advances down stage and creates a telling pause to lend emphasis to his coming speech.

'After his long and distinguished military career,' a slight pause for a sneer, 'Keith must have found difficulty in reverting to our more humble and civilized life.' Pettibone rocked twice and stirred his coffee. 'I wonder what the real facts were behind the inquest at Naraguta which forced the Resident to transfer him to Bauchi? I wonder.'

Constable, reaching out to stroke the majestic white cat, sat back again and twiddled his cigarette. Garrard frowned. Their reaction told Keith what had puzzled him. So it was Pettibone's rehashing of the old tragedy which had been the cause of Keith's cold reception by his fellow guests.

'Try not to wonder out loud, Pettibone.' That was cold warning. 'The facts scarcely concern you.'

'As your senior officer the facts concern me very much, very much indeed.' Pettibone's hands shook so badly he was forced to set down his cup. 'The inquest called it an accident, not suicide. And Petherick-Frost's wife had the sense to go straight back to England to avoid further scandal, further scandal. But . . .'

'Quiet!' Keith cracked out the order. With deliberate care he knocked out his pipe and transferred it to his pocket. He set his cup on the floor. He gave the cat to Constable. He needed time to get control of himself.

Garrard tried to mediate. 'Would it help, Keith old man, if I gave you my word that neither Constable nor I believed a word of the story?'

In silence Keith walked to the door. He whistled for his lantern-bearer. By the time Garuba came, the two gunners stood beside him. They set off home together.

'Sorry about tonight. We ought to have choked the bastard off when he started.' Constable sounded savage.

At his quarters Garrard invited 'Drop in some time and meet the rest of our stable. We don't run a mess up here, or we'd make you an honorary member.'

The *amende honorable*.

The hilltop had been almost chilly, but the rest-house two hundred feet below was still swaddled in the day's left-over heat.

7

Momadu had swept out the goat-droppings, set up the camp-bed, arranged the loads in orderly fashion around the wall, and put some wild-flowers in a jam-pot on the camp-table.

Keith asked if all was well with the household, thanked him for his care, and said good night. After being on his feet since four that morning, even the stocky Momadu must be tired and ready for bed. Keith wished that he were.

He changed into pyjamas, removed the flowers to a tin trunk, and carried table and lantern out into the compound where a faint suspicion of cool air rolled down from the hillside.

He had intended to read, but remembered that his rifle needed cleaning. Passing patch and ramrod back and forth through the barrel wasn't such good mental dope as reading. It left room for unwanted thoughts.

For a man who prided himself on his carefully acquired patience, he had come close to making a stupid scene up there on the hill. His only regret was that his knuckles were still whole. What lay behind his fury was the haunting question which had driven him almost crazy at Naraguta, and followed him relentlessly to Bauchi. It had cropped up on leave, in England.

Had a jolt on the road extinguished the acetylene light on Petherick-Frost's sidecar combination? Or had he deliberately driven off the road, across the storm-water ditch, and into the rock? No one knew, and the Coroner had been merciful. More merciful than Emmy's women friends.

The rifle was as clean as nitro-solvent and patches and Rangoon oil could make it. And a long night still stretched ahead. The physical discomfort of the hot, insect-laden air was not enough distraction from Keith's remorseless thoughts. Like torturers they posed their questions, turned the screw a little more, and awaited the answer which he could not give.

How far could a white man and a white woman be held morally responsible after the tropics had inflamed their senses? Africa was not to blame; with its appalling death-rate it had to replace wastage by the only known means, coition. Natives of Africa through the ages had acquired a measure of tolerance of the

8

constant pressure. Not so the white strangers from the north. Respectable young married women became nymphomaniac and had to be sent home—to recover, as from a bad dream, when their ships met the chill fogs of the English Channel. Their menfolk had to stay on their jobs, and suffer all the tensions of bachelorhood.

As Keith knew he was to suffer tonight. For there was no doubt of the preliminary symptoms. They were as definite and recognizable as the slight ache in the joints and unreasonable elation which warned of the onset of malaria. For malaria one swallowed thirty grains of quinine, drank gallons of weak, scalding tea, and swaddled oneself in blankets. For sex-fever there was no drug, no treatment.

It wouldn't be long now, an hour at the most. Even if he discovered where Momadu had packed the magazines and books, and tried to concentrate. 'They' had been catching up, at each rest-house on the way from Railhead drawing a little closer. Tonight he could almost hear their whispers and smell their perfume. It wasn't fair that it should start so soon after landing, when a whole eighteen-month tour stretched ahead.

Of course it was only imagination; but now you could almost feel them. The throb became clearer. Not footsteps, but a barely audible drum-beat. One of the household had woken, and his fingers were stroking rather than tapping the taut skin. Whoever it was felt lonely in the night, and was talking to himself on a drum.

If you let it irritate you, or if you tried to ignore it, drumming could drive you frantic. Fortunately Keith had always found it intriguing. He felt that if he could learn to understand it he might gain the key to the unspoken feelings of those around him. He welcomed it now, and by listening closely he might keep his own feelings at bay.

It seemed to be the horse-boy, perhaps lamenting that he had been torn away from his gambling. Definitely there was a touch of pathos, of 'how sorry I am for myself' expressed in fading rallentandos—if that was the word.

The drum sighed itself into silence, and Keith's strained attention could catch nothing but the insect noises and the rustlings of the hot night.

Now it began again, murmuring a longing too deep to be identified with regret for a missed social gathering. It spoke of a hunger of the mind and of the body, and of despair since there was no means of satisfying it. Garuba was wallowing in his misery, and rather overdoing it, apparently, for now and then a brisk little phrase of optimism intruded. Garuba wasn't as unhappy as he pretended.

The beat changed. As though the horse-boy had wearied of fruitless self-pity. A certain crispness of fingering made it almost cheerful. With crescendo and diminuendo the drumming advanced and retreated like a courting bird; at each crescendo giving a showy flurry like a mating display of spread feathers; at each diminuendo an invitation. A sophisticated horse-boy calling an unknown woman, tempting her, wooing her in out of the night.

'Come, beloved! Come!' Keith's thoughts, his whole body, repeated the invitation. 'Whoever you are, I need you . . . need you!'

She was coming . . . she was surely coming. . . .

Then irrational hope changed abruptly to panic, and he crouched back in his chair. For she was They, the sex-hallucinations who tempted and tortured but had no means to satisfy.

They came nearer, drawn by the softly-throbbing drum. Coyly withdrawing as the rhythm postured out to meet them; wantoning forward as the drumming seemed to recede. Women he had loved, women he had slept with and forgotten, women he had never known. Even the schoolgirl who had drawn him into a summer-house and demanded that he 'wape' her because 'evwey-body does it nowadays'. They had eaten large purple mulberries and gone back to play tennis instead.

They were about him on every side, as desirous as they were desired, tempting, offering everything yet nothing; for each was locked in the chastity belt of unreality. If they came within the glow of the lantern, and he could seize one in his arms, would that mean that the strain had been too much, and that his sanity had gone?

10

Of desperation was born a fantastic thought. The succubae were answering to the drum, not, as usually happened, his own fevered desires. Would Garuba draw them safely past, to himself? If his reputation were true, that gallant would cope with untold women. Perhaps a legion of she-devils would be no more than a pleasant novelty to him.

The drumming drew them in closer. Yet closer. Now in the darkness beyond the lamplight something moved. He could see it move.

In panic Keith snatched up the Mauser, crammed three rounds into the magazine, another into the breech and slammed home the bolt.

Then, on the still air drifted civet perfume and the scent of woman. Real woman, woman in the flesh—thank God!

'Come!' he called in Hausa, and laid down the rifle. 'I will not shoot.'

Their shapes, blurred by their shrouding outer garments of indigo-dyed homespun, showed no more than that they were Hausa, not Hill women. Two of them. They advanced confidently to the table, sank to their knees, and sat back on their heels as though to gossip. They waited, too polite to speak first.

'Well?' Keith asked sharply.

They reproved his abruptness by offering the correct salutations such as are given to a traveller on his arrival. Keith replied, as good manners prescribed, and more fully than was necessary, to make up for his omission.

They spoke good Hausa, better than Gofwan the Messenger's for instance, and their blue headcloths drawn veil-fashion across their faces showed they were Mohammedan. There was a small trading settlement near by, where Keith's carriers had gone to find food and night's lodging. A carrier or a trader serves as a newspaper. Fifty carriers were practically an up-to-date encyclopedia on the subject of the new *Ba-ture* and his household. So these two women, bearing each other company, had come to ply their simple trade.

That was the most obvious explanation. But there was another. He tested it. 'You seek the one who drums?'

A slight hesitation told that his guess was right.

'The *Ba-ture* has no woman?' The shapeless bundle on the left was spokesman for the two.

The soft rhythm from the horse-boy's hut pervaded the compound. It beat a little faster now, as though impatient.

'No woman,' Keith conceded, aware of his folly.

But the household would approve of the women's purpose, for a man without a woman was unnatural in their eyes. What is worse, such a man sleeps badly and becomes easily angered by the burning of toast or a twisted curb-chain. For he is like a man fasting during Ramadan, tempted by a thirst and a hunger which he may not satisfy.

Momadu always had a wife on hand, pretty and ill-natured. Even Sam, the spinsterish cook with the filed cannibal teeth, often hired a woman for appearance' sake.

From the point of view of the household, there is only one thing worse than a womanless *Ba-ture*, and that is one who brings out a woman of his own tribe. She is in the house all day, having no work of her own; and she calls for one service or another from morning till night, like a child demanding the breast. But a good clean woman of the country is far different. She is no trouble at all, and lends dignity to the home. Also she is better than a dog for keeping away burglars, who know that she may spread her mat in a doorway for the sake of breeze, and are afraid of falling over her and her screaming.

Keith knew all this. Yet he still waited. Hoping that the women would make their offer. As though his agreeing would commit him less than if he made the request and one of them agreed.

He knew that these women, and only these women, stood between him and a night of horrors like those of delirium tremens. He could bear the uncertainty no longer. He had to lick his lips and swallow before he could be certain of his voice.

'I speak, as it were, to shadows. Only your eyes and words are yet known to me.'

They understood. They had only been waiting for the invitation. Each unveiled her face, no darker than those Keith was accustomed to see around him. Since they were Hausas they bore no disfiguring tribal scars, and lips and noses were only slightly negroid. Their dark eyes were adorned by *kohl* eye-shadow. The one on the left wore a small coral stud in the side of her nostril. She was almost a beauty, alert, smiling, and assured of a man's admiration. The one on the right seemed the younger, her face more rounded, and a little sullen. She was only a lumpish girl, and he was no virgin-snatcher.

But he must not hurt the younger one's feelings. He must make her a parting gift. Leaving the lantern to show he would soon return, he gathered up rifle and cleaning-tackle and entered the house in search of some small token. Striking a match, he discovered a newly-opened box of chocolate biscuits. They would do.

They had drawn closer to his chair, and had taken the opportunity to discard their outer garments. Now only a thin cloth, buttonless, tapeless, swathed each of them; wound closely a little over the nipples to half-way down the thighs. Shoulders, and bare arms adorned with silver bracelets, were smooth and rounded. The older girl's breasts were high, forced upwards by the tight folds of the cloth. The younger one's were superb, firm as rounded muscles, needing no support, and with nipples which seemed about to pierce their covering.

Keith's eyes wandered from one to the other and back again. The choice had become difficult.

He offered the box to both, not one as he had originally intended. He started to eat one of the biscuits, to show that it was pleasant. His mouth was so dry that the chocolate stuck to his palate and the biscuit powdered and was difficult to swallow.

The older girl's eyes missed little. 'The *Ba-ture* has only to say "I desire you", and we will say "We obey."' She put a hand to the fold of her cloth. 'Yet if the *Ba-ture* would see more, and judge better, let us enter his house.'

They waited for him to lead the way with his lantern. He tried not to hurry. They followed him closely, and stood gazing at the strange mosquito-net and at the many boxes which must contain a great wealth of goods.

They disrobed, simply and without fuss, and stood waiting. Round their hips each wore the traditional string of black, buttonlike discs made from palm kernels, strung through their centres so closely that each coil seemed a shining black snake. A Hausa woman's most intimate garment; also her savings bank, for each coil has its market value based on the quality and number of discs. The older girl wore seven coils, the younger only two.

Keith remembered. 'There is the matter of payment. I have no coins, but will make a present of cigarettes, which can be sold in the market.'

'If such is the *Ba-ture*'s wish.' A little impatiently.

'But first I must take one of you back to the settlement, while the other waits.'

'There is no need. There is, however, *kumya*, modesty. The *Ba-ture* is a stranger, and this Miriamu has known only boys, whose mating is as the mating of dogs.' The woman placed a hand on the girl's shoulder. 'So I will sit beside her, showing her how to struggle yet allow herself to be overcome by force, and many other ways which will give pleasure to the *Ba-ture*. Thus she will feel no shame, telling herself that it is the will of those older and wiser, to which she must submit.'

To have another woman coaching from the bedside was an original interpretation of 'modesty'! But all that mattered was to get quick relaxation of the forces which seemed to be tearing his loins apart.

He put an arm round Miriamu's shoulders, and felt the thrill of her woman's flesh run through his body. She smiled vacantly, and pressed closer, her odour a superfluous aphrodisiac. He held out the other arm, and the woman slid into it. His fingers toyed curiously with her red coral nose-stud, flipping it, twisting it. The nipples on her bare breasts responded.

'Not yet, with permission . . .' the woman set aside his hand. 'Later, when the *Bature*'s needs are spent. For I am not one to sate desire, but to arouse it. When the *Ba-ture* is rested again, and Miriamu lies as one dead, I will come to him. I will not sleep, for the need of a widow such as I is as the need of many wives and concubines.' She panted, her eyes glistening in foretaste of the coming ecstasies. 'The *Ba-ture* knows already the uses of the nose-stud; some other woman has shown him. But I shall show

14

him more, much more; such things as few women know, and they hide from their lovers lest they be possessed too utterly. All these things shall the *Ba-ture* do to me, though to my hurt. And in return I ask a promise.'

Keith had released Miriamu. It was the older one he wanted, and must have. He managed a grunt 'Ask . . . now . . . quickly!'

'A small matter, costing no money. The *Ba-ture* is the new Judge. Before him will be brought one Salifu Maidugari, a trader unjustly accused of debt. . . .'

Speaking, she sank down to her knees, in the correct pose of a Mohammedan woman asking a favour, or appearing in court. Incongruously naked except for her shining black belt, she lowered her glance, and pled the trader's cause.

Accustomed to taking evidence, a detached part of Keith's mind listened and analysed. Even from this partisan account it sounded as though Salifu Maidugari would be lucky if he were only sued for debt, and not prosecuted for embezzlement or theft.

Keith's mind began to clear. As the pulse-beats in his ears throbbed less loudly he could hear the other drumming, muffled by the walls of the rest-house. Chilled by the woman's crafty bargaining, his ardour began to cool, and he could again feel the thought behind the horse-boy's finger tapping. And the silence seemed to listen. An intricate pause, an abrupt pause. The phrase again, and again the silence listened, waited, hoped.

He took the woman's hands and raised her to her feet, still pleading. She saw his face, yet asked,

'The promise? Is it granted?'

'It is not mine to grant, for Justice is not a trading for profit. Justice is a balancing of word against word, even as a silver-smith weighs coins in his scales.' All Keith could manage was to tell his thought. And it sounded, in the circumstances, pompous and ridiculous.

'Even so . . .' the woman seemed disposed to compromise or bargain. For here was a man, and possible pleasure and profit. 'Yet . . .'

'It is ended between us, though scarcely begun.' Keith forced

15

his difficult self-denial into words, to turn the reluctant, half-formed rejection into a clear and binding decision. He saw a loophole he had left himself, and hastily blocked that too. 'Nor will I take Miriamu to bed.'

But decision had fore-run willpower by too great a lead. His physical and emotional side agonized at his high-minded betrayal of their needs. If either girl made the slightest movement towards him, his body would revolt against the inhuman tyranny he had imposed upon it.

Miriamu vacantly waiting for whatever might happen next. The woman's dark eyes studying him, penetrating the outward firmness to the indecision beneath. In a moment his arms would go out to either of them, both of them.

But now something else had distracted the widow's attention. She half-turned her head and listened. To the call of the drum. It mourned and yearned no longer. Nor did it invite or serenade the object of the horse-boy's desires.

'Come you shall, for come you must!' it commanded. And the woman understood.

'Since the *Ba-ture* no longer desires us, it is permitted . . . ?'

The request was a mere formality, and Keith knew it. 'No harm,' he assented.

He watched them gather up their clothes, and dress with purposeful care. He gave them the rest of the chocolate biscuits. Realizing that they would certainly share them with Garuba and leave the tin as a parting gift, he wondered how he could account for it to Momadu.

Chapter Two

THE tropics are at their most charming in the early morning when, tender-hued and innocently welcoming, they give no hint of the cruelties they intend to inflict during the coming day. The trick of the houris in a Mohammedan's paradise, daily renewing their youth, is nothing compared with the miracle of the harsh day and torturing night transforming themselves into this friendly, gracious dawn.

Reinforced by a cup of tea and two biscuits, Keith climbed shakily officewards. A dog, big, tawny and of unguessable ancestry, lolloped out of the roadside bush to claim Keith's companionship. Collarless, but well cared-for, he seemed to belong to the soldiers.

From the barracks resounded the tump-tump of heavy wooden pestles, and was answered by a similar beat from the Messengers' quarters higher up to the left and hidden from the road. It was easy to imagine a link between the daily pounding of corn and African drumming.

As soon as a small African was born he heard the thud of pestle on mortar. In fact he had been created by what is sometimes called 'pestle-and-mortaring'. Soon, slung in a cloth or goatskin on his mother's back, he danced involuntarily to the rhythm of his mother's body as hour after hour she pounded the family corn or roots. When too big to be carried he, and the family chickens, hung around the clanking mortar. For the accustomed beat said 'Mother is here . . . thump! Safety is here . . . thump! Food is here for hungry little bellies . . . thump!'

All over Africa.

As once he had danced to the swing of his mother's back and the swing of the heavy hardwood pestle, so he continued to hop and cavort to the same sound. He tapped a stick on a calabash,

17

and the beat brought comfort by association with the feeling of love, protection and food. He learned to play real drums and to dance to them. He drummed endlessly, until he became a virtuoso with fingers or sticks, and a connoisseur of other drumming.

Among the more cultured Hausa the butcher drummed to announce that he had meat for sale, the courtier drummed to boast that he and his chief were coming in procession, and neighbours drummed to lighten their toil when they joined together to till each other's farms. Story-tellers drummed to invite audiences, and professional praise-singers drummed accompaniment to their profitable flattery. Among the Hill people a boy might court a girl with wordless drumming; he would dance before her to drumming, and whole villages would turn out to dance on the threshing floor to the same drumming. Men and women, young and old, would travel miles to one of these celebrations, and as they sped through the night would identify their favourite drummers by their intricate rhythms.

In a big modernized African city, prostrate yet sleepless under the lingering heat of the past day, a soft tentative fingering of a drum would ask human companionship in the inhuman night; and lapse into listening silence. And from afar be faintly answered.

Drums were the pulse-beats of Africa. If they were ever silent, Africa would be dead.

No wonder the negro was the world's master of rhythm. And all because of mother's ancestral pestle and mortar!

Anyway, an interesting hypothesis, Professor Keith, and better than dwelling on the horrors of last night. But don't put it into an official report, or your esteemed Resident will burst a blood-vessel.

The companionable dog, at a wild guess part Airedale part Mastiff, discovered an engrossing scent and, recollecting that a remote ancestor on his mother's side had been a hound of some sort, looked back at Keith for permission to follow it. Keith waved him on, and the dog disappeared into the bush.

The mud-built and out of drawing Greek temple, with Messengers already on the veranda, reminded Keith of unfinished business left over from the dinner last night. The time was past for apologies, on one side or the other. If Pettibone had any sense he would see that it was impossible to work together and suggest that one of them must go. Keith, of course, since he was the junior. But would Sharpe, the Resident, agree?

Keith checked by his watch as he strode up the steps. He had re-set it by the gunners' bugler sounding reveille, and apparently it was correct, for the divisional officer, already at his table, looked at his own watch, and seemed disappointed that his junior was on time.

'Good morning . . . sir!' Keith paid the correct tribute to the other man's senior rank.

Silence.

'Would you like me to take over the local treasury and any odd jobs? I've done plenty of that work at Bauchi, and it would free you for touring.'

'I will allocate your duties, Mr Keith,' Pettibone frowned severely, 'in due course.'

The duties turned out to be those more properly done by a Messenger, fetching files from the inner office, counting some pickaxe heads, taking Pettibone's drafts back to the clerk for typing.

The clerk, a Mr Ferguson McTavish, might have been a brother of Mr Samuel Brown of Naraguta, or Mr Ido Carruthers of Bauchi, wearing the same purple ready-made suit, bright socks and a mail-order club or regimental tie. A mournful exile from some coast tribe, more alien to these primitive parts than a white man could ever be, the clerk grew increasingly harassed as the day went on.

Gratefully, but still with that bemused air, he surrendered his museum-piece typewriter. Keith knocked off three brief memos, learned where the carriage jumped several spaces, inked in each missing 'e', and while Mr McTavish took the results to the divisional officer, started work on another.

'Mr Keith!'

Reluctantly Keith abandoned his intriguing toy, and presented himself.

'Mr Keith, I thought I had made it clear that *I* would allocate your duties. They do not include typing.'

After breakfast a minor chief of the Angas tribe and a dozen or so short, lean, tough-looking followers brought in some tax money. In goatskin loin-cloths, armed with bows, arrows, axes and spears, as gentlemen should be when properly dressed, they were impressive after their simple fashion.

As impressive as Pettibone, who remembered how much was due from the village for the year, and how much had already been paid. He sent Keith for the tax register and tax receipt books, so Keith was able to confirm to himself the surprising feat of memory.

To a man who really knows his job much can be forgiven; and Keith was revising his opinion of his senior, when he received his next instructions.

'Mr Keith, you will take the money over to the side table there and count it. The Messengers will check your totals.'

The normal and quicker method was for several Messengers to count, and for the white man to run his eye over the stacks of coins and spot-check a few bundles of shilling notes. The Messengers seemed puzzled, then caught the implication, and were amused at Keith's expense.

He flipped through the silver, alloy and nickel coins and came to the brown shilling notes. Some were in pieces and had to be stuck together with office gum and paper backing. Having been kept in game bags with fragments of rotted meat, and possibly in worse places, they stank to high heaven. Keith lit his pipe.

'I don't allow smoking in my office, Mr Keith!'

It was no worse than being hunted by a sergeant when you were a raw recruit. Stolidly Keith went about the jobs he was assigned. If Pettibone thought he could force his assistant to apply for a transfer to another division, he was damned well mistaken. It was for Pettibone to put in the official request and think up some reasonable excuses.

At ten minutes short of two o'clock, when the local treasury would officially close, Keith wrote out his vouchers for refund of the money he had paid his carriers, and submitted them. Pettibone checked even the carbon copies. Reluctantly he tilted back his chair, unlocked the safe, picked out a bag of coins, and told Gofwan to count out what was due. Another silly pin-prick, implying that Pettibone was above counting money, and Keith not to be trusted to.

Keith put the coins in a used official envelope and wished his senior 'Good afternoon'. He took up his sun-helmet.

'I expect you to turn up for tennis this afternoon.'

It was more of an order than an invitation. Keith went shooting.

He took only three drinks that evening, and no overdose of quinine. He wrote a few letters, closed his portable, went to bed. And slept!

It was incredible. After a bad crisis, such as that of the night before, a slight lull could be expected before the succubae came again in force. But there hadn't even been a scent of one. There could be only one explanation. Pettibone was serving as an efficient counter-irritant. Good old Pettibone! How annoyed he would be if he knew!

It was a genial junior who entered the office exactly on time, and wished his senior 'Good morning . . . sir!'

'Good morning, Mr Keith!' Pettibone condescended to reply.

Recovering from the shock, Keith suggested 'Why not drop the "mister"?'

'Because, Mr Keith, I prefer to do things correctly.'

'Then kindly address me as *Captain* Keith, *Mister* Pettibone.'

That was a stupid retort, and disturbing too. The way it had slipped out was clear warning that Keith's cultivated detachment was only superficial. As counterbalance, Keith set himself to sum up his senior's better points.

Apart from his phenomenal memory for office detail, he had other useful qualities. He spoke good Hausa, better than Keith's at present. Not the classical stuff interlarded with Arabic, such as is used by Emirs and Mohammedan judges, but the ordinary speech of the people. His accent wasn't so hot, though, and for lack of good gutturals his *kha* and *ka* and *ha* were difficult to distinguish.

21

One could appreciate the man professionally, however much one disliked him personally.

On the other hand his Messengers were just a shade too approving of a Pettibone jest, or a Pettibone decision. Just a shade too subservient—to Pettibone, of course, not the new officer. Courtiers, they were, and utterly different from the reserved and fatherly dignitaries who had guided Keith's footsteps as a newcomer at Naraguta and Bauchi.

That was Pettibone's fault, not theirs. He allowed them too much authority, such as permitting an interpreter to interrogate a witness while he went on drafting memos, and later accepting the Messenger's summary of evidence. There couldn't be a surer way of tempting his staff to accept bribes of money, livestock or women.

Pettibone's Pets. One or two of the red-robed local policemen, and the head warder of the small mud lock-up seemed to be part of the privileged coterie. Yet Pettibone wasn't homosexual, despite his long auburn hair, the gold signet ring on his carefully manicured hands, and his spitefulness. Nor did the Pets seem inclined that way, or their gestures, expressions or gait would have shown it.

The Pettibone problem was conveniently absorbing. But there was no sense in letting the man himself become an obsession. Every day, at two o'clock precisely, Keith stopped whatever he was doing, put on his sun-helmet and went his way. Awaiting him at the rest-house were files and a sketch-map which he had smuggled out of the office. He could learn more about the division from them than he could by blowing Pettibone's nose for him up on the hill.

Stretched out in his deck-chair after dinner, pleasantly relaxed by his afternoon's riding or shooting, his new clockwork lamp humming companionably beside, he began, through old official reports, to fit Pankshin into its African framework.

Nigeria, which had started as a few ports and forts for traders in the Gulf of Benin, had developed from a shore-line protectorate into a colony stretching up to meet the French on the southern edge of the Sahara Desert. A few hundred years earlier a Mohammedan invasion had spread west across the Mediterranean coast of Africa, up into Spain, and down through the Sahara to establish Islam in what was now the northern half of the colony.

But nobody had ever conquered Pankshin.

Wave after wave of invaders must have beaten against the rocky Plateau country, and been driven off to swirl around its base and on to easier conquests. The volcanic mass of granite, several hundred miles across, still dominated the northern plains, an unconquered virgin castle. Early divisional officers of Pankshin boasted of this, and used it for excuse when unwilling to enforce too alien ideas upon their primitive charges. Keith found himself sharing their viewpoint, and their pride.

Who lived in these barren hills? Apparently this impregnable fortress had always attracted fleeing remnants of once-powerful tribes. It had become a sanctuary, a human game reserve for many almost extinct races. These had never amalgamated or inter-married. They still spoke thirty or more distinct languages in Pankshin Division alone.

Most used bows and poisoned arrows, but the poison varied with the tribe, and some used barbed iron heads and some a more deadly wooden tip. Some fought with axes, others with long knives, and others with spears. One group were noted slingers, and another relied upon a throwing knife like a non-return iron boomerang.

Religions ranged from pure animism, through ancestor worship to the cult of a tribal ancestor who was in some respects a god. No two people seemed to have the same marriage customs or property laws. They tilled what land they could find, hunted the scarce wild-life, and had objected strenuously to the white man's interference with cannibalism and the gentlemanly sport of inter-tribal wars.

The Hills were a unique ethnological museum. Keith felt that he had stumbled into an isolated stand of virgin timber, or a diamond mine. It would take a man a lifetime to begin to understand just one of these thirty-plus races.

For the present he could only master his impatience, and wait

23

for the divisional officer to get tired of his childish persecution and send him out on tour to be rid of him. Damn Pettibone!

Of course insomnia and the succubae recurred. But they gathered force slowly. The Pettibone problem, hard exercise, and just one extra drink at night seemed to be keeping them down to manageable proportions.

The rudimentary social life of the station might have helped. But with no furniture except his camp kit Keith was unequipped to return hospitality, so he preferred not to accept it. Also office hours gave him as much Pettibone as he could stomach.

And still the divisional officer showed no sign of sending his junior out on tour, or of going on tour himself and leaving the junior to handle headquarter's routine.

Till Constable innocently intervened.

'No, thanks. My scatter-gun would only wound at this range. And he's seen us already, so it's no use trying to stalk him. You do your stuff, Maestro!'

At eighty yards the greater bustard looked no bigger than a domestic goose. Keith sat down, and cuddled the butt of his Ross ·22 to his cheek.

'Call your shot!' Constable insisted.

'Head or clean miss.'

A perfect trigger release, a slight 'crack', and the bird's head disappeared behind the tall grass.

Constable paced the distance. 'Seventy-two yards, and right through the eye. Quite a shot, Maestro!'

'Luck. But a neck-spine-shoulder with only a ·22 wouldn't have been fair on a bird of this size.'

It had been a good evening shoot, with three bush-fowl (Constable's), and a guinea-fowl and this greater bustard (Keith's), for only seven shots.

In contented silence they wandered back through the failing light to where they estimated the horses would be waiting, and hit the right spot on the road within a few yards.

'The bustard's yours, Constable. He's too big for me to eat alone,' Keith decided. 'Garuba, let this *tuje* be given to the soldier *Ba-ture's* horse-boy.'

'Thanks a lot. I'll throw a dinner, and you'll have to come and help us eat it. Time you stopped being a hermit.'

Keith hid his grin by turning to mount. 'Will your spavined old crock fall on his nose if he tries to gallop?'

Constable accepted the challenge and swept past. His Hullabaloo was a fair army charger, a little heavy in the quarters, but a good weight-carrier and capable. Keith leaned forward, and Orion cut loose.

There were no ground-squirrel holes or brush on the wide Panyam-Pankshin dirt road, and Keith rode light for his height. Orion had nothing to fault his perfect stride. He left Hullabaloo standing. Keith had just time to dismount by his rest-house at the foot of the hill, slip the reins over Orion's head, sit down and look bored with waiting, before Constable and Hullabaloo pounded round the bend.

'Did you drop something and have to go back for it?' Keith stood up and stretched. 'Now you're here, how about dropping in for a drink?'

'For those dirty cracks I refuse to drink with you. Unless you come to my quarters where I can put emetic in your glass.' Constable slipped the chin-strap of his sun-helmet. 'So leave your crow-bait and walk up the hill with me. Do you good.'

Keith handed Orion over to the horse-boy's current woman, picked up some more tobacco, asked Momadu to have lantern and mosquito boots sent after him, and walked beside Hullabaloo up the hill. There wasn't much risk of running into Pettibone. His dignity would require a formal invitation, and Constable wouldn't have been out shooting if he expected anyone.

The young gunner was silent on the way up. Arrived at the path which led through a discouraged looking oleander hedge to his quarters, he reined up and slapped his knee.

'Well, I'm damned! I've just remembered. On alternate evenings we all take our drinks on the tennis-court. Scotch club, y'know. There won't be a thing in the house. Hang on a minute while I hand over the nag, and we'll drift along together.'

It wasn't a convincing performance. In fact it was so amateurish that it was disarming. Keith grinned and waited.

25

Constable returned, dropped his cigarette case, and picked up his lines as he recovered it.

'Good idea, a Scotch club, don't you think?'

'We had one at Bauchi.'

'Gives our quarters time to cool off, for one thing. And Griggs and Fletcher like it. Griggs is one of the new breed of N.C.O.s, and isn't sure that commissioned officers are socially acceptable. Sort of reverse-snob. Fletcher's the old kind, who takes everything as it comes. Anything mechanical like a breech-block does just what he wants it to, and he doesn't have to tell the men twice. Wish I knew the trick. But don't ask him to fill out a G.1098 or a nominal roll. It would be sheer cruelty.'

'I won't,' Keith promised.

'Fletcher's old woman is teaching him Hausa, and you might find that easier going than his English. It's taken him nearly forty years to learn his mother-tongue, and he's still got a vocabulary of only two words, *zurr* meaning 'sir' or 'yes', and *ar* meaning either 'yes' or 'no' and hence rather confusing. He's teaching his old woman to knit. She's a market woman from Zaria, who gave up her stall to follow him. Cross-eyed, I'm told, and would make a bishop's lady seem a flighty flipperty-gibbet in contrast.'

The amusing babble, continuous as an incantation which must not be broken lest it release Keith from the spell, stopped suddenly.

Beside the ant-heap tennis-court five candle lamps with their glass globes stood on five low tables each with a bottle and a sparklet siphon. Four men sprawled beside them in deck-chairs. Garrard, cheroot in hand, was saying something to a man who turned out to be Griggs. Pettibone had lifted his legs off the footrest of his chair to tuck white trousers into mosquito boots. Fletcher, swarthily muscular as the proverbial village blacksmith, had fished a flying beetle out of his glass and held it to the light to admire it. No mistaking Fletcher for the paler Griggs with the aggressive little waxed moustache.

Keith dropped into a chair to save Fletcher the trouble of rising and Griggs the painful uncertainty as to whether he should or

26

not. There were two deck-chairs beside Constable's table, and two glasses on it. So the young idiot had planned this earlier in the day.

'Keith, Griggs, Fletcher!' Constable waved a hand in airy introduction and uncorked the whisky. 'Say "when" Keith. By the way, you fellows, I've been telling Keith he ought to turn out for tennis. He put a new string in my racket the other day, and if he can repair rackets he can use them.'

So that was what came of doing the young squirt a favour!

Garrard blew a smoke ring into the warm, still air. 'Come to think of it, a man with the rather similar name of Captain Ian Keith won the Plateau singles cup at Naraguta last year.'

That gave a false impression. 'McLeay should have got it as usual, but he had to ride out to bush on an appendix case. He gave me a walk-over. Rather unfair.'

'Still expecting the world to be fair!' Griggs gave a snort of derision. 'Come to that, was there anything to stop your giving the doctor a walk-over instead of him giving you one?'

Keith let it slide. He sipped his whisky appreciatively. A different brand from his own, sharper and less smoky. But the first drink of the evening was always delicious. With it should go a silence, not of emptiness, but of other men relaxed and at peace beside you. Your head should lean back in the chair, so that the eyes could await and welcome the first glimmer of a star. The whine of a mosquito, and an occasional insect in your glass were almost as necessary to perfect enjoyment. Without them you lost the sense of contrast, and the gift of full appreciation.

'Three times I have invited Keith to play, three separate times. But he prefers to go shooting.' Pettibone's voice jarred on the serenity of the smoothly flowing tide of darkness beyond the yellow candlelight.

Keith felt that a further luxury must be added to luxury to restore his peace. He pulled out a pipe and began to scrape out the bowl with a pocket-knife.

'Ar!' said Fletcher. Meaning apparently 'Here! Catch!' And threw across a leather bag.

'We ought to warn you, as a newcomer, that Fletcher's tobacco will blow your head off,' Garrard said. 'He manufactures it from old army boots and cordite.'

'Ar!' said Fletcher, deeply amused.

It was native leaf, but better cured than usual, and not unlike Boer tobacco. Constable poured Keith a second drink. The first pipe of the evening, when the tar no longer boiled in the bowl, made the second drink almost as wonderful as the first. Pettibone's white Persian paced up from the direction of his bungalow, gathered the lazy attention of the party, then leaped lightly on to Keith's lap.

'Honoured, ma'am!' Keith bowed from the waist up. 'And for the second time!'

Constable, who seemed to consider himself Keith's sole dis-coverer and promoter, produced the story of the greater bustard, shot cleanly through the eye at—the range had gone up—a hundred paces.

A general murmur, which could be taken for mild interest or equally mild doubt, set Constable off again.

'And what's more he's got the fastest mount in the station. I'll back Orion at better than evens!'

'Seen your nag around, Keith. What d'you ride at?' Garrard rose to the challenge.

Keith gave his weight, which he guessed to be about the same as Garrard's, and suggested a short scurry as the horses were in soft condition.

Griggs, who would weigh in a good stone lighter than Garrard or Keith, naturally wanted a longer course. Fletcher, appealed to to make a fourth so that the race could be run off in two heats, there being no room for more than two horses abreast on the Panyam road, was believed to refuse but say he would look to the shoeing.

Pettibone fidgeted. He positively wriggled. Keith could under-stand why the Persian had chosen a more stable lap than her master's. An accomplished actress does not want to have her studied poses broken by being tossed about like a shipwrecked sailor on a raft.

Pettibone was displeased. The cause could be anything. It was the result that mattered. For Pettibone peeved was a Pettibone vulnerable. After suffering his tantrums patiently in the office, why not turn them to account in some way?

The idea dawned slowly. Keith tried to persuade Constable that he was still entitled to race even if he laid the odds. From Constable he turned to Pettibone, the only other man in the station.

'It doesn't matter if the fourth man can ride or not, provided his nag has four legs and can stagger through one heat. How about you, Pettibone?'

Pettibone rose to the fly.

'The race is out of the question,' he announced as to a public meeting. 'Captain Keith is leaving at dawn to repair a bridge on the far side of Panyam. He will not be available.'

Now to goad Pettibone into confirming his hastily improvised orders.

'Isn't this rather short notice?' Keith asked. 'I mean, to get carriers and things?'

'You will be given carriers. You will obey orders. You will stay at Panyam rest-house and also count the near-by villages. My Messengers will show you how.'

Keith couldn't believe his good luck. It was better to make quite sure of it by putting up further protests.

'But I'll need a touring advance, and money for labourers. And tools like saws, adzes, picks and headpans. And a lock-up cash tank for the money, and . . .'

'They will be sent after you. I have said that you will leave at dawn. You understand?'

Chapter Three

OVER dinner, whose all too literal *pièce de résistance* was the recently slain guinea-fowl, Keith considered his next day's trip.

How did one set about census-taking? The idea was simple enough. To count each village, and note each man, woman, child, and any livestock or trades other than the universal farming. Then work out the tax total at so much for each able-bodied male, excluding lepers, blind, sick or lame. But what were the safeguards to make sure that the results were reasonably accurate?

It was a bright moonlight night. Keith finished his coffee, slipped his shoulder holster on under his pyjama jacket, clicked the long-barrelled Luger into place in hope of meeting a leopard on the way, tucked his pyjama trousers into mosquito boots and set off up the hill.

The night-watchman, a red-robed tribal policeman, had just finished the supper his wife had brought, and was stretched out at ease on the veranda. He courteously laid aside his clay-bowled tobacco pipe, gave Keith greeting, and unlocked the door.

In every office there are matches and candles in readiness for the quarterly, annual and estimate rush times, when officials work madly through the night to complete their returns and reports. With their help Keith discovered three six-foot-high stacks of termite-riddled census papers, tied in bundles according to the year.

He slapped off the dust, set aside the bare summaries, and like a good research man concentrated on the original field counts, the most blotched, faded and least easily decipherable. But the marginal comments were rewarding.

'Rainmaker missing. Deposed and apparently eaten.' 'Smallpox epidemic three years ago.' 'Household immigrated from Sanga in next division.' 'Land farmed out and young men leaving.'

'Said to have emigrated to Wukari. Doubt. Check later.' 'Killed by leopard?' 'Started new hamlet ten miles to west as no longer afraid of Ron horsemen.' 'Apparently attracted by milder rule of new chief.' And much more beside, of the all-important crops, of rainfall, of well-digging experiments, and even religion so far as it concerned tribal economics.

This was anything but mechanical counting and tabulating. It was using the census as a means to understanding the people's problems. An asterisk against the name of a householder, who was also the village headman, referred to a footnote: *Ordered to repay those from whom he had exacted extra tax, and given three months hard labour. Messenger three months i.h.l. and dismissed. See Provincial Court Minutes.* Embezzlement in collusion with Messenger, obviously. And Pettibone had said 'My Messengers will show you how.'

Pettibone seemed to have done little recounting in the two years which included his last tour and part of this. He didn't seem to like field work. As Keith didn't like headquarters, between them they ought to add up to one all-round administrator.

He blew out the candle, thanked the watchman, cracked a jest with the man's wife, and stepped out into the cool moonlight with the station sleeping peacefully around him. It must be after midnight, so if sex started kicking up, he could spend the next four hours reading. With any luck this change to Panyam, and new scenes, new thoughts, and hard work in the hot sun should help a lot.

A glare of light blazed out from behind the divisional officer's quarters. . . . House on fire?

Keith broke into a run, leaving the path and cutting through the bushes. It might be only the cook-house, not the main quarters. Curious, no sound of crackling roof sticks, no plume of smoke; and the light was strangely white and bright. He was near enough now to hear voices, so someone was already on the spot, and calmly coping with the emergency.

He stopped and stared, for now he could see round the corner of the main house. The glaring light came from a lantern with an incandescent mantle, and Pettibone carried it.

Before Pettibone six little pagan girls waited in a row, some scarcely breasted, none old enough to wear the string and grass Angas girdle. Behind them, stick in hand, stood Gofwan the Head Messenger.

Pettibone said something in Hausa, which Gofwan translated. The biggest girl, thick-lipped, heavy-browed, scratched herself and grinned. The other five showed a tendency to bunch closer together, as though to lend each other confidence. Gofwan tapped them with his stick and lined them up again.

Setting down the lantern Pettibone took a paper bag from the pocket of his dressing-gown, and walking down the line popped something, apparently a sweet, into each mouth as it obediently opened for him.

A parade of virgins rounded up from some Angas village and brought here for the Greater Judge's bed. Keith turned, and strode off, disgusted.

The regulations, made by people who lived comfortably at home in England with their wives, threatened with dismissal any official who entered into what were pompously called ' quasi concubinal alliances with indigenous girls or women '. But the people who framed the rules had never lived alone in the tropics. So far as Keith's morals and Pettibone's went, there was nothing to choose between them, and Keith had no right to adopt a ' holier-than-thou ' attitude. But at least he had never gone in for young girls. Nor had he employed one of his own staff as procurer. And what continued to anger him was the stick in Gofwan's hand. That savoured of coercion.

It was oven-hot in the dry river-bed, and volatilized Sura sweat was a poor substitute for air. But when a bridge has to be rebuilt from bottom up, with local materials, unskilled labour and almost no tools, someone has to demonstrate, supervise and inspect each stage of the job. And that someone happened to be Ian Keith. To his deep satisfaction.

He had already made some changes, of which Pettibone was sure to disapprove. The old bridge had been sited in the narrowest part of the river, where the pent-up flood-waters tore out the wooden piers. As might have been expected, since there was no dynamite to blast holes in the rocky bed, and no cement to make footings. Keith had hunted for a better site, and found one further down-stream, thereby also straightening out the road alignment.

Crib piers he had judged to be better than the previous tall and tottery legs. That simplified things, as short lengths of wood could be used instead of having to drag whole tree trunks from a distance, without wheels or rollers. Packed with rock, the crib would have no tendency to float loose from the bottom.

'No . . . no . . . no!' Keith took a hand-saw and marked where the ends of the logs should be notched so that they would interlock at the corners. 'Like this!' He had done it scores of times, and would have to do it scores of times hereafter.

An interesting study, these Sura people of Panyam. They were more heavily built than the Angas of Pankshin villages, and distinguishable because they had no tribal cicatrice running from ear to ear like a chin-strap. According to reports they were more litigious and less truthful than other tribes in the division. On the other hand they were said to be better farmers. They looked like good workers, but didn't seem to have much heart for bridge-building. There might be a reason. Why not try an experiment?

'That man with a small drum, up there on the bank,' Keith pointed him out to the bored and dignified Messenger. 'Ask him to come down and play for me.'

To run with a message from the Lesser Judge to a mere Sura was of course unthinkable. The Messenger drew back the chin-loop of his turban, which had protected his mouth from the dust, and yelled.

The man heard. He dropped down the bank, though reluctantly. Keith noted that in addition to the usual goatskin loin-cloth the man wore a twist of plaited straw around his head. A dandy as well as a musician! And obviously a little afraid that he was going to be set to degrading manual toil.

'Tell him,' lied Keith, 'that the fame of his skill reaches far. I would like to hear him.'

For the first time the man seemed to notice Keith's existence. Here, obviously, was a white man less brutish than usual—he

33

liked music! The man squatted on a comfortable rock. Softly, ruminatively, his long fingers stroked the parchment drum-head, as though seeking inspiration.

Then the drummer found his theme. The beat was too intricate for Keith to follow, since he was not an African. But the result was startling.

A man who had been listlessly dragging a log, swung it to his head with a triumphant 'Ha!' and brought it in at a jog-trot. Hand-saws whined like lumber-mills. Battle-axes, cleaning out notches, struck as though driven into the skulls of tribal enemies. Even the men working on the earthwork approaches, and almost out of hearing, moved to a brisker pace. For the first time the Suras were enjoying their work.

'Tell him,' Keith instructed, 'that he shall have sixpence a day as drummer.' Which was a damned good bargain for adding twenty-five per cent to the efficiency of a working force of sixty-two men.

One more lesson had been learned, and the dark fog of a white man's ignorance of Africa lifted slightly at another point. And now for the next test against which to pit his inexperience. The census-counting.

Purposely Keith led the way to a steep almost overhanging bank, and started to climb, the Messenger doubtfully following. The whole native staff needed exercise. They were as soft as they were haughty and overbearing to the peasants; though they themselves must have been lean, tough farm boys before they went to a Mission school and later became government employees.

Anta, the Messenger, gave the white man a sour look, but safely behind his back. This new *Ba-ture*, who seemed of no importance in the office, was starting to be troublesome. For instance he began work before sunrise, and often worked on census papers after sunset; and expected others to do the same. And one did, though intending to refuse. For in his pale goat-like eyes was a knowledge that all would be done as he ordered.

He had no women, which explained why he could not rest. It was not known why he had no women, and questions to his servants were met only by rudeness; Momadu Dangana being by no

34

means patient, as his name *dangana* implied, but saying 'If you wish to sleep with the *Ba-ture*, learn first to wipe your arse!'

This Keeta was goat-like now, in the way he took the river-bank at a run, as though joying in such unseemly effort. In hat, shirt, and shorts, with no covering on his thin legs but shoes, he did not realize that true dignity was judged by the size of a turban, by how many robes a man could afford to wear, one over another, and by one's sword.

Anta disentangled the cross-hilted sword slung from his shoulder on a red woollen cord, raised the skirts of his robes to free his stride, and managed to scramble out of the river-bed, panting and indignant.

Gofwan had said 'I am Head Messenger, and you, Anta, are the husband of my cousin. Therefore if Keeta troubles you, let me speak for you in the ear of Mister Petbo, who is greater than he and has no love for his brother white man.'

But Gofwan had also warned 'Smile not so openly when Keeta is mocked by Mister Petbo. Nor crack twigs under unwary feet. For Keeta is more leopard than goat. It is told by his servants that he bears battle scars. A goat is cut but once, across the throat, and the wound has no time to heal.'

Yet Keeta showed no claws. Even now, finding his horse-boy asleep beneath a tree, he smiled, and himself tightened the girth of his horse. Nor did he strike the boy with his toe. When Keeta mounted, and Garuba opened his eyes to the creak of leather, his master said jestingly 'Rise in haste! It is dawn, and her husband comes!'

It grew hot indeed, even under the protection of many robes, and hotter still for Keeta, who wore little more than did an *arna*, a pagan Hillman. Yet he still rode west.

Before long one said 'This land is forgotten by the Holy Jesus, hard as rock and without water. Also very hot.' To remind Keeta that one was a *Nassara*, a Nazarene, like himself; also that the sun began to pain. That was good, two arrows loosed from one string.

Yet Keeta rode on in silence. It began to appear that he was like the Lame One of Bauchi, also sparing of words. And the Lame

35

One was a *Ba-ture* of great power, whom even Mister Petbo feared. The likeness lay also in Keeta's veiled words. If Keeta were found to be such, one took refuge in Allah, or perhaps the Holy Jesus!

He spoke. 'Now that the bridge is well started, we will help the other Messengers in their counting of heads.'

In haste Anta drove in his shovel-shaped stirrups which also served for spurs, and ranged up alongside. If Keeta had intended to count he should have said so, so that other counts might tally with his. It was unfair, and much harm might come of this!

A reason must be found for leaving Keeta at once, and riding ahead to tell the other Messengers. Though it was already too late to destroy papers, for heads had been counted for three days, and the papers given to Keeta each evening. So does a leopard stalk his prey and spring without warning!

What should the excuse be? Fever, colic, or a sudden pain?

Those pale goat-like eyes in the thin face were watching, as though watching one's thoughts, and the smile at what they saw was as the slight unsheathing of claws.

'You are in health, Anta?'

One answered without meaning to, 'Well indeed, *Ba-ture,* in great health! By the grace of Allah and Jesus!'

Gofwan might be right, after all. As well to crack no twigs under unwary feet. But tonight a letter must be sent to Gofwan, asking him to search the mind of Mister Petbo. For Mister Petbo was the Greater Judge, and Keeta only the Lesser.

Chapter Four

KEITH thrust his long, enquiring nose into the mud-walled, empty goat-pen. By the size and quantity of the droppings on the floor, he judged the tenants to be four adults, one, by the lingering odour, a male, and possibly two kids.

He checked by Tibn's count. Three adults, three kids. Near enough.

With Tibn and the village head tailing behind, he continued his inspection of the huts. Cook fires were easy to distinguish from smouldering smudges designed to keep off mosquitoes. A wooden mortar might be used by as many as three women, but usually only by a mother and her daughter. There were fewer clues to the number of adult males. At first he had hoped that the tobacco patch, close to the house so that it could be fertilized by wood-ash from the fires, would give a rough indication. But old women smoked at least twice as much as men, and completely upset the calculation.

One had to fall back on the actual count of men paraded by the village head. It was likely to be reasonably accurate, since those who paid tax would object to others hiding to escape it. Any trick work would have to be done by the Messenger who counted, with the connivance of the village head.

This headman was a fine specimen, broad shouldered and almost too tall for a Sura. The whole village was above the average, cleaner, its thatch in better repair, more obviously prosperous. Yet the cornbins were small. That was puzzling.

So was the dark mound outside the village, crowned by what looked like small gravestones. Of no importance so far as the count went, it aroused Keith's curiosity, and he led the way towards it. Gravestones and a burial mound in Sura district? Impossible.

The black stain on the hill was charcoal, and a dross crunched like cinders under Keith's feet. The gravestones were small mud walls. In front of each stood a pair of bellows, made of the necks of large earthenware pots half-buried in the ground; with loose drumheads of greasy leather to which were attached sticks like spear-shafts.

Proudly the headman demonstrated his craft. One stood behind the screening wall because of the heat, taking the tops of the sticks in either hand and pumped them alternately . . . thus. On the other side of the screen one put burning charcoal, and iron-stone, pounded to a powder between rocks, also a white clay which had to be brought from a distance. One blew air with the bellows through the pot in which the charcoal and ironstone were, adding more charcoal. By night and day one pumped, by no means stopping. Thus it was.

' And you get iron? ' Keith wanted to know.

By no means. That which was born in the fire was by no means such, until it had been heated many times and pounded between rocks. Then it became pure metal. And so great was the fame of the iron-workers here that each man paid a shilling extra tax each year.

Keith checked Tibn's field-sheet. No mention of iron-workers, or extra tax. So the Messenger had intended to get away with about thirty shillings, and without the headman's connivance, obviously. How?

Riding back to camp Keith tried to summarize the situation. His spot-checks suggested that there was little to choose, so far as honesty went, between his Messengers. All were guilty, in varying degree.

Moman's shifty glance and nervous stammer would convict an angel of halo-snatching, but so far he seemed the best of a bad bunch. He was the only Hausa, the only Mohammedan, in a group of nominal Christians; which meant that the others would be less likely to trust him as a confederate. Of course his difficult position meant that he dare not inform against the others. Anta was related to Gofwan, who as Pettibone's procurer would have Pettibone's ear. Tibn, soft and charming, was of the same tribe, the Plain Angas in Bauchi Division. Loshi seemed a dull-witted lout, but was a hanger-on of Tibn and Anta.

So long as the Pets were in power, and known to have Pettibone's confidence, witnesses would be unwilling to appear against them. How could one break up the conspiracy?

Back at Panyam rest-house was a task at least as important. The administration of justice among the Sura people. As Orion swung lightly over the low mud wall surrounding the rest-house, men in goatskin loin-cloths and women in their puzzling string girdles offered friendly greetings. But the chief and his assistant judges would not be here for another hour. Plenty of time for breakfast.

Under pretence of touring his division, Pettibone had been in the habit of transferring his office to Panyam, the head village of the Sura tribe. With the result that this rest-house was very different from the neglected one at Pankshin.

A garden, empty of vegetables at this time of year, but with a few fruit and shade trees, extended down to a small stream. A delightful place to walk in during the cool of the evening. The rest-house, built on a mud plinth to catch the breeze, with thick thatch reaching down like eyebrows over the encircling veranda, was at least twice the usual size of such home-from-homes.

Momadu, stocky and imperturbable, brought the belated breakfast and his household report. His assistant had been sent to the market to buy cooking salt, to save the white salt which was used at table. Garuba needed more money, as the price of millet-corn on the stalk had risen again, as it always did towards the end of the dry season. The water brought in earthenware jars by the water-girls was muddy. Momadu's wife had been given a kitten by a passing trader.

It was still cool enough for a man to have an appetite. Tea and half a purple-fleshed pawpaw opened the feast. A bush-fowl, and what Sam for want of a more descriptive word called toast, completed it.

Keith glanced around him with a proud feeling of ownership. It was surprising how soon a place became home. A folding cot; a deck-chair to relax in after the day's work was done; a tin travelling bath—also an evening luxury; an enamelled basin on a three-ply chop-box; a line slung across one corner for clothes-hangers, since anything touching walls or floor was liable to be eaten by termites; a few black tin uniform cases; two rifle-cases; and more chop-boxes with imported provisions, books and office papers. What more could a man want?

Momadu reappeared, to announce 'The Sarikin Sura, and his judges.'

'Give greeting, and say I come.'

At first sight the members of the native Court of the Sura tribe were unimpressive. Keith met them on the veranda. The Sarikin Sura, their chief and President of the Court, robed and turbaned like a Mohammedan, was a man far gone in age and drink. The three district heads, in skimpy shirt-like robes, with bow-string guards on their left forearms and hoe-calloused palms were scarcely standard ornaments of the Bench.

Keith greeted them with respect. He knew them. The blear-eyed president disposed himself on a goatskin rug where Keith's breakfast table had recently stood. The other three squatted on the bare mud floor. Litigants, witnesses and onlookers, equipped with spears, axes, knives and an occasional short-handled hoe, crowded in after the judges, and squatted with much rustling of dry skin loin-cloths. Women, girls and children followed, in varying degrees of nudity or near nudity. The packed rest-house began to exhale a remarkable aroma of stale millet-beer, still staler Sura sweat with overtones of rank tobacco.

Moman Wanti, far the most impressive in his turban, gown, and official badge of yellow crown embroidered on black, pinned on his chest like a medal, looked to Keith to open Court.

Keith took his call. It made him feel ridiculous, but the people expected it of him.

'Let only truth be told!' What a hope! 'Let that which has been wrongfully taken be restored! Let all wrongdoing be punished!'

Re-activating the tribal Court had been sheer inspiration. On Keith's arrival at Panyam he had opened his Petty Case book and decided to polish off any outstanding complaints before going on to the more important census and bridge-building. A reasonable idea, it had seemed.

But the first case, over a farm boundary, about an area roughly the size of the rest-house compound, had no less than thirty witnesses, and lasted two full days. With twenty or so cases on his docket, and more coming in before the first land-claim was settled, he grew desperate. Bauchi and Naraguta, where he had served his first tour, had native Courts to arbitrate such matters, and the touring white man heard only more serious criminal cases. Why was there no native Court here?

'Mister Petbo does not desire it.' Tibn was definite.

Further enquiry established that there were four tribal Courts in the division, the oldest here in Panyam. Each member received a small monthly salary, but under Pettibone did nothing to earn it. As few litigants could afford the time and expense of taking their witnesses to the white man, that white man could pose as the fountain-head of Justice, the source from whom all blessings flow. While adding little to his work.

Surely that was a step in the wrong direction? The basic principle of government, here in Nigeria, was gradually to delegate authority to the people's natural leaders. Earlier divisional officers, with far tougher jobs than Pettibone's, had started these native Courts.

Affront Pettibone? Or deny the Suras the homely justice to which they were entitled?

'Four goats were claimed. Two are given by the Judges,' Moman Wanti reported.

Keith duly noted the decision in his court record book, and looked at his watch. Ten minutes to hear and decide one of those small but appallingly complicated cases, where the ownership of a handful of goats is traced back by witness after witness through three or four generations of goats.

The next case was simple. A public brawl with multiple assault and battery. Fines ranging from sixpence to two shillings were imposed, and a witness proved to have lied was led outside and beaten with a whip by a red-robed tribal policeman. All done in seven minutes.

41

Case after case, routine and uninteresting, but any one of which would have taken an ignorant white lawyer a day to settle. Ignorant not of law, but of facts and customs known only to the African.

Then something like a divorce came under review. Separation was proved, and the man claimed return of the money he had paid for his wife, since she remained obdurately with her parents. It sounded simple, until a complication crept in.

Apparently the Suras were in transition between marriage by capture and marriage by purchase. The first custom required the young man and his friends, with the connivance of the girl and her parents, to raid her home with much shouting and threats, and abduct the bride-to-be. With the connivance of the bridegroom the parent would next raid the bridegroom's home, and after much threatening be bought off. The marriage-by-purchase assumed that a girl was the property of her parents, and must be paid for in advance, like a pony or any other valuable property.

Had the man married the girl? That seemed to be the point. If not he had no claim.

He tried to prove he had, because marriage-by-capture was the only true and holy wedlock recognized in his village. The parents made out a fair case that in their village, on the contrary, the old custom was obsolete, and marriage by purchase all the vogue.

Keith lost the thread of Moman's interpretation. The bride's girdle held his attention. What made it stay up?

No doubt by local standards her shaven head and heavy features were attractive. Her slender body with firm upturned breasts, small hips like those of all Hillwomen, and boyish legs, would earn far wider approval. And her girdle, her sole covering except for the straw in her upper lip, would catch the eye anywhere but here.

All Sura women wore the same. Eight strings, stained a rusty red, encircled the lower part of her hips, in rings, one below the other. They always seemed to be sliding off, without visible means of support. Yet quite unaccountably they supported a thing like a double-headed drum-stick. They did more than support it. They strained the drum-stick tightly up into the crotch, so that one of its heads partly hid the *mons veneris,* and the other pressed apart the buttocks at the back.

Did the strings support the stick, or vice versa? When the girl and her mother leaned forward as they knelt, the drum-stick at the back dropped an inch or so. When they leaned back it regained its former position. Had the Sura women some exceptional development, like a very muscular *tablier Egyptien* or *Hottentot apron*, which clamped the drum-stick in place?

It would be easy to find out. Just drop a hint to one of the Messengers and no doubt the girl, or another like her, would arrive at the rest-house after dark.

Thank God the case had ended, and the girl was gone. 'Finding for plaintiff. Gifts to be returned less salt and tobacco, these being gifts to girl's mother, not part of bride-price,' Keith duly recorded.

More cases. The primitive court room rose several degrees in temperature. A woman nursed her child. Flies abounded. Another child, in a skin bag on the back of her elder sister, vomited. A dog chased a goat in, waking a man who hastily drew an arrow from his quiver.

Keith looked at his watch. Three o'clock, and he still had to eat and ride back to the bridge-botchers. He closed his notebook. Moman caught the Sarikin Sura's rheumy eye. The Court adjourned till tomorrow, mounted its saddleless ponies and rode home.

The crib piers were complete, lashed with lianas and packed with stones from the river-bed. Laying the bearers across them brought new anxieties. For lack of jacks or pulleys, dozens of men balanced precariously on crib-heads, hauling on twisted lianas, while scores of men including unpaid volunteers attracted by the excitement stood in the river-bed or clung to the lower members of the cribs lifting the heavy giginya trunks on crooked sticks.

The ant-like method seemed suicidal. One slip and a dozen workers would be crushed beneath the heavy palm stems. Keith supervised each stage, and sweated with anxiety. Probably the

43

rhythm of the drummer did more to co-ordinate the work and save accidents than all Keith's orders. Not a man was injured.

Cross-pieces were laid over the longitudinal bearers, and lashed in place. Over these were laid stout mats, woven out on the southern plain where reed-like grass grew tall and dense. On top came an inch or so of laterite soil for road-surface. Earthwork approaches grew steadily. It was too early to be optimistic, but it began to look as though the race against the rainy season might yet be won.

Census work was less satisfactory. Keith's warning to the Messengers had been met by an united front of injured innocence. Anta, tall, large-framed, and glowering, came close to insolence, saying 'Mister Petbo does not count again what we have already counted. We count well.'

Loshi and Moman took the disarming line 'We will count yet better, now that our faults have been made known to us.' Tibn's blue-black face for once looked more smilingly cunning than smilingly simple. He threw the entire blame on villagers who did not wish to pay tax, so evaded the counters. It was a good line, and he smirked with self-approval.

'In future one of you, each taking turn, shall recount the counts already made by the other three,' Keith decreed. 'Afterwards I will check part of both count and re-count.'

It took them unawares. Keith could almost hear their thoughts racing to catch up.

Drink—and he was up to the maximum he dare allow himself —was no longer a soporific. Because he was afraid to sleep. To twist and turn and ache and sweat was more endurable than the ghastly nightmares, which now ranged the full gamut of physically possible and impossible sexual excesses. Ordure mingled with writhing monstrous female shapes, and disgusting self-abasement with vicious sadism. The Keith of his dreams had no vestige of similarity to the waking Keith. But was this horror the real, the subconscious Keith stripped of his civilized veneer? Or an atavistic Keith to which he would revert if his self-control snapped under the intolerable strain?

Those peaceful moments in the tropical evening, when alien

44

and native alike relax from the heat and toil of the day, were no longer peacefully rewarding. One trouble was the drumming. Garuba had no further need to broadcast his requirements, for his reputation was soundly established and he had no lack of women. But there were other drums, big booming village ones, staidly summoning men and women to beer and dances, growing enthusiastic as the party went on, and driving drummers and dancers into rhythmic raptures until far into the night.

The remedy was simple. Tibn, bringing the day's census papers to be checked and filed, suggested it.

'By Mister Petbo's orders all *kida*, drumming, is unlawful within his hearing. Permit that I carry word to Sarikin Sura that it cease.'

Keith was shocked out of his official tact. 'Unlike Mister Petbo, I do not own the drums and the air of Sura,' he snapped. 'Let the drumming continue.'

The fault lay not in the drumming, but in Keith's response to it. And that could be corrected. At the tiny Hausa market there was certain to be a woman who obliged passing traders. And surely it was better to risk disease than mental breakdown? One thing only deterred Keith from the experiment, a fear close to terror.

Could he any longer trust himself to take a woman in his arms? One of those nightmare scenes might re-enact itself, and he would wake in the morning to find a strangled body lying beside him.

At some point in the past he had gone beyond the safe limit in sexual abstinence. It might have been on the night of his arrival at Pankshin, when the tropics had hit him so hard and so prematurely, and for a ridiculous official scruple he had sent the women away. No use regretting it now.

Or it might go back still earlier, at Bauchi, when young Jenkyns was on the brink of suicide, and Keith had sent the kindly understanding Shetu to him. He had stood in the darkness outside Jenkyns' bungalow half hoping, half dreading, to hear the shot which would announce that Shetu had gone too late, and would return to him.

Into Keith's turmoil, at nine o'clock of a scorching breezeless morning, rode a most unlikely St George to put to flight the scaly dragon of mental unbalance.

His first remark, on reining up at the rest-house, was 'Hullo! Any elephants around here?'

Pinkly fresh from Woolwich, Yeats introduced himself as a replacement for Constable, who was to go down country and take in a refresher course on his way to England on leave. Lanky, with outsize hands and feet, he smiled amiably on Keith's bare barracks of a bedroom, and asked 'D'you have all this to yourself? I mean, it's simply palatial.'

'We'll share it as soon as your loads arrive. Or you can be my guest. Whichever you like. It's a public rest-house,' Keith assured him.

'May I? I mean that's frightfully generous of you.'

Keith tried to break things to him gently. No elephants up here on the Plateau. No white priestesses descended from a long line of English earls. And so far as he knew no King Solomon's Mines waiting to be rediscovered.

Yeats saw through his motives at once. 'Even if there were, you mining johnnies wouldn't let on. And I don't blame you. Don't want the country overrun with other prospecting johnnies.' At Keith's invitation he stretched out in the one deck-chair. 'I'd feel the same way myself.'

Yeats insisted on going round with Keith, and knew enough to be impressed by the crude-looking practical bridge. He wanted to know how long it took to learn the African 'lingo'. He returned to sit, pouring sweat, through the long session of the Court, possibly under the impression that it was some secret tribal ceremony which he was privileged to witness.

Over evening drinks he spoke rapturously of a girl named Helga, of whom he could never be worthy. He contributed a bottle of port to the dinner. It was muddy from travel, but he and Keith finished it to the dregs. He snored without a break for seven and a half hours. Keith woke once to wonder vaguely why nobody before had tried snoring to exorcize ghosts and succubae.

At the crack of dawn Keith helped Yeats get his carriers on the road, and after breakfast cut his usual counting to ride with him and set him on his way. Regretfully he returned to his duties.

Thereby missing Yeats' report to Garrard at Pankshin.

'. . . last night at Panyam. Sort of odd-job johnny there, civilian, fed me and showed me around. Nice old fellow; hands a bit shaky, I thought. Drink, I imagine.' With the innocent virtue of one who can top up his evening whiskies with half a bottle of port and suffer no remorse in the morning.

'Thin, long nose, just under your height?' Garrard played his new second lieutenant along.

'That's him. Talks the lingo, so must have been out a long time. Frightfully dis-what-you-call-it, disillusioned, though. Won't believe a thing the other johnnies tell you about Africa. Looks as though he had seen better days, too. Must be down on his luck to be foreman to a gang of native bridge-builders. He was awfully decent to me. I was wondering if I could do something for him in return.'

Leading the young idiot down the garden path had been amusing. Now Garrard rather regretted it. Yeats' simplicity affected people that way.

'Your down-and-out acquaintance happens to be a brevet major, late of the Sappers. The reason for the battery perching on this godforsaken hill is to protect the person and dignity of His Majesty's representative, the Divisional Officer Pankshin. It so happens that your new friend is due to relieve the present divisional officer this week or the next.'

47

Chapter Five

NEWS travels fast in Africa. All of a sudden sullen Messengers smiled ingratiatingly, doing their best to make amends for past slights. Not knowing the cause, Keith was puzzled.

But he wasted no time on the enigma. It was going to be a neck and neck race with the rains. Right at the bottom of one of the piers the logs had been assembled without those locking notches. With no jacks to take the weight above, Keith had to harden his heart, remove the earth surface, the mats, the bearers and cross-pieces, and take down the pier. And rebuild it all again.

The sky grew brassy, insects began to chirp in anticipation, and the ring of fleecy clouds all round the horizon gave place to a darker concentration in the south. And the south, it was agreed, was the direction from which the grey-clad enemy would come storming up, under cover of the flash and crash of its aerial barrage.

If the bridge once settled, intact, it should last for many years. If! The river was the unknown quantity. Some said that in flood it ran faster than a galloping pony—which was impossible. Some said it outpaced a walking man.

The showdown came without warning, and at night. The solid rest-house with its massive mud walls shook under the first blow. Keith woke, suspecting an earthquake, since there were volcanic craters only a day's ride to the south. He found himself fighting a clammy, invisible enemy, the mosquito net. As he tore clear, the camp bed lifted and turned over. He stood, gasping under the impact of bucketfuls of icy water that someone seemed to be hurling at him. There was nothing to be done in the roaring darkness. Philosophically he groped for the bed, caught it, righted it, and lay down again on top of the wrecked mosquito net poles. His enamelled basin clattered against a tin uniform case. He heard a distant crash through the uproar, and guessed that his table had been blown away. With the first light of a grey dawn came the imperturbable Momadu and his assistant, bringing morning tea, righting the furniture, and with fallen palm-fronds brushing the pools of water from the hollows in the worn mud floor. Water seemed to have penetrated everything except two uniform cases. The light lid of a chop-box—fortunately not the one with his papers—had blown wide open.

Keith carried his teacup on to the veranda, and sipped standing up to be out of the way. Everything would need to be spread out to dry, and much of the stuff would need washing first. Like a husband during spring-cleaning, he could help in only one way—by removing himself. He called for horse and horse-boy.

Orion slithered and stumbled. Pools glittered where no pools should be, and the rest of the track was slimy laterite clay. Garuba Kano, stripped to his cotton loin-cloth, trotted cursing behind. Bare toes grasping the stirrups, shirtless, sodden shorts squelching on sodden saddle, with felt hat in place of his pith helmet which had looked like a decayed toadstool, Keith found himself beginning to sing. In deference to his horse-boy's feelings he checked himself. But it really was a superb day, rainwashed to a brilliancy that almost hurt the eyes.

Huts seemed deserted. Men, women, and children, with hoes, sticks, and anything else which came to hand, were attacking yesterday's rock-hard soil which could no longer resist them. They raised it in great clods, beat them, tore them apart with bare hands. They were already as red-brown as their fields, and must have been at it since the first glimmering of light. They yelled joyously to each other, and called greetings to Keith.

The near-by bridge site was ominously silent. No drumming, no shouted orders, no bursts of cackling laughter. Though there were dozens of finishing touches still to be done. Prepared, now, for the worst, Keith rode out through the strip of bush which still separated the old road from the new alignment. He reined up and stared. Not a soul in sight. The place was deserted.

But the bridge stood!

Below it swirled a roaring red flood. Debris showed that the flood-water was already dropping. Keith handed over Orion, and scrambled down a slippery bank, gripping with his bare toes. For what mattered most was the sub-structure.

One pier had settled a couple of inches, but all stood upright, intact; and the road bearers of heavy palm trunks ran straight as railway lines from bank to bank.

No longer would Panyam and all Pankshin Division be cut off from the north for days at a time. Traders could come and go with their strings of pack-donkeys without being marooned on one bank or the other waiting for the river to fall. No stranger would be drowned by missing the ford-way and stepping off beyond his depth.

This was no graceful structure, no airy cobweb of a suspension bridge, no tricky cantilever or massy satisfying stone arches striding the water. It was as crude as it was useful, as primitive as the people and tools and local materials which had made it. But it was Keith's own work, and his first material contribution to Africa.

But it was time to stop throwing a chest, and to get back to work. He scrambled up the bank, mounted Orion, and was wiping a cut in his foot with a sodden handkerchief, when the horse-boy said reverently:

' By the power of Allah! '

Keith looked back. What had caught the man's attention was no more than a donkey, strolling down from the north with all a donkey's fixity of purpose. It bore no load, and was alone. It might be searching for better grazing, or just be taking a casual stroll to enjoy the lovely morning. Yet, somehow, it had the air of a man with an important duty to perform. It left the old road, disappeared briefly into the scrub, but came out again on the new approach to the bridge. The loose soil had absorbed the rain like a sponge, and the donkey went in up to the fetlock. It skirted a bad gash of erosion. It came to the end of the embanked approach and set foot on the mud-and-mat decking of the bridge itself. This it seemed to consider unfamiliar, puzzling. It lowered its head and sniffed, as though doubtful. But went on.

Keith gave a grunt of relief. So far his handiwork had passed inspection. It began to seem of supreme importance that this, the first traveller, should find the job adequate.

The red flood swirled below, but the donkey trudged purposefully on. At the dead centre of the bridge it stopped again and hesitated. And for no conceivable reason raised its head and brayed!

'*Dandurinwa!*' Garuba Kano produced his favourite expression. '*Dandurinwa! Dan-dur-in-wa!*' His tone was reverent.

It was exactly fitting. It was perfect. The bridge that Keith built had been declared open to the public . . . by a stray jackass!

Keith had barely finished breakfast when the Sarikin Sura and the other members of the Court arrived. They came in haste, to give and receive congratulations on the ample and timely sowing rains. They dismounted and entered the rest-house. The floor was dark but no longer wet. They sat; they talked eagerly of grain and root crops. They waited. They fidgeted.

Keith thanked them and complimented them on their recent work. And adjourned the Court *sine die*. They ran to their ponies, unhitched the single rope reins, leaped aboard. Last seen the old chief was leading by a full length, his unwound turban streaming out behind him.

Not a soul in the compound. Only the Messengers, immune from the Sura farming fervour, waiting for orders on the veranda. The census was complete so far as the immediate neighbourhood of Panyam was concerned. To try to count further afield would be futile. It would be as easy to chase a swarm of bees back into their hive as drive the Suras back to their houses to be counted.

No doubt about it, the labour market for a sober, honest and industrious assistant district officer was highly seasonal. A few days ago four Ian Keiths and a dozen Messengers could have been profitably employed. Today they were useless.

Just one job remained, and that an unpleasant one.

'Tibn, Anta, Moman, Loshi!' Keith called them in, and sat down at his recovered table, its broken leg propped on a box. 'Sit, for our talk may be long.'

The four seemed mildly puzzled. When he reached into his

office box and took out the census papers, a cautious stirring showed that they began to understand. Tibn smiled blandly, and courteously drew the hem of his robe over an exposed toe. Anta frowned, but less belligerently than usual. Loshi glanced over at Tibn, as though waiting for a lead. Moman plucked nervously at his long sleeves, the very picture of guilt.

Basically not bad types. Curse Pettibone for letting them get out of hand! No one could accuse Pettibone of taking a penny of tax money, but his slackness made him almost an accessory before the fact. It was he who should be called to account, not these Messengers.

'It is known to you all that you have counted less than the real number of villagers. You have said that this is because the men hide.'

'The Judge,' Tibn used the formal title, 'Speaks truth, and is merciful.'

'Each man is merciful to himself, and the excuse is yours, not mine,' Keith reminded him. 'But why do more men hide from Tibn and Anta than from Loshi and Moman—three times as many?'

An uneasy silence fell.

'You have no answer? Could it be that Loshi and Moman leave men out of the count by accident, but Tibn and Anta leave them out on purpose? Could their intention be to share the extra money with the village head who collects from all?'

Anta made to rise, but Tibn's hand on his sleeve restrained him. Restrained his rising, but not his outburst.

'Mister Petbo shall be told of this! The Greater Judge is not yet gone. I will take horse and ride to Pankshin, and tell him all!'

Keith checked his own impatience. 'Mister Petbo shall certainly be told, and you shall go to Pankshin this day to answer to my complaint. There is another question which you and Tibn shall answer. Why, when I set one of you to recount the other's count, do you get the same total, though the villagers whom one man leaves out are not the same men that the other left out before?'

It was easy to guess the reason. They had no time to copy out complete lists, and had just made the totals agree. The beauty of it was that it showed clear intent to embezzle. No witnesses would be needed. The lists, in their own handwriting, would convict them.

'That is all. Perhaps it is better that all four go to Pankshin. Loshi and Moman may carry the papers, one guarding the other. The package will be sealed.' There would have to be a covering letter. Keith lifted out his portable from the box. 'Report to me when you are ready to ride.'

Tibn pulled a surprise. The other three were already on their feet when he leaned forward and pressed his head to the floor in the conventional gesture of submission and repentance.

'My wrongdoing is bared, my folly known.'

'The wrongdoing awaits proof in Court,' Keith pointed out. 'It is Mister Petbo, the Greater Judge, to whom you shall say "This I did" or "This I did not do."'

'But you, *Ba-ture*, are now the Greater Judge!' The brown patch of dirt on Tibn's blue-black forehead bore witness to his earnestness. 'Let the *Ba-ture* himself punish the wrong we have done to him.'

Now the other three were kneeling beside Tibn, their brows, too, patched with brown dirt from the floor. 'We repent! Let the *Ba-ture* himself give judgment!' they intoned in chorus.

Tibn's addressing him as the 'Greater Judge' was useless flattery. This was Pettibone's division. The Messengers were Pettibone's. Except for Moman Wanti, who was a precarious survivor from an earlier régime, they had been appointed by Pettibone. This was Pettibone's job.

'Waste no time, or darkness will fall before you reach Pankshin, and flood-waters lie in your way.' Keith spoke more curtly than usual. Why in heaven's name should he feel sorry for them? They had been warned twice. They had chosen to ignore the warning, and had been caught. That was all.

Chapter Six

HE put it to Momadu that evening. The low sun on the west side of the rest-house had turned bedroom and court-dining-room into a steam bath. Momadu had arranged table and chair in the shadow of the east side, where Keith could drip sweat in comparative comfort and await the usual sunset breeze.

'Momadu, when a man has a task to do and does not do it, is he not a worthless fellow?'

Spotless in his white robe and red fez, Momadu considered the glass which he had poured. It was courteous of Keeta to say it in this way, as one asking for advice, not angrily shouting. It was for this that in Bauchi he had been named Mailafia, the Calm One.

'The *Ba-ture* has cause for complaint. We do not do our duty. Is not the sparklet bottle broken so there is no longer soda? Is not the water like mud between the toes? Because of the sowing rains the Chief of the Virgins has run to his farm, and the water-girls, being young and careless . . .'

'There is no blame as to the girls, or the water they bring.' Keith drank a little of his clouded whisky and water. 'But the rains! By the grace of Allah the Bridge of the Donkey is finished, for there are no longer labourers; and the counting is finished, for the villages are empty; and the complaints finished, for the Sarikin Sura and his lesser Great Ones have fled as though pursued by Eblis!'

One waited, forbearing to say that Mailafia should now sit a little, shoot a little, and read a little, until called to his new greatness. Being no longer troubled by such worthless ones.

'We, of our household, are left with no hoes to our hands, no seed, no lands.' Mailafia spoke softly, for that was always his way. 'Useless as handless lepers, begging at the gate of a walled city.'

54

Thus it was with the master of the household when sleep was denied to him. Angered, not at others but at himself; thrusting sharp words into himself, as some holy men thrust thorns. His night would be one of waiting, perhaps for that *Ba-turia* of Naraguta, who had run from him after her husband had died. In the morning little oil would be left in his lamp, and his mosquito boots would show the dust of roads and market-place.

One had pity for his folly, and, since he listened, tobacco unlighted, one spoke to him of the horsemen and warriors of old, whom the rains sent back from their wars. For when the air and the soil grew damp after the long waiting, they raised their noses and, tasting in memory the scent of their own lands—like to no other lands, being home—turned aside their lance-points and wheeled their horses, even in the midst of battle.

One spoke till one's ankles itched, till it became needful to rub each with the sole of the other foot. But at last, not being a woman, one fell silent.

Mailafia said 'There is at times a black dog upon my back, which none but I can see. You have driven it away. My thanks to you for your kindness.'

One gave thanks in return for thanks, as was proper. But as to the black dog, that was doubtless a jest. One saw to it that the whisky was sufficient, that the bottle of water was full, and that the earthen cooling pots in which they stood were damp to the breeze. And went one's way. Wondering, now that it was known that Petbo was to go, why Mailafia did not ride forthwith to Pankshin, and seize the power which was rightfully his. And put chains upon the ankles of false Messengers and others that troubled him. But one reflected 'to each beggar his own lice, to each man his own folly'.

Keith lighted his pipe, and poured himself another drink. Drink, sex, and Pettibone. A difficult trinity to handle. Keeping them nicely balanced against each other was like a juggling act.

To consider Pettibone first . . .

But here came the more amusing water-girls. A little late this evening in bringing the supply of water from the stream. Swaying their bare slender bodies more than was really necessary to

55

balance the clay jars on their heads. Wagging their small behinds, brushing a splash of water from a hopefully forming breast. Adolescent, and very conscious of their bodies. Showing off, in fact.

Six of them, the usual dark-skinned beauty chorus, who put on two shows a day. The bleary old man, ambiguously known as the Chief of the Virgins, who usually shepherded and chaperoned them, was absent. The rains meant springtime, the time of courtship, and set roving six pairs of dark, glinting eyes. The girls drew closer to Keith and his chair. Their gait stiffened, and with eyes averted they passed, demure as débutantes.

Splashing told of water being poured into the tall storage jars outside the kitchen hut. Keith had not turned his head to watch. There was no point in putting added strain on good resolutions.

They filed past again, six straight supple backs, twelve long slender legs . . . remarkably long legs, it seemed, since they were too young to wear the drum-stick-and-string girdle of the married woman. A coil of ochre-stained cord hung at each left hip, the making of the future wedding gown.

They had come a little closer, less awed by the strangeness of a white man. As they would return with another load of water from the stream, Keith felt that it might be a good idea to occupy his thoughts with something else. Not that he was afraid of them, just cautious.

Pettibone should once more serve as a counter-irritant. Set one obsession against another, that was the trick. Divide your emotions and conquer them.

Not once had the man ridden over to inspect progress. Not once had he offered a comment. In return for Keith's progress reports and weekly pay vouchers he had sent the necessary money. That was all. Perhaps that was just as well, but . . .

Damn! Here came the water-girls again, chattering and giggling. Then, at a signal from their leader, growing silent and sedate.

The leading four had straws through their upper lips, the equivalent of engagement rings, to boast that a suitor had already made a down-payment on them. The leader, a little older than the others, deliberately changed direction to pass close to Keith's chair. Her areolae rose like little breasts upon larger ones. As she came near she pinched her nipples to make them stand out further, as a Victorian woman used to bite her lips to lend them fullness before entering a drawing-room. The straw through her upper lip dipped and rose and swung, beating time to her long stride.

They passed, the leader brushing his elbow with her boyish thigh. He found himself flaring out his nostrils and sniffing, as Orion did when a mare passed. Being near to nature it was pounds to pence that the girls scented his need too, as mares did when a stallion was heated.

Renewed giggling accompanied the splashing of more water into the storage jars, and Sam's querulous voice demanded in bad Hausa that they bring still another load of water, so that the mud might have time to settle before morning.

They repassed without incident. They wouldn't have the ghost of a notion what Sam had told them. Anyway, the sun was nearly down, and they would be in a hurry to get back to their village before the men and boys returned from the fields. No risk of their returning tonight, and tomorrow and any following evenings Keith intended to be out shooting until after dark.

Far off to the west a drummer tried a few tentative notes. The villagers could scarcely be home from their hard but joyous day on the land, or have had time to eat; yet one of them was already testing his drum-head. Blast the man! You would think that now the rains had come the people would have no time or energy left for that sort of thing.

A slow steady beat, like the pounding of corn. *Turumi da tabaria*, pestle-and-mortar, the jesting name for copulation. Pettibone was right to prohibit drumming. Keith was a bloody fool. But Pettibone was a louse, a stinkard. . . .

Don't mix up sex and hatred. Use one against the other. If you can't, latch on to the last thing you thought of, and switch to that. . . . The leading girl's lip-straw.

Admit freely that it's a phallic symbol, but treat it purely from the viewpoint of anthropology.

An accepted Sura suitor, in the villages where they had adopted

57

marriage by purchase, set his mark upon his bride-to-be. Whether she liked it or not, he thrust a thorn through her upper lip, and made her keep it there. When the puncture healed he whittled a small peg to stretch the hole enough to hold a straw, or whatever was the fashion in that area. Around Naraguta fashion decreed a polished six-inch nail.

The Pakara people, and particularly the people across the border in French Ubangui-Chad, went to extremes. The first piercing was done with a knife-point and through both lips, and the eager lover kept on inserting bigger and bigger wooden discs to add to the charms of his charmer. Until the distorted lips would rim a good-sized saucer, or rather two. The girl could still eat, after a fashion, or smoke a pipe out of the corner of her mouth if she held the two discs together. But she could not talk. At least none but another Pakara woman could understand her.

It was ornament, of course, *la mode*, like ear-rings. Or few women would have submitted to the process. But it had a further significance. The lips and the *labia* are sexually associated. Only the man who had the right to pierce the former had the right to penetrate the latter. The straw was a symbolic phallus.

And now forget it. File it among less erotic and disturbing practices, such as native burial customs, the sacrifice of sacred kings, or ancestor worship being centralized into what almost amounted to monotheism. And hoes, which varied as much as weapons from tribe to tribe. Now there was an interesting subject. . . .

Oh no! Not the water-girls again!

They lingered, whispering, some seeming to urge the others on. A sharp slap on bare flesh, and a squeak. Their leader enforcing obedience to some new prank she had in mind. She was the kind who would get herself into trouble in any country, from sheer exuberant vitality.

There was something different about their stride, as they advanced. Each had a waterpot on her head. But it was no more than a pretext for another visit, for it must be empty, or it would have slopped over to the dancing step. They were excited, no doubt a little frightened, but scarcely able to keep straight faces. Their attention was on their flauntingly inviting leader, flickering only briefly to Keith.

That ripe young wanton at their head aimed straight at the strange white man. Aimed her whole body, her breasts like the twin muzzles of a highwayman's pistols that ordered 'stand and deliver!'

She must have delayed down by the stream to break off a length of reed. It was far too large for the hole in her upper lip, and the flesh strained up on either side. In time to her swaying dance she waggled the foot-long wand. Not casually as before. With her tongue against the inside tip she swung it like a drum-major's baton, up and down, across and in circles, to catch Keith's eye.

The earlier straw might have been an invitation. This big stiff reed, which drew ever closer to Keith's chair, was a demand. It was more, it was confident expectation, based on the odour of desire her eager young nose had caught when she brushed against his elbow.

The brown beauty chorus, breathing quickly, eyes alight with mischief in the last gleam of the afterglow, penned Keith in. They thrust flat little bellies at him, and overhung him with breasts, round, conical, pearshaped or flat as saucers. While that accursed section of reed, thrust so tightly through the head-wanton's lips, mocked him, challenged his manhood.

Now it ceased waggling and snapped decisively erect, pressed against a small snub-nose. Symbolism could go no further!

Keith called 'Momadu!', and again 'Momadu!', his first attempt being inaudible.

The note of appeal brought the house-boy at a run. He stopped at sight of the clustering water-girls, and advanced slowly, as though reluctantly.

'The *Ba-ture* needs . . . ?'

'Those who have brought water during these many days deserve reward. Let the money be brought. Here are the keys.'

Momadu took his time. Expectancy, and the heady odour of young excited female flesh encompassed Keith in a hunting net of desire. He reached for the whisky bottle, the only deliverance in sight, blindly poured himself a half glass of neat water by mistake, and gulped it down. That didn't matter. Momadu had arrived.

'Let the girls line up, so that I do not pay the same one twice and leave another unrewarded.'

He watched, with admiration, Momadu's casual handling of the enticing bare flesh, as with friendly shoves he got them into position. But of course Momadu had a wife, a charming little creature, also a bitter shrew. And she might be watching.

Keith knew himself for a coward, since he dealt with the youngest girl first. He put silver riches in her hand. She transferred the threepences to her mouth for safe-keeping. After all she had no pockets. He came at last to the leader. Smiling she took the small coins. Still smiling she plucked the reed from her lip and handed it to Keith. She placed one of the threepenny bits in his hand, and pointed to her lip.

He knew what she wanted, and could not help himself. At his first attempt the coin seemed far too large to insert. He could get it half in, that was all. He wet his little finger, thrust it through her lip hole, stretching it to unvirginal size, painfully no doubt, as on the marriage bed. The girl's slender arms, one fist holding the other coins, pressed Keith closer. He forced the coin in, with cruel delight. It held.

The arms about him relaxed. The girl fingered her distended lip to satisfy herself that the token of the man she coveted was secure. With a glance, as a hostess collects ladies from the dinner table, she led away her band of mischievous adolescents.

Keith pulled himself together. 'I will eat dinner, Momadu, when it is ready. Afterwards, since there are no Messengers to do this, I will go to the village and seek carriers. Our work here is finished. We will return to Pankshin. Tonight, if the carriers are willing.'

It could be seen that one had misjudged Mailafia. He desired power more than women. Still women were good. Power was a thorny growth to lie upon, but women . . . !

Chapter Seven

From half-way up Pankshin hill, Gofwan watched the Panyam road. It was unlikely that Mister Petbo's message had reached Keeta before dark last night, and carriers would be difficult to find after the first rains had fallen. But if Keeta—one must remember to think of him as Mister Keeta now—desired carriers, carriers he would get. For that was his way.

It was barely dawn, yet he could be seen, riding alone, and far out on the plain. One would have ridden to meet him, to show him honour, but for fear of Petbo's anger. Instead one would make sure that the wood and water, which one had caused to be set in the rest-house last night—secretly, for fear of Petbo—had not been stolen, and that goats had not sheltered in the bedroom.

Thus it was that one had become head Messenger. Thus it was that one would remain head Messenger. Through knowing when to spread thorns underfoot and when soft carpets.

After a little he came, his nose thrusting forward, his troubling grey eyes drawn back into his head by reason of weariness. Also he was still wet from the night's rain. Yet he slung a leg lightly over his stallion's head, and dropped without stiffness to the ground. And said:

'Greetings, Gofwan! You rise early.'

Giving one opportunity to say, after greetings, 'It would be wrong if the *Ba-ture* should again find welcome lacking, as chanced on his first coming.'

'"Chanced", Gofwan?' he asked. And gave his discomfiting smile.

One walked silently behind him up the hill. But contrived that, when within sight of the other Messengers coming to meet him down the office steps, he should be answering one's enquiry as to the coming of the rains to Panyam. It was right that all should see that one was already close to the ear of the new Greater Judge. Then one slipped aside, lest Petbo glance out through the office door.

Keith could detect no change, except in the attitude of the Messengers. Anta and Tibn were still at large, but that was to be expected, as they had probably arrived after the office closed last night. The only change was in Pettibone. Sitting behind his table he actually volunteered a 'Good morning, Captain Keith.'

A moment now, and he would want to know why the devil Keith had dared to come in without orders. Keith returned a 'Good morning, sir.' And waited.

Pettibone passed the usual lady-like hand over his auburn hair, which was as long as ever. Mr Ferguson McTavish's typewriter clicked spasmodically in the filing room. Tibn was chewing kola nut as usual. All was as before.

'You come very promptly, Captain Keith. I sent for you only yesterday. You must have ridden all night, all night.'

So Pettibone had ordered him to come in. Good. That might save a lot of trouble.

'Until my successor comes, you will have to serve as stop-gap. I leave for Zaria tomorrow.'

'For long? Local leave or something?' It would be grand to hold the reins for a week or two, and find out how a division was actually run. Pankshin Division in particular.

'I have been appointed Station Magistrate in Zaria. You will take over from me here, against my wishes. The two cash-books are closed and balanced. The handing-over certificate is ready for you to sign.' Divisional Officer Pankshin rose from his seat, as though physically vacating his office to Keith, dipped his pen in the inkpot, and held it out.

The two cash-books, one for the local treasury the other for the Native Administration, had been ruled off, and Pettibone had written in his large ornate hand that he had transferred the balances to Keith. Keith had only to sign and accept the keys. The handing-over certificate, a long typewritten sheet of foolscap, was more like a legal conveyance. All Keith had to do was write his short name three times, adding the date, and Pettibone's official tyranny would be over. At least for the present.

'I'll check the cash first. Thirty thousand pounds is a lot of money.' The check was standard routine. 'And I'd like to see your Situation Report on the division.'

'Nonsense, my dear man!' Pettibone still proffered the pen. 'There's no time or need to write a situation summary. You will only be in charge for a few days. A more senior man will then take over, and he won't need it.'

Of course he would need it. And blame Keith for not getting one from his predecessor. Summaries were needed to bring a newcomer up-to-date on such matters as how the tax was coming in, how much of the estimates had been spent, the state of the prison, the courts, and all public works from houses to roads to tools on charge. They ensured continuity of policy, as well as warning a newcomer what was most urgent.

Keith pulled out his pipe and began to fill it. The tobacco in the oilskin case was none the worse for last night's downpour.

'As you know, Captain Keith, I allow no smoking in my office.'

'It isn't your office any longer, or your division. You've signed them away. It isn't my office or my division, as I haven't signed any receipt for them.' The matches in the screwtop box were also dry. The first one lighted. Keith puffed a moment. 'It's a puzzling situation, and calls for a little thought. Like an interregnum in the old days when a king died. No writs were lawful, no one had authority to collect revenue, and in theory the whole machinery of government stopped like a clock.'

'I warn you, Captain Keith. I will tolerate no . . .'

'The divisional officer's chair doesn't belong to either of us now.' Keith was enjoying this. 'Shall we play musical chairs, walking round the table till the typewriter stops clicking, then make a dash to claim the throne?'

'I shall report you for this!'

'Do. But don't forget to mention that you asked me to take over from you blind, without any check. We'll examine the books and counterfoils first, cash later.

Pettibone picked up his hat and left.

Keith missed breakfast. His carriers wouldn't be here for hours, and he was too busy to drop across to Garrard's bungalow and be sociable.

Messengers hastened back and forth from Mr McTavish's office. Piles of dusty counterfoils and vouchers grew tall upon the table, were whittled down, and grew again.

Back to the rest-house for lunch, accompanied by the solicitous Gofwan, who wished to ensure that the household had all that they needed and that all the carriers had arrived. While Keith was eating, a warm invitation came from Garrard, asking Keith to a farewell dinner in Pettibone's honour. He refused, pleading work.

Then back to the office. In the hot afternoon, as a relief from figures, Keith delved into reports, returns, and correspondence, jotting down questions he would have to ask in lieu of the usual Situation Report. He was tired and sleepy after his first meal since dinner in Panyam. Also, now the rains had come, the office was a steam-bath. Reading was an effort, concentration painful, and the reports seemed stupid and irritating. That was only subjective, of course. Normally reports were amusing, intentionally or otherwise.

The briefest on record in the Bauchi Provincial Office files had been written by the present Resident when he was a junior. It dated back to around 1900 or earlier, when an officer was dumped ashore from a river-boat to ride vaguely up country and crack down on slave-raiding, tribal warfare and other popular sports.

Encountered roving band of Fulani horsemen in June last year. Took lance-thrust in knee but managed to unhorse and capture their leader. My down-country soldiers had run without firing a shot. The Fulani leader, Osman Baki, courteously lent me his horsemen to round up my deserters. An excellent fellow, and so is his Emir. Then, rather as an afterthought. *New area brought under administration about thirty thousand square miles and a quarter million people. Excellent site for a polo ground outside walls of city.* And a request for sticks and polo balls.

Pettibone's reports suffered by comparison. The trouble with Pettibone was that he seemed to think he owned Pankshin. 'My division' and 'My command' were wearisomely reiterated. If a chief gave trouble, a village was late with its tax, or a little armed robbery occurred, it was seen as a personal affront to Pettibone. On the other hand he took personal credit for a cattle-thief being brought before him for trial, and even, it seemed, for last year's good crops.

Dazed with lack of sleep, heat, and his recent meal, Keith scratched his armpits and crotch, hoped that he wasn't starting prickly-heat, and tried to understand. Not just condemn.

Jumped immediately into a position of power and responsibility by war-time shortage of officials, Pettibone had developed a swollen head. That could happen to anybody. Pankshin, and previous divisons of which he had been given charge, had become part of his extended ego. *L'Etat c'est Moi!* That sort of thing.

Pankshin, remote from his Resident, where there were no wise old Emirs or Mohammedan judges against whom he could measure his ability, had brought Pettibone's self-importance into lush blossom. As he loved himself, so he loved his extended self, Pankshin. Sex-hungry like everyone else out here, he had indulged himself with local girls. But they were only his occasional concubines. Pankshin was his bride.

There were clear indications of this in his quarterly reports, in phrases which separately meant little, but by repetition became significant, and collectively were enlightening. 'Administratively virgin country' described the Closed Area of Kulere. 'The marriage of production to distribution' was his explanation of building the ambitious Panyam to Pankshin road last year. 'She' and 'her' recurred semi-poetically when referring to the division. There was a lush passage which began 'Comely and blushing as a Venus Anadyomene, the Angas peak rose through a sea of pearly mist to greet me'.

Keith stretched, and looked around the darkening office. And whistled softly as the picture dawned on him.

To Pettibone, in this queer state of mind, had come Ian Keith, officially appointed to minister to the needs of Pettibone's harem.

And now Pettibone was forced to leave his seraglio and hand it over to a triumphant rival!

Whew!

'With permission!' The horse-boy, Garuba Kano presented himself. 'Shall drink and light be brought to the *Ba-ture*? Or will the *Ba-ture* return?'

'The *Ba-ture* will return, since a bath is even more needed than drink or lantern.'

The household at the foot of the hill was in a state of suppressed excitement. Messengers' wives had come to cultivate the acquaintance of the women. They brought news that authority had now passed from Petbo, and tomorrow Keeta would dwell in the big house. Keith neither confirmed nor denied. He bathed, changed, drank and ate sparingly, topped up with two cups of coffee, and went back to work. To the tedious auditing he had shirked all afternoon.

By ten o'clock the list of minor errors had grown long. In pencil in the cash-book Keith entered up eleven refunds Pettibone would have to make, and three sums due to him. The net balance he would have to pay in was less than thirteen pounds; but it showed that, despite the excellence of his other office work, Pettibone was an irresponsible treasurer.

At eleven o'clock, when he was hoping to go home, Keith made the shattering discovery. The Native Administration treasury, which receives half the tax, and pays local salaries and expenses, had transferred one hundred pounds in cash to the government treasury to buy a treasury draft. The draft had been sent off to purchase road tools, red cloth for the uniforms of tribal police, and other things. But the government cash-book showed no receipt of the hundred pounds paid by the Native Administration. Where was the money?

Sodden with fatigue Keith slept gloriously. Neither Miriamu nor the Panyam water-girl approached his camp-bed. Nor did he hear the rain, nor the carriers going up the hill shortly before dawn to pick up Pettibone's loads.

Fee . . . fi-fi, fee . . . fi-fi, fee . . . fi-fi, the whistle of the carriers returning loaded woke him long after sunrise. He gulped his tepid tea, scooped out some pawpaw and swallowed it, dressed, mounted and rode hastily to office.

Escorted by Gofwan and the head warder, five prisoners in their scanty black and white uniforms carried in five padlocked cash-tanks. The native treasury money, kept apparently in the prison. At one minute to seven Pettibone arrived, smart in well-cut riding breeches, uniform jacket and highly polished boots and spurs. He laid a hunting-crop on the office table beside his sun-helmet and a small bag of money.

He gave Gofwan the keys to unlock the cash-tanks and told Keith 'Check, if you like.'

'While I'm verifying the N.A. cash, take a look at the government treasury cash-book,' Keith suggested. 'You'll find a few adjustments.'

Keith checked the seals on the money-bags, and weighed them. The packets of notes took longer. Gofwan and Moman Wanti counted and stacked odd sums. The job took half an hour. Keith locked the cash-tanks, pocketed the keys, sent the prisoners off with the money, and signed the Native Administration cash-book.

Pettibone had inked in Keith's figures in the Government cash-book and was now signing the corresponding vouchers which Mr Ferguson McTavish had prepared for him. Presumably he had paid in the missing thirteen pounds as his small bag of money looked smaller, and the safe door was open. He took up a ruler, to strike another balance.

'Don't do that yet,' Keith warned. 'There's another error. A more serious one.'

'I warn you again, Captain Keith! I have delayed my departure as long as possible, in the hope that my relief might arrive before I leave. Any further obstruction on your part may make me miss the Tuesday train at Railhead, and I shall hold you accountable.'

'You keep the treasury draft-book in the strong-room, I imagine. Check it with your cash-book. Perhaps you owe the government a hundred pounds.' Keith put matches and tobacco back into his pocket, and picked up his hat.

Keith breakfasted as usual in the rest-house. He received Momadu's report that the divisional officer's house looked like a

67

village square after market day, gave permission to engage four women and send them to brush it out, shaved, and set off up the damned hill again, hoping it would be for the last time.

Tibn, Anta and Loshi were missing, presumably sent by Pettibone as escort to his carriers. Gofwan and Moman Wanti whispered excitedly outside the office. They stopped when they saw Keith. Pettibone was in the strong-room. It was a safe bet that he had found no time to breakfast with anyone. Being Pettibone, he still wore tie and jacket, but the tie was awry, and the jacket sweated through. He turned on Keith, as he must have turned on his Messengers.

'I don't know what trick you've played on me . . .'

'Don't be a damned fool, Pettibone. I was playing tennis at Eastbourne on the day you took the hundred out of the N.A. treasury and forgot to put it into the strong-room.'

'I'll make you suffer for this some day!'

The sound of trotting hooves, the creak of saddlery, and Garrard and young Yeats strode in. Garrard as square and red-faced as Keith had remembered him, Yeats tall, eager, and ingenuous.

'Me, I prefer a board on medical stores every time,' Garrard announced. 'The M.O. can usually be trusted to condemn a doubtful bottle of champagne or brandy for the board to test. You look as though you could do with a spot yourself, Pettibone.'

Pettibone straightened his tie. 'I'm in rather a hurry to get off.'

'My levity is suitably reproved! Come on, Yeats. You call out what's on the labels, and see that the bags are correctly sealed. I'll tick 'em off on the register. Be through in ten minutes, Pettibone.'

Keith sat down and lit his pipe. This was going to be interesting.

'Half crowns and florins all correct by book.' Shortly it was 'Shillings all correct.'

Those were the denominations usually bagged by the hundred pound. Still, Pettibone might have overlooked two bags of sixpences.

'Sixpences and threepences all correct.'

68

Smaller coins held out no hope. A hundred pounds' worth of tenths of pennies, for instance, would be twenty carrier loads. Bundles of currency notes were checked twice. A slight pause.

'Register agrees with contents of strong-room, and this is duly attested by the valuable autographs of A. W. Garrard and T. S. Yeats.' Garrard reported. 'And now for the petty cash in the safe. I hope there's a surplus we can pocket.'

Before the Messengers replaced the money-bags Keith strolled over to glance into the strong-room. It held a stack of 'Secret and Confidential' files, a cable code book, the treasury draft-book, a case of obsolete ammunition, and a brass-bound musket probably confiscated from some long-forgotten murderer. No hiding place for a hundred pounds on the concrete-lined walls or the bare shelves.

'Dullest damned board I've ever sat on.' Garrard picked up his riding switch. 'No wine improperly stored in the strong-room, no dirty postcards in the safe. Nothing worth confiscating. Anything else we can do?'

'You might take the keys of the strong-room and the safe.' Keith saw no reason to run uncalled for risks. 'Pettibone has handed over, but I haven't taken over yet.'

'Puzzling, damned puzzling. I'll roll along tomorrow and pay my official respects, Keith, old man. Well, good-bye Pettibone.' He held out his hand.

The office was empty, except for Pettibone, Keith and the two Messengers. Mr Ferguson McTavish, fearing a last-minute rush of work, had already reported sick and left.

'Gofwan, please see if Mr Pettibone's bungalow has been swept. If it has, carry word to my household in the rest-house.' That disposed of one witness to what might become an unseemly brawl. 'Moman Wanti, please go to the Hausa settlement, and find carriers to move my loads up the hill.'

'Well?' the late king demanded.

'If we close the books before you refund that hundred pounds, you're done for. Surely you've heard of auditors?'

'Naturally! In my seven years service, while you were playing soldiers . . .' Pettibone checked himself. 'What do you suggest?'

'Before I stick out my neck I'd like to know what you did with the money.'

The story, punctuated with 'Of course it's impossible to keep strictly to regulations' was typical of Pettibone. Once a week he had balanced his two cash-books, on paper. 'About once a month' he had counted his cash, and assumed that any surplus was due to him for carriers or allowances which he had entered up but not drawn against. The King's Privy Purse!

There was a flaw in the story. No one at Pankshin could spend a hundred pounds in one month. Obviously Pettibone hadn't counted his cash as often as that, though it was supposed to be checked at least weekly. But the confession rang true. As a whole.

'All right. I'll take your word for it.' And Keith, not Pettibone, would have to assume responsibility from now on. 'Your future line will have to be that the board discovered a surplus bag of shillings in the strong-room, and you remembered that it was the N.A. money for the treasury draft. So you now enter up the receipt in the Government cash-book, as you ought to have done before. Of course you'll get a stinker about it when the first auditor comes along. But carelessness isn't as bad as embezzlement. Now all we need is the money.'

Keith gave up his chair. Pettibone sat down once more, smoothed his long hair with a sweaty, dusty hand, tested the pen-nib on the blotter, and made the necessary entry in his florid handwriting.

Pettibone got up, and handed the pen to Keith. 'And now, of course, you'll sign. Naturally I don't carry a hundred pounds about with me, but I have an account with a bank in Railhead. I'll send you the money just as soon as I can catch up with my cheque-book. I'll send Anta with it tonight.'

'I'll take a certified cheque, a cashier's cheque, or hard cash.'

Pettibone frowned. Then changed his mind and laughed. 'But my dear fellow, that's quite impossible! At the moment I doubt if I have even five pounds in my account.'

'You mean . . .' Keith took a breath. 'You mean you would have given me a dud cheque, or' suspicion grew 'not even have sent it, and left me holding the baby?'

70

'I find your suspicions insulting, yes insulting. And coming from a junior officer . . .'

'I'll probably regret this all my life, Pettibone, but I'll give you one more chance. Sell off your kit at Railhead, borrow from friends if you have any, or get an overdraft from your bank.'

'You mean that you'll sign the books?'

'I'll hold up the handing-over papers and certificates for two whole weeks. If you haven't sent me the hundred pounds by then I'll be forced to ask the Resident for instructions, explaining that I can't take charge of the division without a Court of Enquiry being held.'

'I still think you're being damned fussy.'

'Get out, before I change my mind. Out!'

Pettibone gathered up his sun-helmet, small bag of change, and useless hunting-crop. He offered no thanks to his rescuer.

For appearance' sake Keith saw him to the steps, and watched him mount. Pettibone looked round as though expecting touching farewells from his courtiers. But Gofwan and Moman had wisely failed to return.

He risked a final threat. 'There's one thing you forget, Captain Keith. Some day you may be forced to serve under me again.'

Chapter Eight

MUD-BUILT like the office, in what might be called 'Pankshin Palladian' style, the divisional officer's quarters were positively luxurious. The walls and floor were in good repair. There were even wooden shutters to the window-holes, and outside doors which could be closed against intrusive goats or impulsive murderers.

Momadu, very tidy in his red fez and spotless white robe, practically pranced on his stocky legs as he led a personally conducted tour.

'This, with the *Ba-ture*'s permission, is the room where a visitor, a friend of the *Ba-ture*, may sleep. A cloth should be bought to hang across the doorway.

'Here is the place where food may be put on plates, and also the plates washed. And here the small room with a lock where the chop-boxes may be put.'

A few of the better trophies, too old to be Pettibone's, were missing from the walls of the main room. No matter.

'The *Ba-ture*'s own boxes I have placed in the bedroom, with the guns.'

The bedroom, too, had to be seen and approved. It was a large room with two entrances from the dining-room. At one end were four deep alcoves, like bunks on board ship, two of which Momadu had used as shelves. A home-made washstand with Keith's washing gear on it. Also the travelling bath, emptied of clothes, and waiting to be filled. The camp-bed was already set up. And, wonder of wonders, a massive double bed, springless of course, but furnished with a full-sized bat-stained mattress. Both beds had been prepared, mats laid beside them, and chop-boxes to serve as tables.

'Have I in only one day become so great that one bed will not suffice me?'

Momadu gave a short rumble of amusement. 'The big bed is more suited to the *Ba-ture*'s greatness. But the small net is not suited to the big bed, and what do insects know of the *Ba-ture*'s greatness? Therefore the camp-bed and net have also been prepared.'

'And the household?' Pettibone might have seen to his own comfort, but neglected the servants' quarters out back.

'*Ba-ture*, it is like a small village, lacking only a market-place! The cook-house, two stables, the hut of Maigona the gardener whom the other *Ba-ture* left behind, and six more huts. Also a large *itili* tree, in whose shade the women may spin and talk in hot weather. And the well holds much water. And a storehouse for corn, which I had forgotten.'

'Tomorrow I will see if any roofs need repair. Let bath water be brought, also the drinks. And give my thanks to the household. They have worked hard today.'

It was a grand feeling, and a curious one. Like a home-coming; though there was no conceivable reason why it should seem so. The last and only time he had been here he had angrily walked out of Pettibone's dinner party.

He heard lamp and the bottles being set down in the dining-room. He sauntered out, and poured himself the first drink of the evening. And strolled about, puzzling over the phenomenon. Why should this particular place feel as though it had been waiting for him? Why did some muddled emotion suggest to him that for eight years he had wandered about trying to reach this one spot in place and time, and had at last attained some kind of spiritual haven?

A pail of water passed, and then a large sooty kettle of hot water, their bearer Salifu, a gangling, dull-witted youth in a grimy robe and perpetual daze, whom Momadu had engaged as his assistant this tour.

Keith wandered in, set down lamp and glass on a box beside the bath, stripped and folded himself into the cramped space. And reached out for *l'Illustration*, a new copy of which Momadu had set in readiness. The water was warm and soothing, the clock-work lamp hummed steadily. Perfect.

The routine when on tour is to change into pyjamas each night. In the station into tomorrow's clean white office linen. Keith added the inevitable mosquito boots and migrated back with lamp and empty glass to the dining-room.

Momadu appeared, though it was scarcely time for dinner yet. He shifted from foot to foot. Being at soul a perfectionist, in a land of rough makeshift he worried too much. After his beaming triumph at taking possession of the big house, he would be more sensitive than usual to some minor household upset.

Keith tried to help him out. 'The tap of the filter has been left running and there is no more drinking water? No? Then Salifu has broken another cup. No matter. If we grow angry his hands will fear, and he will drop yet more.'

'It is not Salifu, though indeed his hands are as the feet of a *dorina*, a hippopotamus.' Momadu hesitated again. 'It is a trader from Bauchi. He is outside. He begs that you will hear him.'

'Since the man comes from afar, let him not climb the hill in vain. Bid him enter.'

Momadu's legs seemed to approve as he hastened out through the pantry. His legs were the most eloquent part of him. When his flighty little wife misbehaved, or quarrelled with him, he shambled, flat-footed. When angry he stamped along, stiff-kneed. Serving dinner he was a one-man ecclesiastical procession. He had a purposeful stalk when he harried his assistant, or silently nagged Keith into leaving his official papers and eating dinner.

Keith wound up the clockwork drive which blew air through the lamp. It was rather a neat invention, as it dispensed with the easily broken glass chimney.

A rustle at the front door as the trader shuffled out of his sandals. He entered; he made deep obeisance, one hand to the floor, and intoned 'Peace be unto you!'

'And unto you the Peace! Rise, and tell me the cause of your coming, for it is already late.'

An ill-wound turban and shabby purple gown suggested that the complaint would be trifling, which probably meant that it would be wearisome and long. An unclean beard, possibly grey by nature, showing above the chin-loop of the turban, and bleary eyes which shifted furtively about the dining-room, added no dignity to the man's poverty.

A woman entered close behind him. Engulfed by her shapeless indigo-dyed outer garment, with a corner of her headcloth drawn as a veil across her face, only her eyes and one hand were visible. She curtsyed gracefully after the Hausa manner, and her movements suggested that she was young, possibly the old man's daughter or granddaughter.

'Sit then, and let your tale be told.' Keith added water to his whisky, and prepared to be patient.

'By permission of the Judge, my name is Iesufu. I was born in Gombe, but have bought and sold for many years in Bauchi market.' The man was almost toothless, and his mumbling difficult to follow. 'Hearing that by the Grace of Allah the *Ba-ture*, whose wisdom and power are known to all, had gone to Pankshin . . .'

The girl leaned forward, and tapped her companion on the shoulder. 'My thanks, Iesufu, for your services. Accept what was agreed upon, and go.'

Mumbling his thanks to the girl, and parting salutations to the Judge, the man left. Without having stated his complaint. If the girl was the defendant, and had paid the man's claim, it was the shortest settlement-out-of-court that Keith had run across.

The girl showed no sign of leaving. Apparently she had more to say. Keith awaited the next development.

She rose, came closer, and seated herself on the mat at his feet. As a sign of trust or intimacy she let fall the corner of her veiling headkerchief, revealing a charming young face, grave but not frightened, and little darker than Keith's own. A Fulani, to judge by her fairness and clear-cut features. She seemed content to study the white man, and showed no embarrassment at his close scrutiny.

'Well? Tell your tale.' Keith, who usually prided himself on putting petitioners at their ease, spoke sharply. 'Nor think that,

75

because of your youth, your words will come closer to my ears than the words of Iesufu.'

She had the audacity to smile. 'The matter does not concern that one. We hired him as companion for the road, because of propriety. He has gone. He will not return.' Her Hausa, though hurried, was easy to understand; her voice pleasant, though a little breathless.

'I too have propriety. It concerns my duty to give justice.' She looked intelligent enough to understand the hint. 'Such justice is best given in the office, by daylight and openly.'

'Allah separate us from the office! It is no place for that which I have come to say!'

The girl was like nobody who had come before him in Nara-guta, Bauchi or here. They all put on an act. They were ingratiating or indignant or pathetic or repentant, according to the role they had decided to play. But this girl spoke to a stranger of another race as simply as though he were an old friend of the family.

Keith allowed curiosity to overcome caution. 'Be brief, then. Your name, your purpose?'

'I am Hafsatu,' she pronounced it 'half-sar-too', 'a friend of Shetu.'

'Shetu?' Once again he remembered the lone watch beside Jenkyns' bungalow. And Shetu's song, a lullaby such as one sings to children. The agreed signal that all was well. For Jenkins, not for Keith.

He banished the past with an effort. 'But there are many Shetus.'

'Has the *Ba-ture* forgotten the widow of the leather-worker at Bauchi?' The girl sounded disappointed.

'Indeed I have not forgotten! Shetu of the great heart! She is well? She sent news by you? May that news be good!'

'She is well indeed, that kind one. She sent thanks to you, and her greetings. With permission . . . ?'

The girl threw off her voluminous travelling garment, and continued to sit gravely at his feet. Her wrap, the indoor garment of soft blue cloth wound closely around her slender body, displayed

76

smooth youthful arms and shoulders. With the good Shetu acknowledged as a common bond, it seemed that formalities could be relaxed.

'Hafsatu,' Keith tasted her name and liked it. 'We speak together as old friends. I do not know why, since never have we met before. Moreover one is old, the other young; one a man and one a woman. Also we are of different tribes. It is because of this friendship that I speak openly to you, telling what I ought to hide. . . .'

He stopped abruptly, and changed his mind.

The girl waited.

'Let me send Momadu, who is to be trusted, with a lantern to guide your feet safely to the Hausa settlement below the hill. There you will find Iesufu again, to conduct you back to Bauchi and your home.'

Hafsatu remained seated. It was Keith who rose.

'In the morning I will send you money for your journey, and a present and writing of greetings to Shetu.'

Hafsatu waited.

'But, of your kindness, girl, go! I . . . I have no woman in my house. And your beauty troubles me.'

She made a little gesture of outspread hands, which might mean anything, yet was not a thrusting away.

'Your trouble was known to Shetu. As was our like trouble. For this reason Shetu said to us "In the words of the Traditions, the *Hadisi*, for each sword is appointed a scabbard, for each scabbard a sword. For you there is one Mailafia. Mailafia has great need of a woman. Go quickly, before another woman finds him. Even now it may be too late." Thus said Shetu in her wisdom.'

Keith groped for a chair and sat down again. This was a double revelation. He considered the lighter shock first, as the other was still numbing. So his descriptive name in Bauchi had been Mailafia, the Calm or Reasonable? Not ironical, as some of the flattering ones were, nor obvious such as the Stammerer, or the Lame One. And the way the girl spoke the name made it sound like praise.

The heavier shock was the realization that this delightful girl

77

expected no less than he so desperately desired. And had come all the way from Bauchi for that purpose. Nor had she come just to offer a night's pleasure in return for money—what the Hausas called a slap-and-get-up. It was a closer, more enduring relationship which she so bravely sought and offered.

Which she continued to offer.

'We replied to Shetu "But this we cannot do! It would give shame." Said Shetu "There is no shame, but only a need. I would have gone to him long since, but for Ni-Ne who desires me, and whom I still desire."'

Keith smiled. Ni-Ne was another descriptive name. So young Jenkyns was now called It-is-I, meaning the self-important one. The despairing failure who intended to kill himself was now throwing his weight about. Cured by the motherly Shetu and her unmotherly care.

'Then it became known that Iesufu rose to walk to Pankshin with his donkey, trading. He is not old, but he is impotent because of his evil life; and when he loved, loved only boys. So we said to Shetu "No harm! We will go with him." And behold us!'

Dreading that there might still be some obstacle which he would discover only when it was too late, Keith put a few questions. There was a husband? No. Or a case pending before the Mohammedan Judge, and perhaps a marriage portion to be repaid? By no means! There were already children? The girl seemed amused, but again said no. There was health? By the Grace of Allah we had abundant health!

Hafsatu's use of 'us' and 'we' instead of 'me' and 'I' was unusual. But the plural form is used to and by Emirs and other important people. It might also be a Fulani usage. Or she might feel that it leant a touch of formality to her daring proposal.

No barrier was left between them. He could invite her into the bedroom now, before dinner. But beneath her show of courage she might still be afraid. And, more important still, there was the matter of her pride and dignity which she had entrusted to Keith's keeping.

He let go the arms of his chair and stood up. Hafsatu rose too, in

78

one supple movement, like a dancer. He summoned enough self-control to go to his uniform case, take out some money, return and ask her to pay her carriers and any other debts. He offered her a house in the compound where she could receive her friends. He asked her to go down to the Hausa settlement, and, if she still wished, return again to him with her belongings.

Her common sense rebelled against his fumbling tact and lack of caution. She laid the money on the dining table.

'A wise man does not buy a horse hidden under saddle and trappings!' she protested. And made to unwind her wrap, which reached from bosom to shapely knees.

'A beggar such as I does not test the coin as he receives it!' Keith quoted back at her.

'Mailafia is trusting; But he shall find the coin true silver, and unclipped. This I promise.' Her hands left the fold of her wrap and covered her mouth, as she realized the double meaning of her words.

Keith laughed. And her laugh, clear and soft, joined his. As hand joins hand when traders reach an understanding. Both caught the idea, and grew grave. Then smiled—a little shyly now, for the smile was as a betrothal.

Carrying the lamp, Keith showed her out through the box-congested pantry. He called Momadu, and requested that she be escorted to the Hausa village, and be well cared for on her return.

He forced his feet to bear him back to the dining-room to his unfinished drink. Her money still lay upon the table. Shutting his eyes, he could again hear her voice, and take comfort in it. The voice of a girl he had never seen before this evening, whose name he had never heard before.

The next thing was to show her that she was welcome. With flowers? They might mean nothing to her. With refreshments like sweet lime-juice and sugar biscuits? Momadu would see to that, and might resent being told. It was important not to give him any cause to dislike her.

Keith found himself in the bedroom, straightening his tie before the little shaving mirror. As though it mattered! He grinned at himself and looked around. The palm-leaf fibre mats had been shifted. Two stood under the two bunk-like shelves at the end of the room. That was a nice thought of Momadu's. A clue to where Hafsatu might like to sleep, also a tactful 'choose which of the two bunks you prefer'. Not much of a choice, but a delicate gesture.

But those mats must have been placed there when Momadu came to supervise Salifu emptying the bath. Before Iesufu was announced. And the two bunks had been kept clear of uniform cases, and reserved for Hafatsu even before that. So the paternal old scoundrel was deep in the plot. No wonder he had smirked when introduced to the girl!

'Food,' announced Momadu, 'is ready.'

The table had been laid hastily, and in semi-darkness, but when Keith carried in the lamp all was in order, and the soup waiting. He considered a third drink, but decided against it. He didn't need it tonight. Momadu hadn't gone to the settlement. Doubtless he had made other arrangements, more becoming to his dignity.

Hafsatu was a pleasant name, at least as she pronounced it. Wasn't there a queen in Ancient Egypt, with a similar name, who had built a temple under the Sphinx? It wasn't such a wild idea that the girl's name had come from a long-dead queen. Most tribal migrations in the Northern Provinces seemed to have started in the north-east, around the upper Nile. For that matter bleareyed old Iesufu, the trader, was named after Joseph of the Bible and Koran, and Momadu was no less than the Prophet Mohammed.

'No, thank you. No brandy.'

Keith found himself stirring his coffee. Dinner, presumably the standard life-history of the domestic hen, from egg—which meant custard—to death—which meant soup and meat, had been dealt with almost unconsciously, and the dishes had been whisked away. That was a pity, for it would take Hafsatu about half an hour to walk down to the settlement, half an hour to eat and gossip, to pay carriers, and half an hour more to return.

Still anything up to an hour to kill.

Neither Mohammedans nor Hillmen were censorious. Anyone

who wanted, from cook to *Ba-ture*, could make his wants known, pay a woman, risk infection, and thank her and dismiss her in the morning. Chiefs honoured women other than their wives. Traders and other travellers could find a wife in every market. Who cared?

But tonight's adventure would not end next morning. Momadu knew that, as his planning showed. The whole household knew, including assorted womenfolk. By tomorrow Messengers, litigants, chiefs and any others who might be interested, would know that 'Mister Keeta' was as other men. Also that he was now vulnerable. Thank heaven Hafsatu had no compromising family ties in the division.

Damn the lamp. It was smoking again. He carried it over to the stone fireplace, poked the moths and flies out of the base with a match, and shook it. The clockwork hummed again. Strange how you got used to the day and night plague of insects and forgot them, until you brushed your teeth with them, or they choked a lamp.

Hafsatu entered. She carried a cloth bundle, and a rolled sleeping mat of finely woven fibre. She curtsyed.

Keith jumped to his feet and bowed. 'Welcome, Hafsatu!' How feeble were words to translate thoughts. 'You must be hungry and thirsty from your long journey . . .'

'I have eaten, and washed off the dust of travel. There was time, for a horse was lent to me to go and return.'

The horse could only have been Orion. There was no other. Certainly the household had accepted her! No one but Garuba had ever been allowed to exercise him. Nor would many want to try. The stallion could be wilful.

'Orion gave no trouble?' he asked, a little anxiously.

Hafsatu smiled. 'Has not Mailafia heard the Hausa saying "A horse and a cow met. The Fulani were thus born." O-ri-on knew he was of my family.'

It was a brave little jest. He glanced down at her sandalled feet, narrow and straight of toe. 'Yet the feet of this Fulani are nowise like hooves.'

Now, having shared a couple of jokes, they were more at ease

81

with each other. Keith took the lamp and led the way into the bedroom. But he must restrain himself, give her time to make herself at home.

'It is warm, for the walls are thick, holding the heat of the day. No doubt you wish to remove your travelling clothes. Perhaps also to rest.'

She spread her sleeping mat on one bunk, placed her bundle on the other, confirming his guess that Momadu had been consulted beforehand. She removed and folded her outer garment, so he took off coat and tie. She removed her headkerchief. He sat down and pulled off his mosquito boots, and the socks came off with them.

When her hands began to remove her wrap, he could wait no longer. He stripped, back turned to her so that she should not feel shy, his fingers trembling on belt and buttons.

Then he remembered. 'Bodies of my race are white, where they do not see the sun. But this is not sickness of the skin.'

'That is already known to me.' The voice shook a little. 'Also that the scars were won by Mailafia in the *Jihad*, the holy war.'

Shetu had not told her. For all his hot desire that night in Bauchi he had not taken the woman to bed. Momadu, who had often seen him in his bath, must be Hafsatu's informant.

He heard her feet rustle the dry matting. She was coming to him. He turned swiftly. She came closer, unhesitating, bravely naked. More slender, more graceful, more desirable than he could either have imagined or hoped.

His arms clasped her. He felt the pressure of her firm breasts against him, her hurried breathing. He stroked her silken back with clumsy shaking hands. He tried to reassure her with friendly pats. She seemed so young, so innocently yielding.

She threw back her head, and her eyes laughed up at his concern, and banished it.

He tried to be tender and considerate, but could not. This was not love, or even pleasure, but release from an intolerable burden which, awake or asleep, had been close to agony. When it was ended he pulled over the pillow, laid her head upon his shoulder, and still held her close.

82

'The blame is mine. When my need is less I shall be more gentle,' he tried to comfort her.

'There is no blame,' softly she reassured him. 'Since Mailafia desires me, that is my happiness.'

He would have wrapped her around him, like a garment of happiness, if that had been possible. He reached over to turn out the lamp, and regretted that misspent moment of absence as though it were a long divorcing voyage. Every inch of her was a comfort to him, her arms about him, her tightly plaited hair under his chin, her knee pressing between his.

He tried to fight off sleep, as once he had courted it, hungered for it. He lost. Because he had no will-power left, only utter contentment.

Time must have passed. Hafsatu's lips were caressing the angle between his neck and shoulder; like those of an exploring child, who wants, but is not certain what it wants. But he could feel her body begin to explain its needs to her. She shrank away from him, a little frightened of her dawning knowledge. Till, half in sleep, his hands began to caress her.

This time there was no agony of need and haste to force him. This time he could feel each slight response of her body, and tenderly encourage it. Till her tense young body seemed to melt. And she sighed.

'Mailafia, you will not send me away?'

'How could I? At first I was as a man crazed with thirst, who swallows without tasting. This time it was as though I sipped the sacred spring of Zemzem in the temple of Suleiman.'

'Then it is well! Oh, well indeed!'

She left him. But sought him again before dawn, softly sobbing because of her need.

'This is great shame, Mailafia. A woman should not be thus!'

'What harm? "There is no blame, since you desire me". Thus said Hafsatu to Mailafia. Thus says Mailafia to Hafsatu.'

This time he was able to give her full contentment. She slept in his arms, needing the continued reassurance of his body. He thought he understood. According to the woman who had come to the rest-house with Miriamu, a girl's experience with boys

83

was 'as the mating of dogs'. Such experience as Hafsatu had known before had failed to arouse or satisfy her. There were many tragic women in the world, mothers and even grandmothers, whose bodies learned too late, or not at all.

Without fully realizing it, Hafsatu had needed him almost as desperately as he had needed her. It was hard to believe that only twelve hours ago Hafsatu had never set eyes on him, and he had not known that she existed. And frightening to realize what the odds had been against their meeting.

When the warm haze of happiness had cleared a little, he must give his attention to practical matters. And consult her as to her wishes. She was a wise little thing, and would understand. Small as it was, Pankshin station held eight graves, and more people died in England after being invalided. Sam and Momadu knew that if they went to the bank at Railhead six months or a year after Keith's death, they would be given money. The will must provide for Hafsatu's future, too.

Naturally he must give her a small allowance, for clothing and other things a woman needs. And meantime . . .

Carefully he disengaged himself, and slid out of bed. She drew the pillow into her arms, and smiled in her sleep. He stood gazing down upon her. Then, unwillingly drew the sheet up over her bare shoulders.

Keith put on a dressing-gown, and went to intercept his early morning tea in the dining-room. And to puzzle over the amazing stroke of luck which had brought her to him.

Why had she travelled more than a hundred miles into this primitive area to a strange white man? She could surely have married a rich trader, or a dashing young gallant in her own neighbourhood? Why had the kindly Shetu advised her to come to Pankshin?

Chapter Nine

Not at once was the change apparent, even to one as wise as a head Messenger.

Mister Keeta came to office, answered the greetings of 'The Peace be upon you!' entered, and took his seat. Seeming neither pleased nor angry.

The clerk laid papers upon his table so that he might set his name to them. Mister Keeta spoke to the clerk in their language, doubtless enquiring into the clerk's absence yesterday; for the clerk thrust his pen into his hair, laid hands upon his belly, and was understood to tell shamelessly of what is hidden from the sight of man. The clerk withdrew to the room of papers, and sang softly to himself of the Prophet Isa, whom the Nazarenes have made their God.

From this it was seen that the new Greater Judge was not angry, though the other Greater Judge, Mister Petbo, had ridden away without answering his head Messenger's 'May your journey be short! Alight safely!'

It could be judged that Mister Keeta had slept well, and had not walked, pistol under arm, through the dark hours, as often had been his custom. As though he sought an enemy. Little was known of Mister Keeta, for his thoughts were as a robe hidden under four other robes. Which gave great trouble, for those who had once scorned him too openly now feared him excessively. Anta and Tibn particularly. Which was why one had sent them to smooth the path of Petbo to Railhead, giving them safety till Keeta's wrath over the false counting should cool.

Mister Keeta finished his name-writing, for he wrote with speed, not lingering over it with satisfaction, as Mister Petbo did.

He called 'Gofwan! Let the first case be summoned, that some at least of the claimants may start home before the morning rains fall.'

It was the turn of Moman Wanti to interpret, but one listened, seated outside on the veranda. It began to seem as though Mister Keeta had lived in the village of which the witnesses spoke, had walked the boundaries of their farms, and knew the ways of crops, goats, and people. For his questions were such as their own village head would have asked.

Moman came out. It was one's turn to bring in the next case. One whispered 'What is this that happens?' And Moman answered 'Allah separate us from witchcraft!'

The claimant one led in was an old woman, such as Hill villages bred, one who feared neither man nor leopard, but only hunger. When the Judge questioned the truth of her words, she slapped her flat breasts and spat a coarse insult at the Judge. Because of Mister Keeta's strict order that each word should be given, one translated, but feared.

'This she says "I give birth to such as the *Ba-ture* each day upon the dung-heap. But I do not give such turds to suck, nor raise them!"'

Mister Keeta turned to the woman and said 'You are too young, and still too beautiful, to have born or suckled me.' Which again, for fear of Mister Keeta, one interpreted.

'I have born worse!' the woman cackled. And then, as though to another gossip, began to speak truth.

When Mister Keeta went to breakfast, one carried his papers for him, as one had done for Mister Petbo. This he permitted. One went to the back, to the cook-house, to ask water to drink. But learned nothing from his servants except from his cook, who said sharply, 'What is eaten in the house does not come out upon a plate for all to see.'

The word 'eaten' has also another meaning in vulgar mouths. This was made plain when one's older wife, Asamao, came hastening to the office, calling 'Listen! Listen! And what will be my reward?'

One answered, by custom, 'A kola nut.' And, searching in one's sleeve, found one and gave it to her.

'Hear this, then! Last night, to the Judge's house, came a trader from Gombe. Not alone, but with a gift. He left alone!'

One said 'This, naturally, is known to a head Messenger.' That she might tell the nature of the gift. For such is the way of women.

But she was the older wife, and cunning. So she chanted again 'Listen! And again listen! And what will be my reward?'

One answered again 'A kola nut.' But this time, for lack, had to borrow from Moman Wanti. So there was no means of hiding her words from him.

When her tale was ended, Moman said slowly '*Wal . . . la . . . hi!*' and of his own accord gave Asamao another kola nut. And spoke again, wonderingly, 'Two such gifts! This is good news, woman.'

But it is not good news when a happening happens which a head Messenger does not cause to happen.

Pettibone and the gunners had never hit it off. Keith intended to start right. He got Momadu to press his official uniform. It wasn't showy, being much the same as his old army tropical kit, but moss-green instead of khaki, and without badges of rank. It fitted, though, and the ribbons, though undistinguished, had been honestly earned.

He had guessed right. O.C. Troops rode up in style, followed by two mounted orderlies. His sword, his meticulous salute when Keith and his two Messengers met him on the steps, marked this clearly as an official visit.

Keith gave him a chair, the only leather cushion, and his courteous attention.

'Before I forget. You'll need your keys.' Garrard laid them on the table.

'Mind keeping them a little longer? I'm waiting to hear from Pettibone before taking over the treasury officially. Meantime I'm managing with N.A. money.'

Garrard pocketed the keys again. The mild blue eyes in his broad, red face invited confidence. Keith offered his pouch. Garrard fished out his leather cheroot-case.

'Any military-civilian friction, market debts or that sort of thing, for us to settle?' Keith started a safer topic.

'Not that I've heard. No time, what with musketry course, and being changed from mountain-gun battery to trench-mortar unit. The trench-mortars haven't arrived, so Fletcher's having the time of his life training people to drop rocks into the other kind of mortar, the kind women pound corn in. But what I really came to see you about was the flag.' Garrard's jovial face became portentously solemn, and he laid down his unlighted cheroot. 'Did Pettibone leave you any instructions?'

'No instructions. And, by the way, what flag?'

It seemed that a serious matter of principle was at stake. Keith flew the usual Union Jack outside his office, and the gunner's flew theirs above their quarter-guard. Unfortunately there was a flag-staff on the bare knoll which rose above the station. Both Pettibone and Garrard had claimed the right to raise a flag there at sunrise and lower it at sunset. Would Keith, as the new divisional officer, be kind enough to make his official attitude quite clear?

It was the kind of idiotic and pointless dispute between the Civil and the Military which could do a lot of harm, and waste a lot of time.

'If a flag is flown from the knoll, I'd like to see it done in style, with a bugler. And we haven't got one in the Administrative Service."

Garrard stiffened perceptibly. He was about to refuse the loan of a bugler.

Keith didn't give a damn who did what, but had no right to commit his unknown successor. 'Of course I'm lucky, being only acting, not substantively in charge of Pankshin. What I do establishes no hard and fast precedent. How would it be if I sent you an official request, saying that I expected to be out of the station a lot on tour, and would be grateful if the battery would assume the duty of raising and lowering the flag?'

'Weight off my chest. Grand. Meets all requirements.' At last O.C. Troops lit his cheroot. He unhooked his sword and laid it on the table. 'Anything I can do for you in return?'

'You can tell me when it will suit your blokes to come to dinner. Of course it won't be up to Pettibone's standard. No wines or gramophone music. . . .'

'Also no pompous Pettibone! How about next Thursday?'
Garrard picked up his sword. 'I must get back before Yeats and
Fletcher hatch up some scheme to put cordite into those wooden
mortars to lend a touch of verisimilitude to the new drill. I'm
under establishment as it is, and can't afford to lose them. Drop
across to drinks this evening, if you can spare the time.'

Garrard stopped in the doorway. 'Oh, I completely forgot.
Your escort. Can you manage with Yeats and twenty-five rifles,
the minimum? If you want more, I'd like two days' notice,
because of our training.'

'God knows when I'll get out on tour. Not before the end of
the month anyway. Pettibone seems to have kept everything in
his head, delegating nothing, and leaving no notes. It couldn't
be much worse if he had burned down the office.' Keith checked
himself. 'I probably won't need an escort anyway, but if I do
I'll give you plenty of notice.'

Keith stripped off his jacket and tie, and settled down to work.
After last night it should have been a toilsome penance. Instead
it seemed a sheer delight.

Of couse fewer drinks, and the deepest sleep he had ever known
in Africa, might have helped to lift a mist from his brain and give
him this unusual mental clarity. But they couldn't account for
what practically amounted to insight.

He owed it to Hafsatu, he was convinced of that. But it only
deepened the mystery. The Fulani girl was no nearer to these Hillmen than he was, and as a Mohammedan would tend to despise
them as infidels. Except that that tough old harridan from Kwallak
had once been a woman, she was more like Keith than Hafsatu.

The new wisdom, if you chose to call it that, had its limitations.
It helped not at all with Mr Ferguson McTavish, who came in
to report sick because 'his belly fought him'. Nor did it help
with paper-work. Keith sweated and despaired as he tried to discover or establish some office system, and work out a routine so
that some, at least, of the many returns could be compiled before
the month-end rush.

In the late afternoon a storm blew up. Not till the full rains
came in a month's time would the weather establish its regular

time-table of raining from ten to one o'clock each day. Keith clutched at his tableful of papers, saw others whirl in from the clerk's office like a covey of partridges and subside in the pools of water already forming on the mud floor.

It was too dark and windy to go on working. He left the watchman to pick up the papers and weight them down again. He arrived drenched at his quarters.

No Hafsatu.

It would be undignified to enquire for her; distasteful to send for her. And Momadu, supervising the bath being poured, was too cheerful to be the repository of bad news. So all could be judged to be well.

A deep note boomed across from the Angas village on the opposite hill. It was more of a thud than a note; but now it came again, and a little more clearly. The drummer had lighted a straw and trash fire to warm and dry his drumhead, in readiness for a dance on the village threshing floor. So announcing to Keith that the rain had stopped, and that the local weather prophets predicted a clear night.

In rubber boots, for though the rain had stopped the ground was still awash, Keith took a short-cut past the tennis court and through some dripping lime bushes. Garrard's house was almost as large as the D.O.'s, and looked bigger from the side, the rooms being built in line. Though the oleander hedge was less dejected than in the dry season, the lawn on each side of the path still showed no green in the red light of sunset.

The reception of the new divisional officer was unexpectedly formal, even Sergeant Griggs rising at Keith's entrance. To ease the situation Keith dropped hastily into the nearest chair.

'Don't, oh don't sir!' Yeats suddenly protested. 'Not that chair!' and pointed to the revolver beside Garrard's glass.

'What the young idiot means is that you're in the line of fire between me and the fireplace,' Garrard explained. 'The chimney's too wide to draw properly, but it's just the thing for storing bundles of millet. Fill it up from the top once a month, and let the horse-boy come in once a day to draw a bundle out of the fireplace. No pilfering.'

'Bright idea!' Keith agreed. 'But why bait for horse-boys when you can get a more sporting shot at them when they're out exercising the nags in the morning?'

'Rats, not horse-boys, you poor benighted civilian!' The ice had broken nicely. 'They have a regular runway between the door and the fireplace, morning and evening.'

'There's one Garrard particularly dislikes, because he wears a silk hat and a red tail.' Yeats looked suitably solemn. 'Of course he doesn't come till we've gone. None of 'em do.'

In process of apologizing for taking him as a tin miner at Panyam, Yeats latched on to Keith, wanting to know what administration was like as a job. Keith suggested that it was like being a cross between a nursemaid and a bank-clerk. On further questioning he had to admit that he hoped it would turn out to be more like a sheep-dog's job. If he could ever get out on tour.

That set Garrard off again. He wanted to know just how soon Keith would be able to get away, and whether twenty-five rifles would be enough for his escort.

Keith refused to be bullied. 'I might wander off to Panyam for a night, to see if my bridge is still standing up. But that won't need an armed escort.'

Fletcher, stretched out on his deck-chair, massive, taciturn, seemed to be demonstrating to Griggs how anyone could make wire-netting out of enamelled battery telephone wire—presumably to keep rats out of the corn. Griggs said something about 'letting the poor buggers have their whack'. Yeats wanted to know if wireless reception was good up here on the hill. Nobody had ever tried, so Keith didn't know.

When Garrard returned to his fixation about touring and armed escorts, Keith asked for his lamp-boy to be called, and left. Griggs, who seemed to have primed up before arrival, was beginning to be a nuisance, contradicting everyone, and ordering his host's servant about. The battery might like to deal with him in family privacy.

Reading *Punch*, propped up against the porous butter cooler, helped stretch dinner to a reasonable length. It required will-power, though; for Momadu, the household barometer, showed

91

signs of passing from fair to stormy. No, not quite that, but from confidence to anxiety. It was a relief when he and Salifu gave and received their formal good night wishes and went out.

Hafsatu's entrance was as prompt as though she had been waiting in the wings for her cue. It was an exact repeat performance, from her outdoor dress to the mat and bundle she carried. The same courtesies were exchanged, and the same nervous tension built up between them.

Lamp in hand Keith led the way to the bedroom. She dumped her bundle in the spare bunk, as she had on the first night, and spread her sleeping mat in its place with the same deft movement. And turned to face him, waiting uncertainly for a lead.

'You were comfortable in your house?' he enquired. 'Water was brought to you? Food was not lacking? You found friends?'

'All was well. And by the generosity of Mailafia we shall grow fat!' As though encouraged by his thoughtfulness she threw off her outer garment, folded it as neatly as before, and laid it on the other bunk. 'We shall be like horses kept too long at the picketing peg, giving trouble when at last the owner mounts.'

'A trouble which may be cured by riding,' he suggested.

Her chuckle brought them closer. She was unchanged, from the challenging little smile on her clean-cut features to the shapely feet she slid out of her wide sandals. The same youthful shoulders and slender arms displayed by her thin close-wound wrap invited his caressing fingers. The same proud supple figure demanded a closer embrace.

With as casual an air as he could manage, Keith sat on the edge of the big bed and held out his arms. She came swiftly, unhesitatingly. But when he took her on his knees he felt a slight tremor of apprehension pass through her.

'Do not fear. Last night I was as one mad. Tonight will be different, quite different.'

'Different? I would not have anything different!' Hafsatu sprang from his grasp and stood, dark eyes glinting, before him. 'All must be the same. All, all!'

What on earth had he done to arouse this outburst? What he had meant to say was simply that . . .

'Am *I* in any way different?' She snatched off her head-kerchief. 'My hair-plaiting, is it less tight than the other?'

Her *zane*, her wrap, went the way of her headcovering. She stood before him, turning slowly like a model at a dress show, but gloriously without vestige of covering. Graceful as only a Fulani can be graceful. Without scar, or spot, or single hair below her shining kitso to break the smooth bloom of her skin.

'Are not my breasts as hard, my waist as small? Feel for your-self!' she challenged, dragging him to his feet. 'But how shall you feel, wearing more robes than a Caller-to-Prayer upon his tower . . . and as distant!'

Women and their moods! It seemed that there were at least two Hafsatus, and there might be more. But obediently he took off his linen jacket, and unfastened his tie.

He was pulling off his mosquito boots when a light gleamed through the cracks of a window shutter. He jumped hastily to his feet as a voice called 'You in, Keith? Not gone to bed yet?'

Garrard's voice, blast him! This was no time for a social call.

'Front door's unlocked. Walk in. Be with you in a minute.' Keith dropped his voice to a whisper. 'It is the soldier *Ba-ture*. He has perhaps drunk more than is wise. I will soon return.'

O.C. Troops refused to sit down, or to let Keith see if he could find a drink in the pantry.

'Of course I'm butting in, and it's no business of mine,' he admitted.

'I couldn't agree with you more!' Keith made his feelings plain.

'I dropped you a hint in your office, and I've been trying to warn you all evening. Someone's got to tell you.'

'Why?' Garrard didn't seem to be drunk after all. But he was certainly behaving strangely.

'Because, damn it man, if you don't stop it you're going to have a small war on your hands.'

Keith's attention was divided, half on Garrard's puzzling talk, half on the silence of the dark bedroom beyond the open arch. Greek Helen had started the Trojan war, but he could see no grounds for thinking that Fulani Hafsatu would start one in the Pankshin

93

hills. He couldn't remember any hints or warnings either.

'I'm getting annoyed. Supposing you come to the point, Garrard, and explain.'

'Didn't Pettibone tell you?'

How the hell could Pettibone know? 'Tell me what?'

'That they murdered their village head and his assistant, and ate them both. Also all the head's goats.'

Keith lodged his hams on the edge of the table, and felt for his pipe and tobacco. But they were in the bedroom.

'Naughty of them. Dietetic indiscretion too. Seems to make people sick if they aren't used to it. Who did, by the way?'

'The Funyelang people. That's why I've been asking when you want your escort.' Garrard sat down and gave his friendly grin. 'Pettibone told me about it when you were at Panyam, about three weeks ago. Didn't you know?'

He would blister the Messengers for this! But Pettibone's crime of leaving a fire of unrest smouldering in his division was infinitely worse. Garrard was right. Something must be done at once.

'How soon can you furnish an escort?'

'Twenty-four hours notice for the minimum of one officer and twenty-five other ranks.' Garrard looked expectant. 'Just say the word.'

'Too long. I'll take an interpreter and leave at dawn.'

'Suicide's your own business, but why get your carriers eaten?'

'No carriers. Just a quick look-see. Call it a reconnaissance, if you like.' Keith's plans were crystallizing. 'So far as I remember, Funyelang is in Yergam territory in the south-east corner of the division, and hasn't been toured since Pettibone took over. I don't fancy blundering into rugged unknown country with a long string of soldiers and carriers to tempt every poisoned arrow in the area.'

'Makes sense. In a way.' Garrard sunk his chin on his chest and gave way to cogitation. 'In a crazy way.' He thought a while longer. 'I've just remembered that I'm entitled to two weeks' local leave. A spot of shooting will do me a power of good. But you'll never guess where I'm going.'

Keith grinned. 'Not, by any chance, to Funyelang?'

94

Chapter Ten

'LIKE a primitive stone wall, to stop people stepping over the edge and into eternity.' Major Garrard patted a boulder, one of many ranged along the top of the steep trail up which he and Keith had hauled themselves. 'Puzzling, though. From the few glimpses I've had of your friends I shouldn't have thought they'd have bothered about a few lives more or less. There can't be much food up in these granite hills.'

'According to old reports, the boulders are there to welcome visitors.' Keith laid down his rifle, and picked up a rock. He wore several days' beard, bush-shirt and shorts stiff with dried sweat, shoes without socks and an overall camouflage of flies. And was exceedingly contented. Garrard looked worse. His beard was red, his nose was peeling, and he had large sun-blisters on his shins and forearms. He was rather proud of the ensemble.

'This rock weighs only about twenty pounds, but it will serve to demonstrate the principle. I carry it to the edge of the hill, and release it . . . thus. Observe closely where it falls.'

The small rock didn't follow as straight a course as a large boulder would have done, it bounced and zigzagged. But it homed on the one stretch of smooth rock in the pass, and struck it, shivering into a dozen whirring fragments. Just at the point where an attacking force would be unable to find cover.

Flat on his face, head over the void, Garrard was rapt in professional admiration. 'Primitive artillery, no less! Easy as scraping flies off toast and marmalade—in the days when we had toast and marmalade. Of course one co-operates with the low-born infantry, allowing them to threaten a down-hill attack to encourage the enemy to mass to repel it. And there's only one place where the enemy can concentrate, and that's on that flat outcrop. Then heave-ho, the Dallong Gravitational Artillery goes into action; and the useful but unornamental infantry mop up the pieces.''

Keith stirred him with his toe. 'Visitors. But friendly ones, I hope.'

It was Gofwan, the Messenger, his gown torn, his turban little more than a twisted rag. He too had suffered on the forced marches through bad country. With him was a tough old Hill-man, clad only in a goatskin loin-cloth, a dingy brown blanket thrown plaid-wise over his left shoulder, a battle-axe swinging casually in his right hand.

The visitor dispensed with preliminaries. He announced 'I am Pupchina, Sarikin Dallong. The Dallong Hills are mine!' He made a sweeping gesture with his axe and Gofwan ducked. 'My father and my uncle were also Sarikin Dallong. I killed the killer of my uncle and became Sarikin Dallong. Thus it is.'

'Give my greetings,' Keith instructed the interpreter. 'Say that I come neither for tax nor road-making, but wish to pass swiftly through his hills. We have three loads, and since the Angas carriers have run, need three carriers.'

Garrard had rebelled against Keith's original plan to take only one blanket each, a pocketful of money to buy food, and a pocket-ful or two of ammunition. The result had been a compromise of a servant each, a load each, and one load for the servants' mats. Still a compact group, and easy to defend in case of trouble. But dependent upon carriers.

As Gofwan interpreted Keith's reply from Hausa into Dallong, Keith interpreted Pupchina's announcement to Garrard.

'Was that when he got that dent in his skull?' Garrard wanted to know. 'You could lay two fingers in it.' He picked up what resembled a model raft, made of reeds, about one foot wide and two feet long. An Angas harp, bought for a shilling two days ago. Two very long days, Keith felt, for Garrard had been strumming it ever since. 'Ask him if we're any nearer to Funyelang.'

Keith tried. But where people have no units of length such enquiries tend to be useless. Near is near, and far is far, and very far is the same word for far but emphasized by an out-thrusting of the chin and lower lip.

'Sarikin Dallong says that Funyelang is in Yergam, not Dallong territory. Which makes it foreign, and slightly indecent. He has never been there, of course. His stomach revolts at the thought. But Gofwan volunteers the information that it's two sleeps away, is stiff with "bad men" and very difficult going.' Then hastily, for Garrard was starting to strum the harp again, 'Here's some interesting news coming through. You may never have heard of it, because of your neglected education, but the Yergam grow tails!'

Pupchina's social sense told him that he had struck a topic of interest to his guests. He spoke rapidly, giving Gofwan and Keith little time to interpret.

'It's a fact, and Pupchina is prepared to prove it. No Yergams can sit down in comfort without hollowing out places for their tails to fit in. If you doubt this, you can see the holes around every Yergam village, even in the solid granite. But, hold on a minute —not all Yergams, only the men. Their women are usually tailless, just as female kobs are usually hornless. Pupchina can prove this too, because he captured a Yergam girl when he was a young man. He thought he would have to chop her tail off to civilize her, and was quite surprised to find she had none. She's still alive, and he'll send for her if we want to examine her.'

'Keith, old man, it's the sole flaw in my otherwise sterling character, so I hope you won't let it go any further. But the fact is that from childhood up I've never had the slightest inclination to examine an aged female Yergam rump.' Garrard plinked a few sad notes.

After the sweltering plain it was pleasantly fresh up here in Dallong. Pupchina was a remarkable old fellow, and seemed friendly. Gofwan was too tired to play the sycophant. Garrard, war-toughened and cheerful, was just the man for this sort of job. Sam and Garrard's boy Leviticus had shared their masters' discomfort without complaint. As soon as carriers could be found the trek would continue, most likely until nightfall. Meantime, it was restful and interesting to stretch out on a rock and listen to old Pupchina.

'The Yergam are all *masu-dachin-hali*, bitter-hearted. As soon as a boy reaches puberty he becomes touchy. When his father beats him he's liable to wait outside the family hut and, when his old man comes crawling out through the little door-hole, plug a poisoned arrow into him at arm's length. This is considered an unfilial action, and lacking in respect. To avoid it, the boy gets kicked out before it can happen, and having no farm has to live by hunting or robbery. If he's lucky he steals himself a girl.'

Pupchina began to show restlessness, as primitive people are not accustomed to prolonged mental effort. He asked permission to 'go catch carriers'. And the meeting broke up, Gofwan also asking permission to see to carriers.

The head messenger was certainly improving. Unfortunately he knew little about the speech and customs of the Dallong and Yergam tribes, as Anta, now at Railhead with Pettibone, was the expert on this south-east corner of the division. But Gofwan was working hard and willingly.

O.C. Troops had returned to his harp. 'You may not have noticed that the centre string of each group of three is weighted by binding to vibrate an octave lower than the strings on each side.' He pinged one group of three, then another group, to show. 'We know that each octave has twice the frequency of the one below it, but how did the Angas ear make the discovery?'

'God knows!' Keith tore a piece off a dry ball of Angas tobacco, crumbled it in his pipe, and went off to get a light at Sam's near-by cook-fire. The flavour wasn't too bad, though not up to the standard of Sergeant Fletcher's carefully fermented leaf. He returned, to find Garrard still plinking away.

'Of course the octave is basic. But what I want to find out is how they subdivide it.' Garrard mused aloud. 'I think into six.'

'Six and a quarter,' said Keith firmly.

'But that's impossible, because—' Garrard grinned. 'All right. I can take a hint. And now people have stopped strumming their infernal harps I think I'll take a brief siesta.' He laid the harp carefully beside him, put his rifle within easy reach, and tilted the sun-helmet over his eyes. 'If there are any phone calls, take them for me, there's a good fellow.'

Gofwan was the first to return. He had armed himself with a

bow and quiver, in addition to his sword. Behind him came four Dallong men. They saw the white man, dropped back a little, then vanished like lizards among the boulders.

'I bring carriers,' Gofwan announced proudly.

'Where?' Keith asked.

White men are noted for their inability to grasp the obvious. Every little thing must be explained to them, as to children.

'Here!' said Gofwan, with a backward gesture of the borrowed bow. 'There are only three light loads, so four carriers . . .' He glanced behind him, and deflated. 'They fear. They have run.'

'Why do they fear?' Keith wanted to know. 'We are not yet in Yergam country.'

Gofwan looked unhappy.

The old chief with the dented skull knew his people. He didn't make Gofwan's mistake of leading. He drove from behind eight tough looking specimens, all armed and vigorously protesting. By way of reply he clouted the rearmost between the shoulder-blades with the flat of his fighting-axe.

Caught between the white man and their masterful chief, the conscript labour came to a halt beside the three light chop-boxes. Sam and Leviticus lifted a box to load it on a head. But the Chief of Dallong had his own method. He grasped the nearest Dallong man by the neck and forced him to his knees. He lifted a chop-box and banged it down on the man's matted hair, and jerked him to his feet again. The others scrambled for the two remaining loads.

A growl from Pupchina set them moving.

'He says,' Gofwan interpreted, 'if one runs away he give them all shit, he beat them all.'

Garrard rose and slung his service rifle. 'My aunt Clementina had the same idea, but in more refined language. Whenever any of her nieces or nephews did wrong, she spanked them all.'

Keith checked the time by his watch, and the rough direction by his compass. 'If you'll do rear-guard, I'll cut in ahead to keep in touch with the old chief.'

'When in column of route it is customary for the band to lead.' Garrard tinkled his infernal toy harp. 'However, so long as this does not create an official precedent, you may go ahead.'

It began to rain. Not heavily, just enough to cool the air. The narrow track between the boulders widened a little, and there began to be stretches of soil. The capital city of Dallong, of some fifty or more scattered huts, came in sight. Here and there a woman pounded corn in a pestle and mortar somewhat smaller than the Sura kind. A few bedraggled leaves on a string was the housewife's informal morning garb. Babies, slung in goatskins on their mother's backs, lolled helpless heads on thin necks as they rocked to the rhythm of the pounding.

The sound of Garrard's strumming surprised, and apparently attracted. Half a dozen naked and dusty children, with a few goat and dog companions, followed the parade to the outskirts of the village.

Rain grew heavier, making rock and red clay slippery underfoot. Pupchina offered a practical item of advice, in the off-hand manner of 'You can get lunch in the dining-car forward.' Keith relayed it to his rear-guard.

'He says now that it rains we must listen for the sound of bow-strings, as arrows become more difficult to see and dodge. He also warns that morning and evening are the difficult times, as people can then "attack down their shadows".'

'Sounds as though the Sarikin Dallong is expecting trouble.'

'Or hoping for it. He looks positively jaunty, blast him!' Keith wished he felt as happy.

So far no sign of armed opposition. And no earthly reason why there should be any. Dallong had paid their taxes in full last year, and a reasonable amount of what was due this year. Gofwan, questioned, had heard of no trouble. But Pupchina had given clear warning.

Not much farmland in this desolate grey granite. Occasionally a terrace like a window-box could be seen, or sometimes so small that it was more like a swallow's nest clinging to an almost vertical slope. Once Keith thought he caught the odour of native tobacco drifting down-wind from a jumble of rocks beside the path. From another possible hiding-place a mile or so further on had come a click as of a bow or spear carelessly handled. But again there was nobody in sight.

There was scarcely a quarter mile stretch of the trail which didn't offer a tempting opportunity for an ambush, with precipitous hillsides down which boulders could be rolled, or valleys choked with enough rocks to give cover to a whole battalion.

If an attack developed, Garrard and he should be able to cover their servants and Gofwan, abandon their baggage, and perhaps fight their way out. It looked, too, as though Pupchina might help them. It wasn't so much the risk that Keith objected to, it was the futility of the situation. He had no quarrel with the Dallong people. If Pupchina and the carriers were samples, he liked them. They were highly specialized to an environment in which most humans would have starved. In fact a lean bunch of athletes.

It happened suddenly. Pupchina stooped, and without changing pace picked up a large stone and hurled it.

It struck a boulder with such force that it seemed to explode like a hand-grenade. Out leaped a couple of bowmen in full flight.

Pupchina yelled to them. No result. They remembered urgent business elsewhere.

More heads, daubed with red clay, popped up into sight. Two bowtips, then arrows emerged. The column was surrounded.

Keith swung his rifle to the ready, slipping off the safety catch. He checked on his spare ammunition, and glanced back to find cover for his men. There wasn't enough to hide a dog. The ambush had been well sited.

Pupchina halted and shouted. He shook his axe at the fleeing figures, taking no notice of the other ambushers near by.

'He says . . . ?' Keith prompted his frightened Messenger.

'That when he returns he will give his uncle shit.'

A one-idea'd man the old chief. This couldn't be the uncle whose death he had revenged. This uncle wanted to kill him instead. A lively family.

As it couldn't get past Pupchina, the little column halted. Keith called back the news to Garrard, who sat down on a rock, mopped his head, but kept his rifle handy.

Apparently there was something about his own uncle leading a band of malcontents that stirred Sarikin Dallong to righteous anger. He turned it on those within hearing, and expressed himself freely. Still more ambushers broke cover to listen. Two pointed to the fleeing figures and cackled with laughter. Pupchina turned on the two and cursed them—no need for an interpreter to make that plain. The two leaped up on boulders to threaten Pupchina with their spears.

Everybody was having a grand time.

The carriers thought it a good chance to change loads with their reliefs. One of the recent ambushers, eager to earn a little money, knocked down a carrier, grabbed his load and put it on his own head. There was nearly a private fight.

Garrard came up, strumming his harp as he leaped from rock to rock. The service rifle, again slung on his shoulder, bumped against his side. A considerate ambusher took it and carried it for him.

Keith burst into a shout of laughter which was in part relief from his tense feelings. Pupchina had been having trouble with some of his refractory subjects. Like a good host he had taken his guests along to share the fun, as it would be on their route anyway. All the Dallong people had wanted was a little rough sport and excitement, like old English village football, when everybody turned out with clubs and hobnailed boots to use on each other. Life wasn't so sacred in those days, or wounds so important. They and the Dallong tribesmen would understand each other.

The column moved on again, Pupchina at its head still giving short grunts of indignation, like an erratically firing motor-cycle. For lack of other amusement, now that the ambush had fizzled out, the ambushers joined up too. Perhaps hoping that someone would ambush them in return.

The man who carried O.C. Troops' rifle marched proudly ahead of him, turning from time to time, apparently to explain the correct way to play a harp. Since the *Ba-ture* obtusely refused to understand the simplest Dallong language, the only way was to show him. He handed the Lee-Enfield back to Garrard, and took over the harp.

'I don't know if this is your idea of warfare, Keith, but it's getting me quite confused,' Garrard shouted forward.

'We're in good hands. Let's leave it at that. I'm going to sleep on the hoof. Wake me when we get there.'

'When we get where?' Garrard enquired, reasonably enough.

A healthy animal has eyes in its feet. Keith's legs took the shock of a drop, sprang up and across to the next rock, without his having to guide them. The drizzling rain seemed to stop, and may actually have done so. The heat seemed to lessen, though this was unlikely to happen around mid-afternoon. The ambushers had brought their own personal supply of flies, all of which seemed to realize that until they had tasted white men they had led thwarted, frustrated lives, which might easily lead them to the psycho-analyst's couch. They set out to remedy this. Some just stamped and quarrelled over their prey. Others, more practical, dived right in to tear Keith apart, vulture-like, and smack their lips and dribble.

They, too, began to recede from Keith's consciousness.

A wonderful feeling of relief. Perfect!

Perfection became personalized. About five feet four inches of slender dignity winding on a close-fitting garment of blue, as Keith lighted the lamp to dress by.

'When the Emir assembles his horsemen in his war camp outside the city walls, it is not the custom of a Fulani woman to say to her man "Stay with me! Do not go!"' Hafsatu spoke like a Roman matron, proudly giving her son to the defence of the Republic.

Sam had coughed discreetly outside the front door, to imply that load and carrier were waiting. Keith filled his pockets and picked up his rifle.

'Only great need would take me from you. That you know.'

'That I know.' She smiled up at him. 'Return safely. Victory be yours!'

A truly remarkable girl, or woman. Her standard might be hard to live up to. Undoubtedly one should return to her in flowing robes, on a black charger with colourful trappings, with a troop of mounted trumpeters galloping behind. One should rein the charger back on his haunches, lower the tip of a slender steel lance, and deposit at her feet the blackened head of the principal rebel.

Chapter Eleven

THE Funyelang Reconnaissance Force was still on its way. Keith's legs seemed to have been walking for ever. But he had a hazy impression of spending last night in a village where he, Gofwan and Pupchina had settled disputes while others slept.

Shortly after dawn the column had hurled itself over a precipice, as though intent on mass suicide. But this was only the Dallong idea of how to descend a more than roof-steep slope in leaps that only a klipspringer should have attempted. Keith had burst a shoe, and Garrard complained that his long intestine had got wrapped around his kidneys.

Down here in the plains the track was level, but that was all that could be said in its favour. It was a twisting, rain-eroded ditch, perhaps a game-trail cut in the slippery laterite soil. It required a tight-rope-walking technique, swinging one bruised foot directly in front of the other.

Vicious thorns snatched at you as you passed, ripping shirt and shorts, and breaking off to rankle in the skin. Voracious as leeches, ticks thumbed a ride on the human dining car. Yellow butterflies rose daintily from a blob of bush-cow droppings. It was hot and humid after the Dallong hills, in fact typical malarial country. The tsetse flies might not be the kind that carried sleeping sickness, but they drove home red-hot hypodermic needles. Flies and sweat-bees were rather worse than usual, no doubt because you stank so invitingly.

You couldn't defend yourself. But if you had any sense you learned to detach yourself.

Keith began to dissociate his mind. The first stage was the most difficult. Bodily discomfort seemed to increase, as though in protest against being abandoned. The feet stumbled. But gradually, like one officer relieving another, the subconscious took over command of the body, and the conscious mind could retire, withdraw.

The rustle of leather loin-cloths, the click of one weapon on another, the tinkling of the toy harp—Garrard or his new instructor seemed to be attempting a march tune—faded into the distance of past or possible future. The present had all the charm of going under a general anaesthetic.

Sheer bliss. And naturally his thoughts turned to Hafsatu, for Hafsatu and bliss were the same thing.

He had seen Garrard to the front door, leaned against the doorway remarking upon the beauty of the night, confirmed the dawn rendezvous outside Garrard's quarters; and given, he hoped, an excellent portrayal of a man with time on his hands and no engagements.

Hafsatu had dressed again, but was waiting. In her dark-lashed eyes a challenge, in her trim little mouth curling a little at the corners, a lurking invitation.

'There is unrest in Yergam country,' he explained, 'and in the morning I must leave you. But now?'

She came a little closer.

Keith stooped, hauled off his mosquito boots again, and by custom stood them beside his bed. She slid her feet out of her ornamental indoor sandals, and waited for his next move.

Her heavy silver anklet hung askew. He bent and straightened it for her. She smiled more openly.

He pulled off his shirt and cast it aside. Her eyes took in the strange colour of his skin, but her hands did not falter as she unwound her soft blue wrap and folded it. Her angry disrobing earlier in the evening seemed now to be turning into a matching strip-tease. Except for the scanty skirt-cloth which clung to her slim hips, she was bare, and utterly desirable. Her lips were parted, and her breasts stirred to her quick breathing.

'Now only my *fatari*, my skirt-cloth, is left between us. It is you who shall unloose it this time. That is my right!' A little arrogant, a little frightened.

Stooping he removed the last covering, and kissed her flat

stomach. It took her by surprise, and he heard the quick intake of her breath.

Harshly he seized her, carried her, laid her down. Her eyes opened wide in surprise, but she did not struggle.

It was unfair that she should suffer this madness twice. If Garrard had not come, and the delay had not allowed his desire to build up to such frenzy he could have controlled himself. He was being cruel again, when he had wanted to be kind. . . .

Hafsatu asked only 'It is no different, Mailafia?'

'Praise be to Allah!'

'Then I am happy! And no longer doubt or fear.'

Her unaccountable dread that tonight would not be as the first night was groundless. The pattern repeated itself, exactly. Her body began to stir and awaken to her needs as it had done before. Also she came to him, and again found full contentment.

So exact was the repetition in each detail that Keith was puzzled. She had shown that she was no ignorant Victorian maiden, and he had scarcely expected her to be a virgin at sixteen or seventeen, or whatever her age was. Yet there had seemed to be a slight obstacle to intercourse on the first night, and tonight there had seemed to be rather more than less.

He had not spoken, but she stirred a little at his side, and asked 'Mailafia?'

'How does virginity renew itself, and in so short a time?'

'With the houris of Paradise, daily, or at will. For the pleasure of True Believers!' He could feel her silent chuckle.

'But I am a Nazarene, not a follower of Islam. Also I am not dead.'

'And I am no houri,' answered a sleepy voice, 'but only Hatasu!'

Hatasu or Hafsatu. One might be a pet name for the other; like Lizzie for Elizabeth.

Thinking back he realized that he had been anything but clinically calm at the moment of his observation, so he could easily have been mistaken. In fact he must have been wrong. Unless it was explained by some ingenious trick taught to Fulani girls

107

by their mothers. That was possible. Some tribes not only had regular courses of sex-instruction in connection with initiation ceremonies, but anthropologists had recorded some remarkable variations on the circumcision of boys and the excision of girls which seemed designed to make each sex more attractive to the other.

There was another possibility, though the time-limit of twenty-four hours seemed to rule it out. It was fairly common, though not among the northern tribes of Nigeria, to sew girls up to ensure they remained virginal until marriage. Arab slave dealers in the old days had used the same method to preserve the full market value of the girls they bought or captured. A middle-aged woman was pointed out in Bauchi as having had herself stitched up and sealed when her husband refused to take her with him to Mecca. The idea may have been to guard herself against passing temptation, since adultery would be far more sinful when her husband was on pilgrimage.

Sewing up was said to be no more dangerous or painful than circumcision. In France, Spain and Italy steel chastity belts, sometimes called Paduan locks, had been used instead, either as a defensive armour against rape, or as a portable prison for reluctant virtue. The famous silversmith Benvenuto Cellini made at least one, noting in his diary the design and the name of his customer. So they must once have been very fashionable.

'The River of the Canoe. There!'

Keith missed the rest of the announcement. The head Messenger was pointing with his bow to a belt of dark green foliage. The trees looked lush and noble after the stunted bush around and behind. Obviously they had their roots in year-round moisture.

'It is said that Mister Heathcote struck the boundary here, between Dallong and Yergam. After, the other river, the one at Lankan, drowned him.' Gofwan added the rest of his small stock of local knowledge.

It was a warning. As the limit of Dallong authority, the River of the Canoe was the place where the Dallong escort would have to be sent back home, however reluctantly.

'Tell Pupchina that we will rest in the shade of the trees, and drink of the water.'

Sarikin Dallong's growl was not encouraging.

Gofwan interpreted. 'The chief says better we go on. Funyelang is still far.'

Looking back, Keith could see the long dark line stretching back to Garrard's sun-helmet with its yellow oilskin cover. A hundred warriors, or two hundred; silent, grimly silent, he felt. All hoping to be led to battle against their hereditary enemies the Yergams.

Something must be done at once, for the belt of trees now lay only a few hundred paces ahead. Keith plunged from the trail into the bush, lowered his head to protect his eyes, and drove forward as a bush-cow does, but without a bush-cow's thick hide. He rejoined the trail, ahead of Pupchina, but with no definite plan in mind.

He must get to the boundary river first. Then think of something. Fall down as though his ankle had twisted, and so hold up the march long enough to argue with Pupchina. Perhaps threaten to cut his monthly salary?

The deep shadow of tall trees closed around him. At any other time it would have been as welcome as a draught of cold beer. A slight break in a low bank, where, by the tracks and droppings, it seemed that beasts went down to drink. The River of the Canoe turned out to be barely a fair-sized brook, which he could almost have jumped.

He didn't try to. For very good reason.

His ears had caught the faint rustlings on the further bank. His eyes began to clear themselves of glare-blindness, and penetrated the shadows across the rippling water. A bow-tip, several bow-tips, showed above and around bushes.

Strictly speaking not another ambush, but a neatly sited outpost, ready and more than willing to let fly arrows at any who might be stupid enough to try to cross the twenty yards of bare banks and shallow water.

'Yergams!' said Gofwan. And shrank back behind Sarikin Dallong.

The fact that the Yergams had no possible means of knowing that the *Ba-ture* was coming, and therefore no foreseeable reason for being where they were, was no valid excuse for Keith's bungling. It was a hell of a shame that so many Yergam and Dallong warriors were about to die, because of his mistake.

Chapter Twelve

Arrows rather than men seemed to be watching him. That gave an impersonal effect to the situation, as though it were a mechanical mousetrap which would snap shut if one touched something. One second for an arrow to be drawn, released and strike. Five minutes for the poison to do its work, if it was reasonably fresh. According to accounts the strophantus numbed almost at once, and there was little pain. That was a comforting thought.

The game was lost already. But Keith intended to play it out until the whistle blew 'time'. That would give Garrard and the Dallong men a chance to organize a rear-guard action, and protect Gofwan and the two servants. Thank God for O.C. Troops' experience and discipline. A younger man would dash impulsively forward and make the mess far worse.

Deliberately—for a quick movement will startle a dog and make him snap, or make bees sting instinctively—Keith laid his useless rifle down on the bank and took out his notebook. With his compass he sighted back along the way he estimated he had come. Just as though a route-traverse could do any possible good.

The action gave him time to re-assess the situation. It was worse than before, for arrows now bristled behind him, Dallong arrows. The damned fools hadn't taken the opportunity to retreat, as they should have done. Instead the column had deployed to line the northern bank, prepared to dispute the Yergam crossing, or even to attack.

White men are always puzzling, but this one was more so than usual. Like an experienced leader he had been the first to smell danger, and had forced his way forward to confront it. That was good. And reasonable. But why had he laid aside his weapon? And what was the meaning of his looking through that small thing, and then writing?

III

Now he sat down on the bank and took off his sandals, sandals which tied to the feet and had to be untied. Now he fastened the ends of their strings together and slung the sandals around his neck. Now he rose again and, picking up his weapon, scratched between his shoulder-blades with the end of it. And grinned at the pleasure of the scratching, just as one did oneself. Which was a good sign, for when angry one does not feel an itching, nor enjoy a scratching. Perhaps soon he would give the word for the fight to start.

Keith felt that the first tension had abated a little. Drooping arrows, and the occasional careless exposure of a warrior's whole body suggested a growing uncertainty of purpose. Which was what he intended. There began to be a faint chance that he could impose a sort of armistice, and perhaps get the Dallong tribesmen to go home.

But he must face another fact. Unless in reading old census summaries he had confused Funyelang with another place, it was no more than a small hill hamlet, and quite unable to furnish as many warriors as lined the far side of the stream. Which meant that Pettibone's delay had allowed the revolt to spread. Since Keith was now expected, and had lost the tactical advantage of surprise, there wasn't a hope of finding Funyelang unprepared, or even of reaching the place alive.

But first to get out of the present mess. Or at least try to.

He stepped down from the bank, and began to wade across the shallow boundary stream. It was only ten paces or so to the south bank, but tricky going. For, if he stumbled on a stone or slipped in the mud and whirled his arms to recover balance, the Dallong might take it as a signal to advance, or the Yergam as a threat to attack. As he set foot safely on Yergam territory he gave himself even chances of survival. And relaxed a little. Since every delay would help, he stooped, carefully wiped his feet with a sodden handkerchief, and put on his shoes.

The Yergams were breaking cover, cautiously. One came from behind a tree-trunk. Another, camouflaged by dappled sunlight and deep shadow, seemed to rise right under Keith's nose. No way of judging their intentions by their expressions, for they showed none. Small receding skulls, massive frontal bones and heavy cheek-bones made the Bitter-Hearted look more brute than human.

A little old man in a white fez and scanty green robe bowed slightly, twiddling his fingers above his dingy cap in the age-old gesture of casting earth on his head as token of submission. But that submission wasn't to be counted on. The situation might deteriorate with startling suddenness. Just one arrow, released by itching fingers on either side of the narrow stream, would do the trick.

Keith greeted the wizened ancient in Hausa. The man replied in what no doubt was Yergam speech.

Then came Garrard, splashing across the boundary, herding an unwilling Gofwan in front of him.

'Had a job catching him, or I'd have been here before,' he explained. 'He had an acute attack of home-sickness, but I thought you might like an interpreter so you could make an oral testament before a few Yergam witnesses. Just the usual stuff, whom you want to leave your aunt Tabitha's patchwork quilt to, and what lucky legatee gets your liver to eat.'

'Christ Almighty! Why didn't you see—' Keith checked his useless outburst. No rifle left to cover the servants now. The only chance left was to send Gofwan back to Pupchina with orders to rush Sam and Leviticus back to the safety of the hills. He had counted on Garrard showing more sense, and not behaving like a gallant damned fool!

And now, before Keith could amend his plans, another gallant damned fool, Pupchina himself, came splashing across the River of the Canoe, battle-axe in hand.

An ominous readying of arrows on bows showed that distracting action must be taken at once.

The little old Yergam must be someone of importance, to judge by his faded green robe. Keith grasped him firmly by the hand and, not stopping to remove his shoes this time, led him across the river to Dallong territory. Puzzled the old fellow might be, but he offered no resistance, and picked up his robe with his free hand like a lady managing her train.

Each leader was now hostage for the other.

Keith waded back into mid-stream, swallowed and licked his lips to bring saliva back to his dry mouth. He had not realized how scared he was, until now.

He made a speech. 'This is a sign that a man may cross the River of the Canoe in peace and friendship. This is a sign which your own chiefs have given to you, men of Dallong, and men of Yergam.'

Gofwan did a double translation, the one presumably into Yergam slowly and haltingly. The two chiefs looked supremely indifferent. Pupchina stropped the edge of his axe on a horny palm. The other man blew his nose, one nostril at a time, in quite unladylike manner.

'This is the sign that where I stand runs the rule of the *Tura-wa*, made many years ago, that none may pass in anger or in war.' Keith emphasized. 'This is the Peace of the River, which your chiefs and I pledge. Let none break this Peace!'

The water was pleasantly cool around his legs, but he couldn't stand here for ever. But chances looked more hopeful. The silence of waiting had changed to the murmur of conversation on both banks. No battle cries or taunts. But still an impasse.

He put it to Garrard. 'I don't know what the Yergams want, but it doesn't seem to be our heads, or they would have butchered us some time ago. Are you willing to take a gamble with them?'

'You mean join up with our new stone-age friends and push on? Might be rather fun.'

'It'll look a lot better than running home to mother because they made nasty faces at us.'

'They don't *make* those faces. They couldn't without rock-drills and blasting powder.'

Keith turned to the mild little man in the green robe, and hoped that he might have some influence over his fellow tribesmen, despite his insignificance. 'The people of Dallong have carried our loads since dawn. Now, since we enter Yergam land, it is the right of the Yergams to carry and earn the reward.'

Gofwan bowed to Green Robe and translated, softly, deferentially. His recent scare seemed to have done him good. He wasn't usually so courteous to village heads and minor chiefs.

Gofwan turned, and translated Green Robe's brief reply. '" The Yergams shall carry." So says the Sarikin Yergam.'

The Tribal Chief? Keith stared. This little man, who bore no weapon, and shyly twiddled his toes—could he really be that warrior of warriors, the autocrat of the bitter-hearted Yergams?

If so, how did he stand in relation to the Funyelang murders? Were they done by his orders, or against his wishes? A hell of a lot would depend on the answer. But now was no time for tactful interrogation while hereditary enemies faced each other across a narrow stream.

Pupchina stopped putting a final edge on his axe, and called. Sam came up with the three Dallong carriers, and in exact midstream helped Keith transfer the light boxes from clay-matted Dallong heads to clay-matted Yergam ones. The cook postured a little, being downstage centre, and in the public eye. Leviticus was more retiring. Keith opened a box, paid off the Dallong carriers, and gave them the usual thanks.

There remained the two unconscious hostages, Sarikin Yergam and Sarikin Dallong, each on the wrong bank. Keith led each across by the hand and something in the ceremony or symbolism appealed to the spectators. Arrows went back into quivers, and with the letting down of the recent tension several warriors felt the demand of their bladders, and relieved themselves.

The new column of march had a different 'feel', to one who was sensitive to impressions. The Yergam stride was different, their toes didn't seem to grip the ground as did those of the rock-dwelling Dallong. Their odour was different, because of race or diet, or both. But the game-trail was the same as ever, with thorn brakes which reached out cat-like claws; and so far as Keith could tell the insect pests had merely changed trains at the last stop.

Garrard found his way up the column to ask a question. ' I don't ask for a formal introduction to your new pal, but should I address him as Miss or Mr if we chance to converse? '

' That quiet old gentleman mincing along ahead of us has killed more men in battle than anyone else in the division.'

' A hobby of his, like stamp-collecting? '

' More like office routine. The Yergams talk with weapons, and he answers them in the same way. It's a little unfair though, as he's well known to be unkillable. One of our early divisional officers saw him hit by a couple of arrows—barbed of course. The Sarikin Yergam ordered his men to hold him upright, and tap the arrows till they stuck out through the muscles of his back. They snapped off the heads, and then pulled the shafts out through the front. Of course the arrow poison must have been stale, or else he had an antidote.'

' Let's find out how we stand with him, and where he's leading us.'

Keith called forward in Hausa ' What brought Sarikin Yergam to meet us? '

After a slight delay Gofwan answered ' The message of the dog.'

A slight slip in translation, no doubt. Gofwan's Yergam wasn't very good. Keith rephrased his question.

Back came the answer ' The dog told Sarikin Yergam you were coming this way.'

' What dog? ' The crux of the misunderstanding was the word ' dog ', so it seemed a reasonable question.

' The *Ba-ture*'s own dog, the dog of the Judge of Pankshin. So says Sarikin Yergam.' Gofwan, too, sounded puzzled.

' But I have no dog. You know that,' Keith pointed out. And summarized briefly in English for Garrard's benefit.

' I caught the word " Pankshin " and the Hausa for " dog ". It was Garrard's turn to be puzzled. ' There's only one dog in the station, and that's Griggs' yellow mongrel. I never heard that he spoke Yergam.'

Gofwan must have caught the word ' Griggs '. He saw the need to correct a misapprehension. ' Mister Keeta's dog. The dog of Mister Keeta.'

' What kind of a dog? '

Gofwan referred the question to the Sarikin Yergam. Back came the answer ' A white man's dog.'

' How does Sarikin Yergam know that it's a white man's dog? '

'Because it is white.'

'Rubs against his master, I suppose, and some of the white comes off on the dog.' Garrard tried to rationalize Keith's latest news bulletin. 'Of course this sort of chit-chat enlivens the march. But we would like to know if we're walking into a trap, or just walking because the Sarikin Yergam thinks it's good for our health and pallid complexions. Wants to see the roses back in our cheeks again, particularly Gofwan's.'

Caught between the ludicrously irrational and the pressing need to plan some course of action, Keith made another effort.

'Ask carefully, Gofwan. Where is this dog? May we see him?'

Sarikin Yergam waved gracefully forward as he replied.

'The dog waits,' said Gofwan.

Keith lifted his sun-helmet and ran his fingers through his sodden hair to cool his head. This was getting him down. 'All right. What's he waiting for?'

'For his master, the Judge of Pankshin. For you, *Ba-ture*.'

In England it would be perfectly safe to say that such dogs do not exist, and that such things could not happen. But Nigeria had taught Keith to keep an open mind. In this instance one had a choice of believing that the old Sarikin Yergam was a clairvoyant, or that the dog was.

In favour of the hypothesis that the dog had this uncanny faculty was the fact that Sarikin Yergam seemed to accept it without question. Against the hypothesis was the doubtful assumption that he could understand dog language, or that the gifted dog spoke Yergam. Of course one should reserve judgment. So far one had only heard Sarikin Yergam's side of the case, not the dog's.

The stagnant heat of the late afternoon grew almost unbearable. The red laterite game-trail was a red hot treadmill which turned beneath the feet yet took them no further forward.

There seemed no point in continuing to endure the vivisection of sadistic insects without anaesthesia. Keith availed himself of his old technique and submerged. Almost everyone seemed to have the knack, but, perhaps because most people lived most of their lives in comfort, few seemed to develop it any further. It didn't, in his case, offer any defence against really extreme pain or really bad worry. But it was handy.

Had it any connection with Yoga, or with martyrs being able to walk composedly to the stake? More likely with the absent-minded professor who forgot his notes and took the morning paper to his lecture hall. He mused awhile.

It was a shock to surface again into reality, and receive the impression that time had turned back. Surely he had left that dark belt of trees behind many hours ago? But the sun was unmistakably on the right, so they were still heading south. And faster now that shade and water lay just ahead.

Keith called back to Garrard, consulted, and when they came to the new stream ordered a halt. It was a small stream, possibly dry for most of the year, and seemed to have no name. Sarikin Yergam sat down with his back against a tree, Gofwan beside him. Keith and Garrard stretched out and took off their shoes. Sam brought water in an aluminium saucepan, which was passed round like a loving-cup. Leviticus asked if the *Tura-wa* would take lunch or dinner; but though pre-dawn breakfast lay in the remote past, it was still too hot to eat.

Of his own accord Sarikin Yergam brought up the subject of Funyelang. He made his points clearly, and the *Tura-wa* listened in respectful silence.

If the Funyelang unrest had stopped at the killing of the village head and his helper, Sarikin Yergam would simply have outlawed the killers and hunted them down at leisure. But this the killers had anticipated, and provided against. Konkrip, their moving spirit, had given a great feast, mingling the meat of the dead men with the meat of the dead men's goats. Thus there had been enough for all, and all were implicated, for all had been forced to eat, even the women and children of Funyelang.

Keith and Garrard nodded understanding and sympathy with the Sarikin Yergam's difficult position. No doubt an enlightened chief does not like to outlaw a whole village for the wrongdoing of only two or three. The viewpoint did him credit.

Someone brought the old chief his pipe, with a black pottery bowl as big as a pint mug and a stem like a spear shaft. He stirred its contents with a skewer, added a handful of fresh leaf from a bag hidden under his robe, and mixed that in too. He allowed a warrior to top it up with a handful of embers and wood-ash from a travelling fire-pot. He sucked contentedly, belched out enough smoke to quell a colony of wild bees, and handed the pipe to Keith.

'I sent word to the *Ba-ture* when there was talk that a killing would be done. The *Ba-ture* did not come. I sent word when the killing had been done. The *Ba-ture* did not come.'

Keith drew cautiously on the portable incinerator. The chief's accusation was plain. The white man had let him down badly. Whether Pettibone had shirked danger, or wanted nothing to delay his getting away, or hoped to let his successor in for a mess which might easily blight his career, didn't matter. The point was that, so far as the Sarikin Yergam was concerned, Pettibone and Keith were the same, the divisional officer.

At least it was a relief to find that you and this remarkable man were on the same side, and that the escort, who sat around digging a thorn out of a calloused sole with a knife-point, scratching themselves or just silently glaring, were also friends.

'Say this to the Sarikin Yergam, that though we come late we will strike swiftly,' Keith instructed Gofwan. 'If it be his wish, tomorrow before dawn he shall set a ring of warriors around the village, let the innocent pass out, and we will catch and bind the killers.'

The chief nodded encouragingly. 'Me they expect, because they know my anger. When it is nearly tomorrow I will climb Funye-lang from the south side, and, seeing me, they will run north. Now you they will not expect. Even I would not have known of the coming if the dog had not told me of you.'

'The dog again!' Garrard noted, as Keith translated. They both tried to look intelligent about it.

'I placed the dog in hiding, lest he tell others. But now that you are here I have sent for him.' Sarikin Yergam still stuck to his story. 'Tonight I will set you beside the path on the north side of the hill where the villagers will run. Some you will only wound, for they will be many, but I will leave with you some men to kill these too.'

The chief mistook the reason for Keith's silence, and went on to cover what might by a fellow tactician be considered a weak point in his plan. 'I will see that they take the death path by sending some of my men to run with them and lead them into the trap.'

'And I suppose it wouldn't matter if we shot a few of those Judas-goats too. Anything to make a good bag!' Garrard looked as though he were going to be sick. 'Hullo! What's this I see?'

Garrard's sharp surprise made Keith jerk round and lay hand to rifle.

A black and white fox-terrier trotted into view, followed by a small boy in the remains of an old dinner shirt.

'Timmy!' said Keith, unbelievingly. 'What the hell are you doing so far from Bauchi?'

A black ear cocked, then a white one. Then Timmy raced forward. He flung himself on Garrard, yipped apology for his mistake, shot into Keith's arms and licked his chin.

'Dog!' announced Sarikin Yergam, with a wave of his pipe-stem and the air of a conjurer who has just pulled off his most telling trick.

'Who on earth's the young Neanderthal?' Garrard wanted to know. 'I thought the breed died out soon after the last Ice Age.'

'Dog-boy, car-washer, and general pain-in-the-neck to Medical Officer Bauchi. His name is Nyenyam, which incidentally is a nickname meaning "cannibal". I'd forgotten he came from one of the Pankshin tribes.'

Somewhere between ten and twelve years of age, a skinny little runt with large hands and feet, and a face which made even the Yergams look like Greek statuary, he stepped forward, and without warning presented the point of a barbed throwing spear at Keith's stomach.

Wrapped around the shaft, just below the evil-looking barbs, was a paper, secured by two rubber bands. Keith unrolled it and read aloud.

'I'm going on leave, and may not be allowed to return, unless I can bluff my confrères at the Colonial Office. So will you keep Timmy for me? Some rumours of Sharpe retiring. Jenkyns is poisonously exuberant. I think his former melancholia was easier on his friends. Vince died of cerebral haemorrhage after a hot afternoon in the sun teaching his schoolboys football. We miss him. Not much happening. If all goes well I may want Timmy back. But for heaven's sake keep Nyenyam. As justifiable homicide appears to be fashionable in your new division, the boy need not trouble you for long. "Be good sweet child, and let who will be clever!"'

The letter explained a little. Nyenyam, in his smattering of sing-song Hausa, explained more. When nearing Pankshin he had heard from a returning trader that the long, thin *Ba-ture* had gone south with another *Ba-ture*. It was already known that there had been some killing in Funyelang. Since the smell of dead bodies draws white men like vultures, he knew where he would find the long thin one.

'Your little cherub might have omitted the vulture part,' Garrard protested. 'But I suppose the dog "told" the old chief in the sense that a fox-terrier could only belong to a white man, and so confirmed your little cherub's story. But I still don't see how they guessed our route.'

Again the explanation was simple. '*Tura-wa* travel by easy paths,' Nyenyam pointed out the obvious. 'There are only two. One, long, which they take with horses because it is flat. I did not overtake them. So they had climbed the hills. This I told the chief of Yergam when I stopped to ask food.'

'Does this child mean he just trots around the countryside with a dog and a throwing spear?' Garrard demanded.

Nyenyam must have caught the note of surprise, or perhaps he had picked up a few words of English when at Bauchi. 'I am a man of Tal!' he boasted.

'The Tal, who live west of here, are an evil people!' Gofwan broke silence. 'It is the Tal of the Plains, who are called Montoil, who tore Mister Maltby from his saddle, and tore him apart with their hands. They do not kill for anger, but for pleasure. Worse than the . . .' Gofwan glanced about him, and subsided.

Pleased by this unsolicited testimonial Nyenyam drew himself up. 'That is true!'

Bored by so much talk, Sarikin Yergam abandoned his pipe for one of his warriors to pick up, and rose and walked.

Chapter Thirteen

Use of Armed Force, Keith typed the heading.

The murder of the Funyelang village head and his assistant occurred during the first week in June. It was not brought to my notice until July 8th.

There was no point in saying more. The Resident was capable of drawing his own conclusions.

In consultation with Major A. W. Garrard, R.A., Officer Commanding Troops, it was decided that a preliminary reconnaissance was desirable, so that we might learn the nature of the terrain, and how far the unrest had spread. These considerations would dictate the size and nature of the military force which might later be required. Major Garrard and I left at dawn on July 9th.

Pupchina, Sarikin Dallong, gave us every assistance in passing through his territory, and in effecting a meeting with Sarikin Yergam at their mutual boundary.

All very nice and official. The least said the soonest mended. Also the soonest typed, which was important since Mr Ferguson McTavish had managed to put the office typewriter out of order, and had reported sick the instant Keith had arrived at Pankshin. Keith's own portable would make only one blurry carbon, and six copies of the report were needed when, as in this case, casualties had occurred.

Even the august secretary of state in England had to have his copy, signed by Keith, which he could compare with the comments of Keith's Resident at Bauchi, the lieutenant-governor at Kaduna and the governor of Nigeria at Lagos, based on their respective copies. Unlike Sarikin Yergam, officialdom took death very seriously. A half page more, including,

An alternative plan offered by Sarikin Yergam was tactically more apt, but would have resulted in greater casualties, perhaps among the innocent. It was therefore discarded.

No sense in horrifying nice old officials with details of the proposed human battue. They might think that Sarikin Yergam was a bloodthirsty old tyrant, who ought to be deposed.

A little local colour about the ascent of the hill at night and in a blinding rain-storm, the discovery of a balanced stone slab designed to clank when anyone stepped on it and so serve as a door-bell or burglar alarm. The watch-fires at the top deserted, and no more than sodden ashes. The cordon thrown quickly around the offending hamlet, just before dawn.

Again, omitting Sarikin Yergam's practical suggestion of setting fire to the dry underside of the thatch and killing the smoke-blinded people as they ran out. Noting briefly that Garrard and Keith had entered the two door-holes on opposite sides of the honeycomb of adjoining huts.

By the time Garrard and Keith crawled out again dawn had risen over a deserted village. Garrard spat out wood-ashes, and Keith had scorched his hand, crawling low through hut after hut. The sleeping fires had still smouldered. One of Sarikin Yergam's own men must have slipped forward through the darkness to warn friends or relatives.

At this point movement was noted in the bush outside the village. Heads seen above the rocks wore the ochre-matted hair of warriors, not the shaven scalps of women. Trouble was expected. This became more probable when our own volunteer bodyguard was seen to be disappearing by twos and threes. Their reason for joining the Funyelang men might be friendliness or simple curiosity, but it reduced our numerical superiority.

Asked to recall his men, Sarikin Yergam showed no sign of doing so. He refused to answer questions, or reply when spoken

to. It must be taken into account that he was piqued at having to abandon his plan which, though costly in lives, could scarcely have failed in this way. The chief of the ' bitter-hearted' Yergams remains paramount only by continued success as a fighting leader. Our failure had seriously undermined his prestige.

Keith hoped that would be understood, back in the land of safe ballot boxes. It was as clear as Keith could make it. No point in mentioning the abandoned loads, Gofwan looking about for cover, or Nyenyam trying to borrow the Messenger's bow and quiver.

Before the situation should deteriorate to the point where it became advisable to retreat, Major Garrard and I decided to examine the site of the cannibal feast.

In reality the move was intended to show independence of the Chief, and to regain the initiative. Both were important, but the need was difficult to explain to people who weren't used to rough-and-tumbles in the Pankshin hills.

The sites of seventeen small cook-fires could be traced on the grass-topped knoll overlooking the village. But all bones had been removed. (As souvenirs, like signed menu-cards. The cannibal feast would be something to boast about for months to come.)

On our return down the knoll, the Yergam warrior walking between Major Garrard and myself was hit in the left elbow by a poison arrow. We cut out the point with my knife, and Major Garrard and myself took turns in sucking out the poison. We estimate that the man became unconscious in two minutes, and dead in three more.

Nyenyam had stirred the corpse with his toe and remarked nonchalantly 'He's done.' The man's friends refused to carry the man down till Keith insisted. Irrelevancies, and not worth typing.

It was agreed that Major Garrard should follow the party down while I waited behind for the killer. By this means one or other of us might get an enfilading shot. The killer raised his head incautiously, and we both fired.

It was a snap shot, and to make sure of results Keith had splashed his ·30-06 bullet on the rock just under the man's eyebrows, and lifted his cranium off like slicing the top from an egg. Nyenyam and Timmy had bounded forward. Nyenyam stabbed downwards with his spear and again announced 'He's done.'

Sarikin Yergam had been pleased as a girl with a box of candy. He let out a long-drawn howl for food and beer, and miraculously it appeared from nowhere. Sarikin Yergam said 'Pong!' and made a gesture of slicing the top of his head off. His warriors cracked their sides with laughter, and he gave a repeat performance. Yergam laughter set one's teeth on edge, and it was a merciful dispensation of Providence that it occurred so seldom.

But this was an official report.

The customary inquest was held on the two deceased. It transpired that the dead killer was Konkrip himself. Evidence was adduced that he was earlier the murderer of the village head, though less certainly of his assistant. Had he been able to kill one of the white men at whom he loosed the arrow it would have enhanced his prestige to the point where, it is believed, he could have gathered a big enough following to challenge the supremacy of the present Sarikin Yergam. It is, therefore, fortunate that he failed. His bow-string bore a tuft of cotton such as is used by hunters and outlaws to silence the twang, and enable them to get a second shot. There seems little doubt that he was a troublesome character.

The secretary of state doesn't want to hear about bow-string silencers. Get back to the point, or you'll be typing all day.

The villagers who came in with gifts of food and beer were at first frightened and sullen. By administrative decree Sarikin Yergam set them to demolishing their houses and burning their own thatch. They seemed to consider this an expiation of their wrongdoing, and all but one or two aged women became friendly.
The people of Funyelang have made good the loss of goats

which Konkrip had seized from the relatives of the late village head and his assistant. They express willingness to pay their arrears of tax as soon as their harvest is in. It is recommended that no further action be taken against them.

That seemed to cover it, except for typing those extra copies. They could wait.

Next for a quick glance at the official mail. Pettibone's certified cheque had come. No note with it, not so much as a grudging 'thank you'.

The handing-over certificate and similar things could go off with the Use of Armed Force report. The latter would seem to explain the delay in the former. That was a stroke of luck.

Better put the cheque in the safe. No key. Go over and get the keys from Garrard. And see how O.C. Troops was getting on.

That was a strange business. Perfectly fit and cheerful all the way to Funyelang and back. Right up to the moment when he raised his hand to acknowledge his quarter-guard's 'Guard . . . present . . . arms!' Then collapsing just as though he had put a pistol to his head and pressed the trigger.

'No, Moman. I hear no cases today. Tomorrow, I hope.'

Keith remembered his rifle. 'Anta, take this to my house. Also tell Momadu that I will soon return to eat.'

For Momadu, read Hafsatu. But propriety required that the message should not be given direct. This was the second reminder.

He smiled wryly as he found his feet leading him and Timmy to his own bungalow, and had to remind them that he was going to reassure himself about Garrard first. Also it was a sound Mohammedan custom that after absence a man must give a woman a full day's warning before he returned to her. To the cynical it might imply distrust of how a woman conducted herself during her man's absence. More charitably it could be taken to assume that a woman might need to go marketing for more food, and need time to titivate and look her best. A new hair-do, a little more *kohl* eye-shadow . . . that sort of thing.

He hoped that Hafsatu would consider a few hours' notice

127

sufficient. After all he had been gone a bare fortnight. It would be interesting to see what she thought would enhance her charm. No Paris gown would do it.

The tennis-court would need complete resurfacing after the rains ended. No small pug-marks in the softened surface. This year's crop of baby leopards might still be too young to take advantage of the children's play-pen which the white men had so considerately levelled.

The lawn in front of O.C. Troops' quarters needed cutting. In Pettibone's régime the prisoners in the local lock-up used to do that once a week. The practice must be continued. Good food and plenty of work were what murderers and goat-stealers needed just as much as divisional officers and soldiers did.

'You in, Garrard?' If any damsel were bathing his fevered brow the hail would give her time to clear out.

'Where the hell d'you think I am? Climbing trees?'

The snarl was reassuring.

Yeats, always a little taller, more youthful and eager than one remembered, grabbed Keith painfully by the hand, and drew him in. 'So worried about the old skipper, y'know, clean forgot to welcome you back when you carried him in.'

There were more magazines and official memoranda on the sick bed than bedding, and the patient seemed to be suffering from high blood-pressure due to suppressed emotion.

Yeats put a large hand to his mouth and whispered 'Sunstroke, I'm much afraid.'

Garrard jerked upright. 'Sunstroke! Hear what he says, Keith? Sunstroke! Young man, hasn't anyone ever told you that we're not allowed to have sunstroke out here? It's contrary to official policy! I'm not even sure that the word 'sun' is admissible. Malaria is grudgingly granted us, but it's far safer to stick to the well-tried English illnesses, coughs, colds and pneumonia. For the adventurous, perhaps frost-bite. But sunstroke! My God! Don't you know that the White Man's Grave is now officially a health resort?'

'O.K., Skipper!' Yeats almost saluted.

Keith appealed to Garrard. 'You've got to have something.

How about calling it nervous prostration? People get it in England from the shock of seeing the sun appear.'

Yeats grabbed at the chance. 'Thanks a lot, sir. I'll go and put it down in my daily report before I forget it. How d'you spell . . .' He caught Garrard's glare, drew himself up and saluted. 'Very good, Skip . . . Major!' He did a stiff about turn and departed.

With an injured air on his large red face O.C. Troops relaxed backward onto his sweat-stained pillow. 'He's taken to calling me "Skipper"! Also he refuses to bring me any papers which may cause anxiety, and has warned Fletcher and Griggs that worry may prove fatal. And what makes the imbecile think I have a young sister who would like to know, I quote, "your gallant exploits in Funyelang"?'

'A sister?' Keith was beginning to see light.

'As a matter of fact I have one. But I haven't told Yeats.'

'You don't need to. He's read about her. D'you happen to know Edgar Wallace's yarns?'

'Heard of him. But I don't like detective stories, too blood-thirsty or brainy, sometimes both.'

'This is one of his West African tales. That's why Yeats has fallen for it.' Keith was enjoying himself. 'You'd better reconcile yourself to the fact that you're really Captain Hamilton of the African Rifles, referred to by his subaltern as 'the skipper'. And I'm that poop Sanders of the River, district commissioner and so forth. Through the loyal effort of the worthy Lieutenant Tibbets—for whom read Yeats—Captain Hamilton's sister comes out on a visit and marries Sanders.'

Garrard brooded awhile.

'I'm not saying anything against young Liz or you, Keith; but there's no future in a monomaniac ice-skater, almost up to Olympic standards, marrying a half-crazy tropical administrator.'

Keith nodded solemn agreement. 'We'll have to set our faces against the match. Marry her off to young Yeats instead. That ought to keep him out of mischief.'

'Sure you don't mind, old man? Actually Liz is rather a decent kid, and she might easily get to like you. Girls are funny that way.'

It was grand to be home again, and to receive the cheerful welcome of the household, Momadu in spotless white at their head. Garuba Kano must be on a winning break, for his turban and gown were fit for an Emir's court, and one of his women was new. Momadu's wife was beginning to look like the scold she was. The gardener and his wife, following custom without waiting for orders, had gone to plant up Panyam rest-house. Salifu seemed as half-witted as usual.

Since they were all assembled he paid them their week's wages ahead of time, and explained that the new dog and dog-boy were now part of the staff. They gave thanks and left.

Nyenyam would shake down all right. He and Sam had struck up an ill-matched friendship on the road. To a hard-boiled youngster who ate anywhere, any time, and anything he could force between his jaws, a cook was a friend worth cultivating. Sam's attitude had been less predictable. That snarling male spinster had become a sort of bachelor uncle to the Tal boy, showing him how to clean a cook-pot and chatting, actually chatting with him on the march. Perhaps in the way Timmy's attention flattered Nyenyam's self-esteem, so Nyenyam's dog-like and calculating devotion ministered to Sam's. An odd pair, all right.

Hafsatu appeared, and all else was forgotten. The same Hafsatu, wonderfully the same.

Keith rose from his chair and answered her curtsy with a bow, exchanged the correct greetings, seated her on a leather cushion beside him, and hastily demanded more personal news.

'All was well. Well indeed. But for the waiting!' He had forgotten how pleasant her voice was.

'The days were as long in Dallong and Yergam. And the nights empty as my arms.'

'Thus was it with us, Mailafia! Even the skies were not more empty than our hearts. Till this morning!' Her dark eyes, shadowed with *kohl*, searched him from scuffed, broken shoes to the white rim of forehead which had been protected by his helmet. 'Mailafia, you are unhurt? You have no fever? There is no hidden wound?'

'The arrow hit another.' Keith misunderstood. 'We killed the killer.'

'That we heard, only after we knew that you were safe. But before that came news that the two *Tura-wa* had returned, one dying, and the other carrying him into the nearest house. We waited, saying "It is of course the soldier who dies, for it is the soldier's house. It cannot be our Mailafia!" But you did not come.' A depth of tragedy, so recent that it still lingered in her tones. A hand was laid on his knee, as though she still had need to reassure herself. Keith took it between his own.

A bell chimed in the pantry, or rather someone had struck a glass with a knife. Hafsatu rose in haste.

Momadu thought it time to serve lunch, curse him! He should be more considerate when his master had been away and had only just returned.

But apparently Keith's guess was wrong. For Hafsatu came again. And if the whole rigmarole didn't have to be gone through again, from the greetings to the enquiries. As though she could only content herself with an exact repetition. Women were inexplicable creatures.

Again he took her hand, and this time drew her up from her cushion and seated her on his knees. Just for a moment he knew the blissful comfort of her body against his. Then she leaped as though she had sat on a thorn, and said accusingly 'It was not thus the first time!'

He let her go. Puzzled, and a little hurt, he saw her collect herself, curtsy and withdraw.

Lunch was magnificent. Even the final coffee was drinkable when doctored with brandy. But what had offended Hafsatu?

The afternoon's work in the hot, silent office was just as satisfying as lunch. And one could forget about Hafsatu for the time being. Sitting in a chair was a luxury. Keith finished the Use of Armed Force report. He found time to transcribe the pencil jottings in his note-book into formally typed inquest proceedings, and sent them off by the same mail runner.

As a public servant, Keith's movements were of general interest. So it was no surprise to find his bath already poured as he entered, and Momadu prepared to pour a drink. He shed his torn rags for Salifu to pick up, climbed into the soothing warm water, and lathered himself all over before holding out his hand for the glass.

His stern self-denial at midday had been worth the effort of will. A bath, like a whisky, should be taken when one can relax, and that is impossible until evening. Only Hatasu—or Hafsatu, whichever she preferred to be called—was lacking to make satisfaction complete. He had expected her to be here, awaiting him, in spite of her newly acquired coyness.

He was a little concerned about that. Also over her wanting everything to be repeated twice, like an exact drill. Come to think of it, this morning wasn't the first time that had happened. Her second night, by chance and also by her wish, had been remarkably like the first. Perhaps a psycho-analyst could explain that by some childhood experience which had left its mark on her. He would be patient, and hope that it would soon wear off.

He washed off the lather, and put the full sponge on his head for the childish satisfaction of feeling the trickle down his shoulders. Everything within sight was exactly as he had left it, even to Hafsatu's gear in her two bunks. It all added to the feeling of home-coming, of taking up exactly where he had left off. Hafsatu had obviously been on a buying spree with the money he had left her, and had wisely brought her purchases in here rather than leave them in her deserted house during the night, and had tidily arranged them beneath the blue coverlets of the bunks.

One of the coverlets stirred. Timmy? It couldn't be. The fox-terrier, his official duties done for the day, had gone out into the compound to cultivate new and profitable acquaintances at their evening meal.

Out of the shadowy bunk stepped a voluminously clad figure, which despite a newly added white veil and the dimming evening light was unmistakably Hafsatu. Just what was needed. So she had been there all the time, the little minx.

Out of the second bunk, equally shrouded and veiled, stepped another Hafsatu. Heavens above!

They joined forces, as though afraid that Keith might be angered at the jest. And produced a weird effect as though a touch of the sun or a fall from a horse had temporarily given him double vision.

A man in his bath with a ridiculous sponge on his head is a man taken at a disadvantage; but full uniform would have left Keith feeling just as helpless. All he could do was watch the dark muffled figures glide towards him, pick up his towel and kneel at the foot of his bath.

'Who are you? I mean who is the other one?'

'It is the custom' 'when the master of the household returns' 'for the old women' 'to rub weariness from his feet.' Sometimes they spoke separately, sometimes in unison, but in the same voice. 'We are those old women.'

Hafsatu and her friend, whichever was which, seized his feet, lifted them out of the water, dried them, and began to knead them with small but certainly not helpless hands.

They were enjoying themselves. And so, regrettably, was Keith. All the same, the situation required clarification.

'I see no old woman in this room. Only Hafsatu, and one hidden under a veil and many garments whose voice is as Hafsatu's.' Not that he had the ghost of a notion which of them was the real Hafsatu. Now they had finished kneading, and were pulling the toes. 'There are five toes to each foot.' He suggested. 'Make sure that they are all replaced.'

They giggled. He had hoped that though they had learned to imitate each other's talk, they might have forgotten to rehearse a laugh. But the two giggles were identical.

By now he was sure that he knew the simple explanation. A Mohammedan wife will often insist on her husband taking a second wife, so that she may have a companion, or someone to share her housework. Or for prestige, like having two cars in the garage. Hafsatu had been lonely while he was away, and had found a friend of her own age down in the Hausa settlement. And the two of them had hatched up this plan.

If that was what they wanted, it was worth considering. Hafsatu had certainly seemed prim this morning. She, whichever she was, wasn't being so prim now. But steady competition might keep her up to the mark.

They planted his feet on the mat on each side of the bath, ran round, clasped him under each arm, and lifted him out. It wasn't a standard way of leaving a bath, nor easy. Their thin veils fluttered under the effort, but they succeeded. Determined little females!

They rubbed him down. They took the clean shirt Momadu had laid on the bed, and tugged it onto him. Both of them had trouble with the unaccustomed buttons, but they managed somehow. Next one of them clasped him firmly to her, while the other lifted one of his feet and inserted it into a trouser leg and a mosquito boot. Then the other seized him. Again he put his arm round a girl, as though to steady himself, and tried to compare her shape with the first one. But the tent-like outer garments defeated his purpose. His other foot was inserted through trouser leg into boot, and the trousers pulled up. Triumphantly—he could feel that.

If the second girl were Hausa, not only would she be more solidly built, but her nose would be flatter, her lips fuller. All he could see above the flattering white veils were four mischievous eyes. His attempts to peer under or round the veils were tactfully thwarted.

Lamplight showed through the arched doorway. The table was being laid in the dining-room. Co-operatively Keith held up his trousers while twenty hurried fingers and thumbs struggled with the fly buttons. The light silver bracelets on one girl's arms were the same as those on the other girl's—and the same number. The young conspirators had certainly been thorough.

The trousers were fastened. Dark eyes consulted with dark eyes in alarm. But silently, for now there were ears in the dining-room. The shirt tails were outside the trousers, and shirt tails should be inside! To unbutton and rebutton was unthinkable. Dinner would be on the table at any moment. Each thought of the same original expedient. Each pulled up a linen trouser-leg as high as it would go. Each knelt, thrust back her bracelets, and wriggled a hand up inside. But the arms were too short, or the trouser legs too tight. Keith tucked his own shirt in, to save tomorrow's office wear from looking like an accordion.

Nobody remembered the tie. Hafsatu, or it might have been

134

her friend, held up the jacket, while the other loaded tobacco pouch, two pipes, matches, thirteen rounds of ammunition, a prismatic compass and a paper-weight which happened to have been beside them, into the side pockets, as into donkey's panniers. They got him into the jacket. They patted him approvingly, and stood back to admire their handiwork, rather breathlessly to judge by the fluttering of the white veils.

A soup plate clicked. Momadu announced 'Food is ready.'

The amateur valets made a last attempt to smooth down the rumpled linen, then stood aside.

Tieless, hair unbrushed, but fortunately without a forgotten sponge on top, Keith summoned an air of nonchalance and entered the lamplight.

'A little early?' Keith looked at his wrist-watch. No wrist-watch.

Momadu didn't crack a smile.

Chapter Fourteen

THE last dish had been washed and put away. Momadu had exchanged 'good nights'. The house was silent. Purposefully Keith took up the lamp and returned to the bedroom. But he must be careful not to hurt the new girl's feelings. Having nerved herself to this adventure, she would still be a bundle of doubts and hesitations.

They dropped lightly from their bunks. No, he still could not tell one from the other. Their height was the same, their dress the same, even their step the same.

'I ask a favour of you, Unknown.' He spoke the words he had planned.

'It is granted!' Both answered in the same words and voice.

'Then, of your kindness, Unknown, retire to the house where you have passed the day.' He was careful to look between the two. 'Tomorrow we will take counsel together. But tonight there is only one thought in my mind, only one love in my heart, for Hafsatu.'

'Or Hatasu?' they suggested. And with uncertain hands began to remove their outdoor clothing.

'Or Hatasu,' he agreed. He turned and hung his office coat on a chair-back. 'Please go. I will light your way with a lamp.'

'Mailafia does not know?' Now they lifted their veils and laid them aside.

'But . . . but . . .' Keith gaped. But this was impossible!

Slowly, as though disappointed at having to prove what his affection should have revealed to him, they unwound their wraps; as reluctantly discarded their scanty skirt-cloths, and folded and laid them aside on the other garments.

Keith stared, hoping to discover some mark, some gesture, some shape of breast or mouth or limb which did not belong to the girl he loved. There was none. From gleaming plaited hair to shapely toes there was no difference. By some miracle one girl had become two. And both were real. And each was the one for whom his body hungered.

Tears gathered in their eyes, but bravely they challenged him. ' Which will you drive away, Hafsatu or Hatasu? '

Not one girl, but two identical girls all the time! Hafsatu first; then Hatasu, demanding that her night should be exactly like her sister's down to the smallest detail. What had seemed a strange need to have news of the Funyelang trip repeated twice was now explained, for Hafsatu had wanted to be told what was told to Hatasu, or the other way around, and had escaped from his embrace since he had not embraced the other first.

Only one thing could make this impersonation possible. They must be identical twins, looking alike, speaking alike, even thinking alike. Though it seemed against all the laws of nature, or of chance, that perfection could be thus repeated.

' I cannot part with either, for I desire both, and equally! ' he blurted out.

With his shirt cuffs he tried to wipe away their tears. The sleeves were too short. He pulled off his shirt, and now he could tend both faces at once. Tears still gathered in their eyes, but smiles trembled on their lips. He found a clean handkerchief and blew their noses. Now their eyes smiled too.

' Mailafia forgives, even before our tale is told! Indeed he is not Eblis! Indeed he is not! '

' Eblis, the Devil? Why should I be? '

' When Shetu learned the curse of our twinship, that by law no man might take us both into his house, she said " Alas! For there is no remedy." We said " Woe to us, then! For if we are parted, we die." '

The twins spoke separately or in unison, and Keith could not tell one voice from the other.

' Shetu saw that our words were true. She said " Have patience! " We waited. After many days she said " I have sought far, and questioned secretly."

' We said " accept our gratitude! " But we waited.

137

'She said "There is still one, I think, who will dare your love. He is clean, strong, and not too old. But he is an Unbeliever."

'We said "Though he be Eblis himself, we will go to him; if he will not part us asunder."

'"Not Eblis, but far otherwise." The good Shetu smiled, with a smile which was like the licking of lips on sight of a comb of sweet honey. "Once he broke the custom of men, leading me to another when he desired me greatly for himself. But what you ask of him is yet harder, that he break the law of both Nazarenes and Believers." And again she took thought.'

Keith drew them to the big bed and sat down, perching them one on each side of him. He could guess what they meant by the 'curse of twinship'. Sisters, or mother and daughter, or cousins were not allowed by Koranic law to be co-wives or co-concubines.

'We answered "Let his punishment fall upon us, here or in the hereafter, if only he will take us! Tell us his name and dwelling!"

'Yet Shetu was troubled, saying "Perhaps I requite white with black, and return him evil in exchange for his good. Your desires are as the quick flame of thatching grass, for you are young. How can I be sure that you will give him love, which is as the comfort of a cooking fire in the cold season?"

'We said again "We will go to him though we search the whole world, for in all the world there is none other for us! And our desires will turn to love, and by the greatness of our love cause him to love us too."' Hafsatu-Hatasu turned earnest young faces up to Keith's. 'And this we seek to do!'

'It is done already.' He put his arms about their bare shoulders.

Embracing two delightful women at the same time produced a strange sensation, which increased when four slender braceleted arms slid under his and wrapped themselves around him. If this had happened when they first came to him as strangers it would have shocked his conventional way of thought, and no doubt added an appealing spice of wickedness. But now he felt only a strengthening of the wish to cherish and protect. As though his love for them had doubled, even as they had seemed to double.

'Mailafia forgives that we are twins?'

'Even as a beggar forgives, when expecting only one coin he receives two!'

'Oh, but we dreaded! We could not be sure that Mailafia would understand our need. Therefore we said to each other "For the first time in our lives we must be parted. We will go singly to him. Then if he love one he will love the other. If he love each separately, he will love both together."' The twins ended on a note of triumph, 'And thus it was, and thus it will be!'

He stroked their silken backs, and they tried to wriggle even closer.

'To my great happiness,' he assured them. 'Yet we must give each other counsel, so that no unhappiness or jealousy shall arise between you.'

'Is one eye jealous of another, one ear of its fellow? No more could one of us envy the other one. And now the love of Mailafia has drawn us yet closer together!' They hugged him convulsively. 'Once it was Hafsatu-Hatasu who were one. Now Mailafia is part of us, joining us more closely still.'

So much was at stake, such unexpected, and so far as he was concerned undeserved, happiness, that Keith wanted to take no avoidable risks.

'Men wiser than I have made the custom that a man shall take one of his wives for her appointed days, then the next wife, and the third and the fourth. Until it is again the turn of the first to sleep in his room.'

'Woe to us, if Mailafia is so cruel!' He could feel their young bodies grow tense. 'When he parted us before, even though he did not know that he did so, it was like the sickness of death. Not till the whole day had been passed behind the closed door of our house, telling of every word that had been said, of each thing that had been done, did our tears dry.'

'Yet if all is seen by both, and all heard by both, it may be thought that by accident I love Hafsatu more than Hatasu, or Hatasu more than Hafsatu.'

'This we have given thought to, for we know the ways of women, being women. But with Mailafia's permission, he shall never know which is Hafsatu, and which Hatasu!'

That might be a little awkward at times. But it was a small risk to take. He hadn't the least wish to part them. Ever. This close union in mind and body with two women at once was something he had never heard of before, and had not imagined could exist. All the more reason to make sure that nothing should dissolve it.

'Even though I do not know which of you is which, it may be that my body will draw closer to one than to the other. I would not wish this to happen, but it may.' If he could be certain it would not happen, his last unwilling doubt would be laid to rest.

They knew that they had won. One tightly-plaited hair-do butted him softly under the chin on his left side, the other on his right. Four lips nuzzled his neck.

'How shall Mailafia tell the difference between two sips of water taken from the same bowl? We are only one bowl.' Now each was straddling a knee, and pressing closer. 'Taste both again, Mailafia. And judge!'

It was first dawn, but some time before sunrise, when Keith heard the whisper of sound. He slipped into pyjama shorts, and taking his long-barrelled Luger went to the front door.

Nobody. But something stirred at his feet. So the sound had been a feeble mewing, not a cautious whistled signal between burglars. He picked the poor beast up. It weighed little more than its clotted fur, which had once been white, long, and silken. The Empress.

He took her to the pantry, poured a little canned milk into a saucer and with his finger mixed in some water from the filter. The Empress tried it, coughed till she seemed about to fall apart; then finished the dish, slowly and as though painfully.

Momadu and the rest of the household were likely to be still asleep. Perhaps the twins would look after the waif, until he came back from early morning office and could make other arrangements.

The twins looked rather like kittens themselves, curled closer together to fill the gap left by Keith's absence. They were still sleeping, yet when he murmured 'Hafsatu-Hatasu', their eyes opened at once.

'Here is one, a traveller, and in need, who asks our hospitality.' He laid the disreputable object on the bed.

'Mailafia's guest is our guest.' Their hands went out to it, hesitated, but overcame their repugnance. 'We will care for it.'

'Of your kindness. She is Petbo's cat. Perhaps she strayed when Petbo went to the train, and because she had shown friendship to me he did not cause search to be made.'

He was unaware that he had said anything remarkable, but Hafsatu-Hatasu were staring at him.

'This we did not know! This was not told to us!'

'Of course not. It is unknown. It is only my thought.'

'It is Mailafia's hot anger which was unknown to us. Petbo's hatred is spoken of. He hates many, Moman the Messenger, some chiefs of tribes and villages, Mailafia himself, the big Sergeant, and sometimes carriers and even prisoners. But Mailafia's hatred was unknown, even to us.'

'Unknown, even to me. This is foolish talk.'

'The talk of women is as unwinnowed corn, much chaff but some grain. And this we think is grain. That the anger of Petbo falls on many, like the flat of an ill-wielded sword. That the anger of Mailafia is as the point of a sword, more deadly, yet which only one need fear—Petbo!'

Keith finished a brief wash—shaving was done at breakfast time—and brushed his hair. He laughed to show he did not take the twins' idea too seriously. 'Petbo is in Zaria, and safe from swords. Not even an arrow flies so far.'

A cup clinked in the pantry, and the twins ran to their bunks for clothing. 'We came from Bauchi to love and be loved. So Petbo will return from Zaria to hate and be hated. This we believe.'

'Tell none but me such foolish thoughts.' He hugged them both together, put the Empress in their arms, and shooed them out.

One sat on the veranda of the office, waiting. It was said that yesterday Mister Keeta had concerned himself with writing, as he had done before going to Funyelang the Accursed. Today, perhaps, his face would be shown more clearly.

He came from his house whistling, which was his custom so that robes and faces might be straightened at his coming. He exchanged greetings. He asked after one's illness of yesterday, and gave thanks that one was better. Then said to Anta and Tibn 'Come. We will speak together.'

Together they took the path which circles the Hill of the Flag, and were lost to sight.

They returned.

Mister Keeta said 'The clerk has not come?' and turned his feet towards the house of the clerk. One made to follow, but he ordered 'Rest, Gofwan! Funyelang was far, and you are weary.'

One asked Tibn and Anta what words were spoken upon the path, and they replied 'Not many!' It was as though they held a secret.

They did not sit, but leaned against a pillar. No whip had been taken, so a bamboo had been cut. Sweat was on their faces, and Mister Keeta's face had been cool. It became clear that for their folly in the Panyam counting they had been set to beat each other.

One said 'A great wrong has been done to you! Beating is not permitted. Also many papers are necessary, and the permission of the Resident, before punishment is given.'

Tibn answered 'And for each page in writing, a month in prison! What ignorance is this that you teach?'

And Anta said 'Blind are your eyes and deaf your ears, Gofwan, my relative by marriage, if in walking to Funyelang and back you did not learn more of Mister Keeta than we did walking round the little hill.'

Soon came Mister Keeta again, with the black-man-of-no-tribe hurrying behind, for Mister Keeta's pace was long and swift. The clerk's feet were bare, and under his coat he wore no shirt, nor a coloured cloth around his neck. It was clear that he had risen in haste, perhaps from bed.

Then it was quiet, and even before the morning meal many people brought complaints and were heard, and writing was put to many papers.

Having eaten, Mister Keeta returned, his small writing machine in hand and with him the small white dog, which lay down beneath his table.

Loshi took the machine. Mister Keeta did not seat himself. He said 'I will walk again. Come Gofwan! Come, Moman Wanti!'

One followed, remembering the walk he had taken with Anta and Tibn, and fearing. Moman whispered 'I have done no wrong, or only little wrongs. I place my trust in Allah and Mohammed, his prophet!'

One answered 'It is perhaps worse than a beating. This path leads to the prison. What has he learned? Who has told him?'

It was not fair that a *Ba-ture* should be like this one, showing no anger, nor shouting. For how can a Messenger shape his speech if he does not know whether anger, sadness or pleasure is needed? Words, like food, should be salted and flavoured, with something left out and something added.

Then one remembered that much profit can be made by standing between wrongdoing and punishment. One said 'Permit that I be the forerunner, to see that all is swept and ready.'

Those words were folly, and went unanswered. A leopard does not send warning when he is about to spring.

The prison was no bigger than the office, but with walls too thick to dig through in a night, and a roof of beams, close and well plastered. The path led from the back, so Harar the head warder was found seated in his deck-chair outside the door, a bowl of food on his knees, and the woman prisoner fondling his feet. He rose slowly, his mouth open in fear.

Greetings were exchanged. Mister Keeta said 'The book. The warrants.' They were brought in haste, and Mister Keeta entered with them. The prisoners rose from their mats and made obeisance. He spoke with each, asking his name and crime, and with pencil made mark on warrant and in book. He tasted their food and spat it out. He ordered that the head warder should eat what the prisoners could not. He ordered that Harar's food bowl be given to the prisoners, and that more be cooked.

He found two prisoners who had been held more than their appointed time. He found that one prisoner was absent without due permission. He sent the women prisoner running to call a smith, that leg chains be struck off from those who should be freed, and from others whose wrongdoing did not call for chains. Harar had chained all, for hardship makes men willing givers and afraid of authority.

Much indeed was done, and briefly as a woman brushes dust and scorpions from her floor. But the matter of the head warder still cumbered the threshold. He clasped the knees of Mister Keeta saying 'I repent! I repent! It was by the order of Petbo! All was by the order of Petbo!'

Mister Keeta summoned one of the two prisoners who should have been freed. He was a good man, though he had killed. Mister Keeta asked 'Have you a wife? Can she cook for many? And well?'

It was so.

Mister Keeta said 'When a man has been long in chains, he returns to find his land unhoed, and his goats missing. It is better to be a head warder than to starve. Send for your wife. Take Harar's robes, which are not his but the government's, and wear them.'

The man, whose name was unknown even to a head Messenger, was unwilling to be head warder! He asked 'How is it known that I will not seize the woman prisoner and sleep with her? As this . . .' he pointed an insulting toe at Harar, 'did?'

'Because your wife has hungered, yet not sought another man. That woman is well loved by you.'

It was true, for the man smiled as though Mister Keeta had acknowledged his riches. Yet it was still as though Mister Keeta begged him, a man still in chains, to accept greatness, and he was still unwilling. For he said 'What if I take the iron boxes of money that are kept here, and run?'

'I will pursue and, Allah permitting, capture and punish.' It could be seen that Mister Keeta grew impatient. 'But these are idle thoughts, and shall not break my sleep.'

The nameless one gathered his chains in hand as though they were a robe of honour bestowed by an Emir. He made obeisance neither unduly high nor low, and said:

'I accept.'

There was much to consider on the way back to the office. Said Moman behind his sleeve as he straightened the tying of his turban, 'Only a little, and chains would have been about our ankles! It is no longer wise to hide what is known to us.'

One demanded 'Who told him of Harar? Someone has his ear.'

'He has also eyes, and a nose. And his nose is long.'

That was a strange thought, but no stranger than others. How had he known that the killer was honest? Because he too was a killer, and like spoke to like? And why had he shown mercy to Harar?

Keith, back in the office and trying to repair Mr Ferguson McTavish's typewriter, found himself asking the same question. Why had he? The head warder should have been formally tried in the provincial court. Once under arrest there would have been plenty of witnesses against him. If anything stank in Keith's nostrils it was breach of trust and abuse of authority towards people like helpless prisoners. Cowardly crimes of the meanest sort.

Pettibone was the answer. The man had invoked Pettibone. The head warder was one of Pettibone's Pets. You didn't fight unarmed underlings. You kept your sword for their master.

'Sword'? What a damned fantastic idea! But of course it was the twins who had put that into his mind. They had Tennysonian ideals of chivalry. If someone in the station happened to have a copy of the laureate's poems, he would borrow it. The twins might like to hear a translation. It would be right up their alley.

Chapter Fifteen

DURING the weeks when he was not out on tour repairing roads and rest-houses, collecting taxes and settling disputes, Keith found plenty to do in reorganizing his headquarters. And discovered an unsuspected talent in that direction.

Flattery he could detect. Praise glanced off him harmlessly. Too many people in his past, schoolmasters, sergeants, right up to the snarling old Resident Bauchi had ensured that he should cherish no illusions about himself. What worried him was his long string of successes.

They seemed to say You can't get around facts. You really are damned smart. You say that office work isn't in your line, but did anyone before you get it so organized that they could do more than half of it out on tour? And so far as practical administration goes, how about your new dodge of getting the lesser chiefs to sit with you as assessors when you listen to village cases? Saves you making any amount of fool mistakes, adds to the chiefs' prestige, and gives the people their own kind of justice, not English law.

Or training that Hausa, who doesn't know a word of English, as scribe for the Native Administration treasury. Certainly it's meant a lot of extra work for you, but it's going to save you and your successor a lot more in the end. And it's long overdue. Other divisions have had native treasurers and people for years. See what I mean?

Deflators of swollen egos are almost essential to those in authority. Emperors have been known to keep jesters whose main function was to mock the pretensions of both Emperor and courtiers. Religious men and women sometimes slept in their coffins to remind themselves of their mortal natures. The sacred King of the Jukons, in the next division to the south, carried the skull of his predecessor along wherever he went, though possibly not for the same reason.

Keith's deflator was a rusty, mildewed typewriter with an iron-hard and corrugated platen, whose every letter was out of alignment and whose carriage did all but jump the rails. He patched it and repaired it with all the skill and ingenuity at his command. He knew he was licked from the beginning, hopelessly outclassed. And wondered if that was its fascination.

It was no longer the fault of Mr Ferguson McTavish. He mourned with Keith over every failure, triumphed with him over every temporary success. It became a bond between them. While Keith tinkered, Mr McTavish confided his innermost secrets. In no other mortal body, it seemed, did bowels, kidneys, liver and stomach fight a more devastating civil war. Sheer anarchy reigned within. Daily, sometimes twice daily, striking developments called for new war bulletins. Sometimes they were typed and sent to Keith on tour with the official mail. One was nearly sent in error to the Resident Bauchi.

Mr McTavish was lonely. He despised the Messengers as illiterates, feared the soldiers, and classed all Hillmen as heathen cannibals and subhuman. Keith was his sole recourse. When Keith was in the station, the clerk took to coming early to office. He lingered over jobs when the office closed in the afternoon.

Being a born worrier, and having nothing to worry about, Keith worried about having nothing to worry about. Things were going far too well. There was something fishy about it. On a day when the letter ' e ', the most whimsical part of the office typewriter, had continued to function for a whole week, he felt a crisis had been reached. And decided to seek advice.

Momadu and Nyenyam had locked up and left. It was a warm night, and Keith wore only pyjama shorts and slippers, the twins their house-sandals and their coquettish little face-veils which emphasized their lack of other clothing—as no doubt was their intention.

The harsh frenzy of the strange triple relationship had softened into a deep contentment. So long as they were together, touching if possible, the three were one. Keith, knowing his duty, had

147

admired their new hair-do. Each plait had been teased out and replaited again from the hair roots, so mercilessly tight that it drew up the outside corners of their eyes. They had placed his hands on their heads, and he had wriggled the shining black helmets, and said that they were as tight as shells on nuts. Apparently the right comment, for they suddenly hugged him.

And now came what Keith privately thought of as the Children's Hour. He led the way into the spare room which he had turned into a home office. The Empress followed them. Timmy, who out of envy of the Empress had taken to sleeping in the house, gave a bored yawn and followed the Empress.

The Empress curled up on the table among the files. Timmy relaxed with a thud under the table, where careless feet would not interrupt his slumbers. Keith dropped into a large chair, and Hafsatu-Hatasu disposed themselves by custom one on each knee, trying to tickle him with their veils against his ears.

The girls didn't mind what he translated for them. Written words were wisdom, far removed from idle conversation. By being read to, the twins were absorbing culture. And they adored culture.

They held the book for him with their unoccupied hands, his being around them. When he said 'Now', they impressively turned a page. He finished the story: 'And thus it was that Odysseus slew those who had courted Hafsatu-Hatasu during his long absence.'

The twins wriggled happily. That trick of running their own names into a story never failed to please.

'And now it is I who seek knowledge.' Keith moved them slightly so that their hip-bones should rest on a different part of his lean thighs. 'And it is you, of your wisdom, who shall inform me.'

The idea amused them. 'It is enough that we have found Mailafia, who has made us one, and who still desires us. What use have we for wisdom. Let Mailafia be wise for all three!'

'Yet still I ask. Since, as you say, we three are one, let the three heads which are one consider what puzzles one-third of the heads. As a man lifts with both hands what is too heavy for one hand to grasp. As day follows night, so in my life have good fortune and bad always mingled. Yet now, in my eyes, there is only good fortune. Can this be, or do my eyes no longer see what I do not wish to see?'

They did not understand at first, and he had to give instances of his long run of good luck.

'All things are possible, under Allah.' They nodded sagely. 'And the ways of Allah cannot be known. There is a foolish story such as is told in market-places. Does Mailafia wish to hear it?'

Mailafia did. Very much.

'"What is this thing called 'rain'?" asked the Old Sandal. "For forty years I have travelled and traded, and never seen it. Yet you, who do not stir from your dung-heaps, speak of it as familiarly as the dust between your toes."

'The villagers tried in vain to convince him that there was this thing called "rain". For indeed he had never seen water fall from the skies. His loads, and almost his life, had been lost in flooded rivers, his sandals had trodden upon paths still running with new-fallen rain, and in his passing he had brushed fresh rain-drops from the bushes. Yet Allah had willed that never where he walked, nor where he made night-stage, should rain fall. Thus it was.

'And thus it came about that wherever he went he strove to correct the folly of those who believed that water could fall from the empty skies wherein are no rivers or wells, or so much as a calabash bowl to store water or to empty it. Great, he declared, was the blindness of people! Could they not see that what they called "rain" was made by trees, and dripped from trees on to the ground below? Moreover the land itself bore witness, for where trees were thick, then was the land always moist below them. Where there were lines of trees, at their feet flowed streams and rivers. Where there was only bush and grass, man had to dig wells. And he himself, going on pilgrimage, had seen lands where, for lack of any trees or even bushes, no water could be found for several days' journey.

'Speaking thus, angrily, in the big city of Kano, the other traders mocked him, saying "This man is surely mad!" The tale was carried to the Emir for his amusement.

149

'The trader, the Old Sandal, went his way.

'The next day rain fell upon Kano. The Emir gave order that women should wash well their bowls and set them out. He caused the rain to be collected. He caused a thousand horsemen to carry two thousand calabash bottles of rainwater, and ride swiftly, and overtake this trader, and show him, and cure his madness. Or slay him.

'When he heard the hooves, the trader ascribed greatness to Allah and to the Emir as is due. Also, fearing for his loads, to the captain of the horsemen. He took the calabash that was given to him, and poured water into his right palm, and tasted, and drank. Then fear left him as his anger burned. "This is a jest you play, Chief of the Horsemen, thinking I lack understanding. Often have I been told that this 'rain' of which you speak is in pieces, small as millet-corn grains, each apart from the other. This is in one piece. It is only water!"

'The chief of the horsemen drew and smote.'

As usual, the twins summed up their story with a maxim.

'From this comes the saying "To Allah all things are possible; but to the Emir of Kano only the taking or sparing of heads."'

Keith chuckled appreciatively. It was well told, as were most of the twins' stories. Then he caught the implication.

'If in forty years a man may never see rain, though rain fall all about him, a month or a year of good fortune need not trouble me?'

The twins turned adoring eyes upon him. They had the womanly faculty of believing that their man was a paragon of wisdom, and at the same time a slow-witted babe in arms. And seemed to have no difficulty in admiring him for the one and cherishing him for the other.

The household had its ups and down. A run of bad luck in gambling reduced the horse-boy to only an occasional woman and no gown. Orion's supply of corn began to melt away, and Keith was forced to keep count of the bundles. The horse-boy appeared in a gown again, and his wife had a new and larger silver nose-stud. For the time being Orion's feed would be safe.

Salifu, the second house-boy, 'ran' without any explanation,

150

and while three days' pay was due to him. Last seen, he was heading back to Railhead.

As dog-boy, Nyenyam claimed that the Empress came within the category of dogs, rather than horses which were Garuba's, or humans which were Sam's and Momadu's care. With teeth and large gentle hands he teased out the burrs which the cat collected daily, and the Empress recovered her looks and dignity.

Then Nyenyam fell from grace. Apparently out of curiosity he had occasionally helped Salifu with minor indoor jobs. When Salifu 'ran' Momadu promoted the small Tal tough as substitute, until someone better could be found. Returning from office to shave before breakfast, Keith walked in on the denouement.

A scowling Momadu, pillow in hand, pointed to a hole through sheet and mattress which the pillow had hidden. An equally scowling Nyenyam denied that he had tried to kill Salifu. He had been helping Salifu to make the bed, and had lifted the pistol which the *Ba-ture* kept under his pillow. The pistol had gone off.

As the revolver was an old army model it was surprising that Nyenyam had been able to pull the stiff trigger. But it explained Salifu's hasty departure.

Nyenyam was fined half a week's pay, but at Momadu's request given second-house-boy's rank. There was a sort of cock-eyed justice about the promotion. After all, Nyenyam had arranged for his predecessor to vacate the post.

The Resident's comments on the Funyelang expedition came in. Keith read them with foreboding, then re-read them to make sure he hadn't missed a touch of irony, or a negative or two.

By their prompt action, disregard of personal comfort and safety, and remarkable grasp of a very difficult situation, these two officers averted the need for a small punitive expedition. I recommend that the valuable services of Major A.W. Garrard, R.A., be brought to the notice of his military superiors.

The opportunity was too good to miss. Keith trekked across and found O.C. Troops in the battery orderly room.

Garrard caught sight of Keith's solemn expression, and sent his orderly room corporal out on a job to count equipment.

'Trouble?' he asked.

'For you. And I'm afraid the lieutenant-governor, the governor, and the secretary of state all concur with the Resident.'

Garrard read. He looked blank. He looked surprised. Then a grin spread across his red face.

'You're right, without knowing it. My commandant. He's a first-class soldier, polo and bridge player. But he's got a misguided sense of humour.'

'I don't see what harm that can do. You pulled off a tidy job. That's all.'

Garrard considered. 'How would you like to be tagged with "Killer Keith, the Tribal Tactician"? I can just hear my boss referring to "Gallant Garrard, Foe of the Funyelang" or some such horrors. Why do you damned people have to write reports?'

Keith's touring had developed along two different lines. One was the armed patrol, to places long unvisited where the attitude of the people was doubtful. With the aid of a few red gowns to make the actual arrests, it could be turned into a police raid to catch a wrongdoer whose own chief found him too hot to handle.

This type of patrol travelled fast and far, often under cover of darkness or rain-storm to secure the advantage of surprise. The soldiers in the ranks lapped it up, as a relief from barracks and parade-ground. Dan Beki Kano the battery sergeant-major, Fletcher, Yeats and Garrard took to it as a new, and reasonably dangerous sport. Griggs had to be different, of course, and in his cups referred to 'bullying the poor bloody nigger'.

This was the 'picnic' as Fletcher called it. It announced quite unmistakably 'I do not fear you.' And let it go at that.

The second, the 'circus', said 'I come in peace. Do not fear me,' and was a logical follow-up to the first. The two were complementary, and far more effective than an attempt to combine both.

But it was the peace mission, not the raid, which demanded most of the divisional officer. Travelling traders who accompanied the circus to convert corn, red peppers, and various oddments down to an occasional roll of webbing-like cloth into money which could be used for paying tax, tried to set up monopoly prices, and had to be closely watched. Wives of Messengers and tribal policemen, who were allowed to come along to advertise that the party came as peaceful friends, tried to seize food and private property and refused to pay for the scarce fuel they used. And they all, including small children, straggled on the short slow stages of a march, and strayed in the villages, blindly confident that it was the divisional officer's duty to see that they came to no harm.

Usually it was the first day out which was the most trying, but on this occasion trouble started on the second day. Keith had personally inspected each donkey before starting, but a trader had added two more, one horribly galled, and the other with a part-dislocated hip. Keith ordered the man back with his whole string, and sent a red-robe along to see that he complied. Two women came to blows, a child fell sick, a load was smashed, someone muddied a drinking pool before water could be drawn . . . just the usual things, but more of them. Keith had to ride herd all morning, and reached Panyam with a blistering headache and the tingle in his joints which meant a touch of malaria.

Possibly the fresh fruit and vegetables of Panyam rest-house disagreed with his heavy dose of quinine. Diarrhoea embarrassed the start of his next morning's march. It cleared up, but his head began to spin. He tried walking, he tried riding. It was no place to fall ill, this no-man's-land between the Sura tribe to the east and the Ron tribe to the west. By guess he had only five miles to go to reach the first Ron village, when he fell flat on his face.

It was malaria all right, plus a probable touch of sun. From time to time Keith was aware of Momadu piling on more blankets including Orion's, and Nyenyam bringing hot, tasteless tea. Hafsatu and Hatasu claimed the night-watch, and his babbling quieted at the touch of their hands.

When his mind became receptive again, he learned that he had ordered the circus to return to Pankshin, but Moman Wanti had ordered that brush be cut and shelters made for the *Ba-ture* and his household. Which was as well, for it had rained. How it had rained!

Malaria leaves behind it appalling depths of depression. The recurrent bouts of high temperature and hazy happiness grew shorter, and the intervening stretches of grim misery more prolonged. No one with any sense, Keith began to feel, came out to West Africa, the notorious White Man's Grave. Two of the ten who had come out with him were dead already. But not Ian Keith. Oh no. That meddling fool was still messing about with poor devils of Hillmen who only wanted to be left alone to lead the life they had always done. If that was what he was here for, he ought at least to get on with it.

He told the twins, in a voice that seemed to belong to a stranger, 'We must get up and go. I cannot die here in the mud.'

They said gently 'Rest, Mailafia! There is no thought of dying.'

He decided to be firm. 'Of course there is. There is even a need for me to die. Though not here. I grow angry at your foolish talk.'

They lifted the mosquito net and placed their heads upon the mildewed pillow beside him. 'Let Mailafia's anger fall upon us! But rest! Rest!'

He must have rested awhile. But when Momadu came with some very salt soup made from canned beef, he remembered his purpose.

'Let carriers be sent for! We move at once.'

Momadu exchanged glances with the twins, and answered. 'I will tell the Messenger.'

Before Moman Wanti entered the twins found time to put on their veils and outdoor garments. There was no place where they could hide, but Moman's glance seemed to pass over them unseeing.

Keith rose on an elbow and repeated his orders.

Moman said 'Tomorrow, or the day after, the carriers shall be brought. There is no village near.'

'Now! At once!'

The Messenger looked frightened, but obstinate. 'Let me send first for the soldier *Ba-ture*.'

'There is no need for soldiers. Unless you disobey!'

'With permission of the *Ba-ture* . . . I thought . . .' Moman's stammer grew worse. 'There is a man . . . Tagwal . . . who killed in the next division . . . and fled to the Ron tribe . . . perhaps with the help of the soldiers . . .'

'No need for carriers or soldiers. We will go ourselves and capture Tagwal.'

Keith called for his clothes. In vain. He crawled to a uniform case and found an office suit. He felt a little stronger after that success, and stood upright, supported by the twins. Tactfully Moman went out into the rain. The twins dressed him over his pyjamas, but it was he who had to remember the shoulder holster and the heavy pistol. He took no sun-helmet. He went out into the rain.

People tried to stop him. Sam ran up with a part-eaten leg of goat and tried to give it to him. He brushed them aside, but they tried to follow.

There was no need for them to die with him. He loved them all, even Sam, who made such salty soup. But he must hide his affection, for now was the time to be stern. For their sake.

'Let none follow!' His voice had a thin, reedy sound, but it was the best he could manage. 'And when I am gone, let Allah keep you and protect you!'

It was a difficult march, though mostly on the level. Whenever Keith fell, he whimpered in his weakness like a puppy, and had to go on all fours like a puppy till he could again force himself upright. Then it was only rain, cold, and misery beyond belief. And the reluctant passing of the miles.

Moman Wanti fell from a bridge. As the bridge was only a palm trunk, smoothed by the passage of many feet, and slippery with mud, it was excusable. Keith straddled the log, reached down a hand but missed Moman's grasp. The Messenger, robes floating up around his head, was carried away downstream. Keith sat there, regretting that a life so full of stupidity should culminate in such a stupid mishap. Moman was undoubtedly worth ten of Keith, or ten hundred, or ten thousand. Anyway, it really was a pity he had drowned.

Then Moman reappeared, said 'Come' coaxingly, but had to balance out again along the log, and help Keith hitch himself onward to the far bank.

It went dark again, and Moman had to lead Keith by the arm. It was most undignified. But catching Tagwal would justify it. Catching Tagwal would atone for much folly.

The march came to an end. It was still dark. By the smell they were in a goat pen. It was dry. Keith tried to withdraw his senses from his misery, but failed. That was all he had ever done or could ever do—fail. Why had he never realized that before?

Moman was missing. No matter. Keith would rest and charge up his willpower again. It had run down like a battery, and wouldn't stir his self-starter. Of course it was possibly he and not his battery which was dead. He could not be sure.

Moman came back and touched his shoulder.

'It is now, Ba-ture. The sun will soon show.'

Then it was simple. A child could do it. Keith had tried it first in Funyelang, and picnics had improved his technique. There was a round hole, hip-high, in a hut wall. Keith put his ear to it, then his pistol, and followed his pistol in with head and shoulders. Moman knew the drill and lifted Keith's legs in after him. Moman gave a groan. Keith must remember to warn him not to do that, for this was the most dangerous moment, when you were helpless, and outlined against the dawn.

After that you lay still, and listened. Then you crawled round, tight up against the wall so no one could get behind you, and to avoid crawling through fires. Often you stopped and listened. But could only hear the quinine bells.

No one. Nobody at all, except a man in the second hut. He was dead. Fresh-dead by the blood smell.

Keith crawled out again.

In front of him was the brass spur-anklet of the Sarikin Ron. His followers wore iron ones. Yes, it was the chief himself, naked except for the yellow straw penis case which waved under Keith's nose as he tried to stand up. There were other Ron elders, their marital ambitions boastfully displayed, tall, gangling, in-toed, their ponies waiting beside them.

The situation called for an assertion of dignity on the part of the divisional officer.

156

'Chief of the Ron people, I came here to seek one named Tagwal. There is also the matter of some unpaid tax.'

No one could accuse the Sarikin Ron of smiling, but one of his toes wriggled enjoyably.

He said 'Your coming has increased our crops. Our goats and our women will have many young. Tagwal gave trouble, choking a woman who would not take him, so that she died. When the rain stopped we would have blocked the door of his hut and set fire to the thatch.'

'Where is this Tagwal?'

Sarikin Ron rocked from foot to foot. Ron men find it painful to stand. 'Your Messenger is in my house. We have drawn out the spear-head.' He patted his thigh to show where the wound was.

'But Tagwal? Where is he?'

Sarikin Ron pointed with his short heavy stabbing spear to the hut. A Ron man translated 'There. Dead.'

Keith's mind took one plodding step at a time. 'The Messenger Moman. Show me. I have practice with wounds.'

It took many steps to arrive at understanding. Moman had known that his *Ba-ture*, weak and deafened by quinine, was in no state to meet a killer in the darkness of the man's own hut. So the mild, shy little Messenger had gone in first, armed only with his usual bracelet knife, to make the killer harmless. Then, badly wounded, he had lifted Keith in, and gone off to call the tribal chief to look after his fool of a white man.

It became necessary for that fool white man to live. He owed so much to so many people, including Moman Wanti.

Chapter Sixteen

THE strange thing was that neither pneumonia nor the more dreaded blackwater fever followed chill and extreme exhaustion on top of malignant malaria. Perhaps the bugs didn't think Keith worth while. What was left was scarcely alive, or conscious.

Nursing, of a type impossible in a modern hospital, kept him from fading out altogether. No amount of blankets would warm the chill grey body. Hafsatu-Hatasu stripped him, rubbed him with hot cloths, stripped themselves and lay beside him in the narrow camp bed, enwrapping him with their arms, trying to pour their love and warmth into him.

For a day and a night it seemed hopeless. Then he stirred a little, and it became possible to feed him. One twin would throw on a garment, take the bowl of hot pepper soup from Momadu at the door, and return swiftly before her side of Keith could chill again. Each in turn took a mouthful of soup, opened Keith's lips with hers, and forced it into him. Like feeding a nestling bird.

There came a time when he tried to speak. But it was also feeding time, and the lips of the twins joined his, and he drank instead. The twins discovered that even soupless lips quieted him, and so added another technique to their nursing repertoire.

He had to get up. They set him on the edge of the bed, and ministered to his needs. Blackwater had not clogged his urinary passages. With enormous relief he let himself be rolled back into bed between his nurses' comforting bodies.

When he wanted to talk, they told him stories instead. The low-comedy one of the virgin pursued by a pumpkin, the macabre one of the Gwari woman who hid her child in the oven, and the contest between the man who claimed he could outrun raindrops and the one who claimed he could dodge them.

'There is one story which I have long desired to hear,' Keith suggested. 'But only if you are now willing to tell it.'

'With gladness, if it is known to us.'

'Tell, then, of the birth curse—as Shetu called it—which fell upon Hafsatu-Hatasu, separating them from suitors of their own race and faith, and driving them into the arms of Eblis himself, whom some call Mailafia.'

The twins chuckled softly at the old Eblis–Mailafia joke. 'But that was long ago, and while Mailafia lives can no longer trouble us.' They were amused, and mildly surprised at his request. 'How can a tale be made of foolish maidens—for that was all we were till Mailafia gave us love and womanhood? Yet we will try.'

Keith lay back on his pillow with a deep sigh of relief, and closed his eyes.

'Twins, as Mailafia knows, are a great misfortune, both to themselves and to others. Twin girls, not even boys, and as like as two eyes in one face! Out of kindness to our mother the neighbours spoke little of it. Nor did we know, but grew to be happy, like other children.'

From their account theirs was a contented, busy family, neither rich nor poor. Apparently the misfortunes which should have been brought down upon the household by the birth of mischancy twins did not occur. Smallpox left them without a mark. They grew straight and strong, so that they were sought in marriage before their friends, and by traders richer than their father. Since they did not wish to be parted, they agreed, secretly, that both should marry the same man. But, as Mailafia knew, this was not permitted!'

The signs that they were now marriageable came to them on the same day, almost at the same hour, and they rejoiced at the new bond. But mourned that childhood was ended, and that they must now be bedded separately. For their mother, who had before been patient, grew angry at having to refuse and return the gifts of suitors. She made their father beat them. He beat them equally, which was a comfort even during the pain; and not too harshly, for he loved them.

Their mother ordered them to choose their suitors, for she too loved them in her way. But, when they still delayed, called them unnatural, and bade them begone. The whole village turned against them, saying they were as women of the Shuwa Arabs, who loved each other, and took their husbands only after being beaten or bound.

'But Mailafia knows this is not true! Indeed it is not true! It was only that we could not part from each other.'

Keith had good reason to believe them. Feebly he stroked them to show his sympathy.

'When our father was away trading we ran, in the night.' He could feel their bodies stiffen, as they recounted the desperate deed. 'We came to Bauchi, to the tanners' quarter, asking about bleaches and stains. With these, and if need be with knives, we would alter our looks so that none would know we were sisters. Then we would marry the first man who asked us, blind, lame, or old. But not a leper.

'Thanks be to Allah the Compassionate, we spoke first with Shetu. She said "Show me the goat skins, for no two are alike as to dyes." We could not. And that wise one said "Come to my house, that we may eat while talking. I am a widow."

'We spoke truth to Shetu. She took thought and said "It may be there is another way, needing neither dyes nor the cutting off of ears. As well as true Believers and Infidels, there are also Nazarenes, who lie somewhat in between, being people of the Book. Perhaps they do not have this law which troubles you. I will ask. One of them is well known to me."'

Their bodies relaxed. Past horrors were fading, and relief was in sight. But not quite yet.

'She left us. We traded for her, one at a time, in Bauchi market. We are traders, born of traders. We made good increase for her. She came again, the good Shetu, on the day of prayer. We showed her our gains, which were hers. She said "That is good." Scarcely looking, and not counting at all. "But there is something better."

'We had steeped the henna and made it ready for her. We bound the cloths around her feet, and set her arms in the calabashes, that the dye should make her beautiful for her Nazarene. And waited. She said "There was one called the Calm One, but he was not calm when I sought him once, long ago. I would seek him again, but that I love and am loved."

'We took the name Mailafia, and tasted it. And found it good. Yet we knew him not, and were afraid. So we said "You have given us safety in your house. We are your servants. We will make great profit for you in our trading. Send us not away!" We made excuses, saying "Who will trade for you and guard your house if you send us away?" Thus we said, being but foolish maidens.'

Hafsatu-Hatasu were enjoying their story now, and Keith's body shared the happiness in theirs. For all was going to come out well.

'We made harsh voices when trading in the market. We rose, as with difficulty, giving grunts. We limped, leaning a little on one side, and wore rags that none should know us for the daughters of our father, or desiring us enquire our names. Yet we ourselves began to desire, and yet more strongly. So that in the house we wept together, asking "Must we always be virgins? Woe to us!" And Shetu at her comings spoke of this Mailafia and his great need for women. That his hands shook with his desire and his voice trembled. Yet he would not send for a *mare-ki-tashi*, a slap-and-get-up, from the market. Also that he was as a stallion of breed, strong and lean and hard, with good eye and skin. Oh . . . that Shetu!

'Till at last we said to her "Where is this man, that we may find him? Our need is as great as his. Also two women will not burden him!"

'She said "He is gone to the Hills. Perhaps the naked heathen have already eaten him. Perhaps he has at last taken a woman." Then seeing our faces added "But two weeks ago he was alive and womanless." Oh . . . that Shetu!

'And the rest—by the Grace of Allah—is happiness.' Keith's hands gave their amusing helmet-like coiffures a gentle wriggle, and felt strength begin to stir within him for the first time. 'We must write our thanks to Shetu, and send a gift.'

'It was done. Since all need not be told to a scribe, it was written "To Shetu in the quarter of the leatherworkers, greetings. Also this gift. Both skins arrived in good condition and sold separately to same purchaser."'

161

When Keith tottered out to the living-room, fully dressed and wrapped in a blanket, to give his first public audience, Moman Wanti, limping only a little, was pleased as though at a baby taking its first upright steps. There is nothing like having your life saved by a man to attach that man to you. Moman had joined the household syndicate, and obviously felt he now owned common stock in Keith. The rest of the division could be considered bondholders, with no personal claims on him so long as he met his obligations promptly and in full.

A quaint idea. His brain seemed receptive to any absurdity. The sensible thing was to occupy it with something useful. He found that making a list of Ron words, for comparison with those he had collected in the eastern part of the division, was a sound occupation for a convalescent.

It was as interesting as census analysis. All sorts of deductions could be made. Where the same object, an animal or a tool for instance, had a different name in different tribes, it suggested they had known the object for a long time. Where the object had the same name, it was likely to be a recent introduction. They had different names for their own half-wild dwarf cattle, but the same word for the big humped Fulani beast who was domesticated enough to be milked.

Occasionally the answers were puzzling. The Ron said they had a name for lion, though none were known up here on the Plateau. Keith asked the Sarikin Ron to describe the beast.

'A leopard without black spots.' The tall bow-legged man settled the brass spur-greave on his left ankle, and thought awhile. 'Bigger. Harder to kill. Now there are none.'

Just possible. The Ron lived on a high-level plain, not among broken hill-tops. 'When was the last lion seen?'

The tall horsemen with their long sword-like knives, heavy stabbing spears and flaunting penis-cases, consulted together.

'I was chief, so it was not long ago. We hunted, galloping perhaps ten of us in line, catching guinea-fowl or lesser-bustards in our hands as they rose, or spearing them. A lion ran. We rode her down and speared her.'

That sounded a lot too easy. 'The lion did not fight?'

'A little.' Sarikin Ron scratched his scrotum to aid memory. 'She killed two men and a horse, and the leg of that one' he pointed with his chin at a follower 'broke and shrank. Other wounds healed.'

About the only thing the Ron cared for was horsemanship. Compared with the other mounted tribe, the Sura, they were rotten farmers. They didn't walk a yard if they could help it. They tethered a pony on its single long rope rein to the nearest tuft of grass when they had to dismount to eat or sleep. They mounted again as soon as they could.

They were tough cavalry too. Keith asked 'The wild Kulere people to your south, do they give trouble?'

Sarikin Ron patted his heavy spear. 'When they come out of their hills we hunt them.'

'But their arrows, with the poison-which-never-heals?'

'The poison is slow. We kill first, and die after.'

A mail runner came in with the Pankshin bag, the first in two weeks since Keith had left headquarters. It included a note from Garrard, worried over some garbled version he had heard of Keith's collapse on the road outside Panyam. The bulk was official memos.

Keith checked and signed, drafted some replies for the clerk to type, typed some himself. In answer to Mr McTavish's latest horrendous health bulletin he recommended a pint of warm water with a little salt, to be taken internally four times a day. He reassured Garrard, and asked for an armed escort, probably in two weeks' time. To Kulere, he hoped.

He was fit enough to convene the Ron court, and help decide the disputes which came before it. They were few, for warriors are seldom litigious. He borrowed a sure-footed local pony— Orion would have broken a leg—and took part in bare-back hunts. He tired quickly, but otherwise was back to normal.

Hafsatu-Hatsu, who were good judges of his form, resumed their provocative little white veils, and inflicted on each other the painful-looking hairdressing in which they took such pride.

Keith's own hair was almost as long as Pettibone's used to be, and it would be a week, at least, before he was back in Pankshin, and could get Fletcher to operate with the battery mule-clippers. But he had some scissors here at Ron. The idea came to him before lunch one day as he duly admired the new coiffures.

'They would turn aside the sharpest sword-blades!' He had run out of stock compliments, and tried a new one.

Above the veils, the twins expressive eyes showed that he had blundered badly.

'Also they would turn towards them the dullest eyes!' he tried again.

They hugged him closely. They were a demonstrative pair.

'And now you shall do my hair. Not with plaiting,' he added hastily, 'but with cutting.'

They protested, but he wrapped himself in a sheet, and they took up the scissors. Their method was unusual. One took a snip off one side, handed over the scissors, and ran round to watch the other take the next snip. They then reversed the process.

Like all barbers they talked as they worked. They wanted to know how Keith would like them dressed as Ron women, for a change. With shaven heads and each with a small round mat hung on her tail.

Keith wouldn't like it at all, and said so. But his anthropologist's curiosity was aroused.

'Why do they wear only one mat, and hung from a string behind?'

'For sitting. All women fear that a snake may enter them, and they will go mad.'

That agreed with Hausa stories, and with folk-lore in other countries. The European woman's dread of mice had its African counterpart in this fear of snakes. Snakes were generally taken to be phallic. Things which are feared are often worshipped, and it was notable that snake cults were usually served by priestesses, from Knossos to the present day.

An interesting line of thought, and worth following up. 'Is this fear taught to girls by their mothers?'

He was aware of silence. No snipping scissors, no answer, no twins. To his quinine-muffled ears came a rhythmic beat, as of hooves. Yet not the gait of a Ron pony.

'Are you in, Keith?'

Keith ran a comb hastily through his hair, threw off the sheet and went to the steps.

A short, thick-set white man slid off a saddleless Sura pony. Garuba Kano ran up, bowed remarkably low, and took the rope rein. The man limped forward.

Sharpe, Resident Bauchi!

'Heard about you at Panyam. Left my car, and rode out to bury you or give you hell. Hasn't it entered your thick head what trouble you'd give your successor if you died or got yourself killed?' He threw off his sun-helmet and slumped stiffly into the one deck-chair. 'Having your hair cut, I see. Carry on.' Still in the well-known snarl.

Keith noted an ornamental sandal, abandoned in the twins' hasty flight.

'Would you like me to show you the famous stone bridges?' Hafsatu-Hatasu must be given a chance to escape before the Lame One decided he would like a wash. 'Nobody knows who built them. Certainly not the Ron. They're supposed to be unique, and they're not far away.'

'She can come out. I won't bite her.'

Blast the old man's quick eyes! The best thing was to set the tone of the inevitable meeting with something better than a blunt 'Come out!'

'Hafsatu-Hatasu! Here is one with whom, if you wish, greetings may be exchanged.'

They appeared in the soft blue wraps which clung flatteringly close to their youthful shapes, dignified by the formality of their veils. They curtsyed, and in so doing one deftly recovered her lost sandal.

The Resident was a gentleman. He rose, with difficulty because of his stiff knee, and bowed.

'Welcome! Rest from the weariness of travel!' said Hafsatu-Hatasu.

'The weariness is gone with your coming,' said the Lame One gallantly. 'It is my wish to thank you for your care of Mailafia. Guard him well.'

165

'That is our desire.' They curtsyed again, and left.

Sharpe hobbled to the bedroom, leaving Keith a little breathless. A tough old Resident and two young Fulani girls had met without constraint, and approved of each other. Like spoke to like, strange as it might seem. As—Keith recollected—thirty years before the same man had met a Fulani leader of horse in battle, been wounded but unhorsed his opponent, and in friendly fashion had borrowed the other's cavalry to round up his own deserting infantry.

The Resident returned. His sparse grizzled hair was brushed, and he cleaned his nails with a match-stalk. But no washing could remove the purplish tinge of his swollen nose, or the mottled sword-cut which had barely spared one eye.

At Bauchi the Resident had smoked a pipe. Keith offered his pouch.

'Not allowed any longer. Doctor's orders.' He kicked a chop-box along as foot-rest for his stiff leg, and settled back into the deck-chair.

'Don't want to spoil your lunch, Keith. Get it over first. You and Pettibone have no use for each other. Old story. The lion and the unicorn fighting round the town.'

So that was what had brought the Resident to Panyam. A drum started up in the near-by village. It seemed to chuckle derisively. A purely subjective impression, for it was no more than the primitive sort of strumming that you would expect of these penis-proud Ron. Annoying, though, when you were trying to guess what was about to happen.

'Zaria lost three out of a staff of five in one month. Lowry took an overdose of some sedative—very unusual. Simmons and Pearce invalided, Simmons buried at sea. Bauchi Province had to spare them a man.' The staccato snarl was back, after the gracious Hausa greetings. 'I sent Pettibone. Had unfavourable reports on him by the man who knew him best—himself, of course. Fool hadn't realized that when he reports on his junior he's also reporting on himself.'

Keith said nothing. You didn't waste the Old Man's time.

'Bank at Railhead confirmed my opinion, when they wired me

for authority to grant him an overdraft. I'm not asking you any questions.'

Because he had added that to the delay in receiving the handing-over certificates, and knew the answer.

'I sent you to Pankshin to help Pettibone open Kulere. As a soldier you would avoid useless killing. Wasn't so sure of Pettibone. He might get excited, or something. Done anything about the Closed Area since he left?'

Telling about the careful training of the picnics would only seem like an excuse. 'No, sir.'

'Damn me, I asked you a civil question! Give me a civil answer!'

'Very well, sir.' Keith explained his ideas and his training. He had no need to elaborate. Sharpe had been an expert at the game almost before Keith was born. There was a story about his capturing a village single-handed, by crawling into it under his travelling bath, arrows sticking in it on all sides.

'Reasonable.' So far the Old Man seemed to approve. 'What comes next?'

'My idea is to nibble away at the corners of Kulere—'infiltrate' might sound better on paper. A force small enough to be compact, carrying its own rations. In and out again, a few days at a time. And keep on doing it until they get used to us.'

Sharpe nodded. 'Adapt to conditions as you find them. No cast-iron plan. Expect some casualties, and perhaps you won't get many. Of course you know why the Kulere have been left alone so long. Some of Carlyle's soldiers died weeks after from the arrow poison.'

The Resident knew. It saved a lot of words.

'That's the main reason why I don't like Pettibone's plan for what amounts to a small invasion. It's bound to scare people, and give villages time to combine. And two hundred soldiers with around a hundred carriers in single file on hill paths would stretch . . .'

'Asking for trouble. He's done the same in Zaria.'

'But his plan's authorized officially, and mine isn't.' Keith's mind took in the word Zaria belatedly. 'But I thought he was acting Station Magistrate?'

'He is. He has also spread himself around and asked for trouble. I don't blame Resident Zaria for insisting on returning him.'

Momadu came in with a tray of gin and kola-bitters. He remembered the Resident's usual midday drink. Sharpe, taking his glass, said 'Thank you, Momadu Dangana.' And Momadu grew an inch in stature.

Sharpe put his glass aside. Apparently that, too, was now prohibited.

Keith was sure, afterwards, that he had known what was coming. The sound could scarcely be called drumming. A simple tap . . . tap . . . tap . . . tap, unvarying in tone or timing as the beat of a pulse. Yet here, quite recognizable, was the final count to zero, the zero which would demand that you tear yourself from the comparative safety of a trench and voluntarily expose yourself to danger.

Five . . . four . . . three . . . two . . .

'Well, Keith, do I send Pettibone to one of the other divisions or let him return to Pankshin?'

It had happened.

'If you mean it's for me to choose, sir . . .'

'That's exactly what I mean. Can't you understand plain English?'

'I have to take your orders, but I'm damned if I have to be your conscience!'

'Unfortunately you do. Only the two of us know the facts of the situation. For purely personal considerations, which cannot concern you, I find it necessary to disqualify myself from judging. That was why I was on my way to Pankshin, to see you.'

The defensive snarl, as much a part of Sharpe as his stiff knee, fooled nobody who had worked for him. Keith had no difficulty in guessing those 'purely personal considerations'. When working in the Provincial Office, Keith had been aware of the organized pressure of mining interests upon the politicians in England, a pressure duly passed on down to the governor and the Resident Bauchi.

An opportunist would have bowed to the pressure, have asked

for a battalion with machine guns to supplement the mountain-gun battery, and beaten Kulere into submission. The tribesmen's natural self-defence against invasion would have supplied enough 'provocation', and the ghastly effect of a few unhealing wounds caused by their poison arrows would have gone far to disarm criticism. In so doing, at no cost to himself, the Resident could have earned the approval of those on whom his future depended.

But Sharpe was no opportunist, or he would have been governor of this Colony or another, instead of being under threat of invaliding or compulsory retirement. Mrs Sharpe was buried at Bauchi. He had no children, or other links with England. All his interests were out here. Yes, those were the personal considerations which Sharpe had refused to mention.

He had left Pettibone free to take milder and more humane action. And Pettibone had done nothing.

'Let's put it this way, sir. I think I can run the division better alone.'

Sharpe did not wince. He said calmly 'I agree.'

'But it would take longer for me to open Kulere. If Pettibone could run the division, and leave me free to spend all my time in Kulere we might be able to open it in six months. Of course that's only a guess, but—'

'So Pettibone is to return?'

The drumming had stopped when Sharpe first put the question. In the silence Keith heard himself confirm the decision he had known from the first he would have to make. 'Yes, sir.'

A hand, mottled with brown liverspots of age, went out to the brimming gin-and-bitter glass, and carried it to the heavily moustached lips without spilling a drop. The empty glass was set down with what sounded like a sigh.

'You insist on being a damned fool.' The snarl was a release from emotion, and Keith welcomed it. 'There used to be a lot of damned fools in the old days. But the breed's getting rare. Now, if your camp-bed isn't full of women, I'll take a siesta. Have to start back immediately after lunch.'

Chapter Seventeen

RIDING bare-back into Panyam to return the Sura pony which the Resident had borrowed, Keith suffered more than mere physical discomfort. He had a kind of moral hangover from the overdose of idealism he had poured himself the day before. A man should learn just how much he can take of highfalutin virtue, and keep within safe limits.

In the rest-house compound only alien wheel marks told of the Resident's momentous visit. These and a folded note which the rest-house keeper proffered.

Grateful for your loan of Orion. Perfect gait and manners. Grateful too for your difficult decision. A. J. S.

When Pankshin hill came in sight the morning after, Keith was in a better mood. After his day's rest in Panyam, Orion had danced the first mile, then, given his head, had swept along like a bird. All that was left of Keith's remorse was the simple conviction that he had been a damned fool, but it was too late to do anything about it.

O.C. Troops was out, said by his house-boy to be breakfasting with the tall soldier. Keith left Orion with the groom, and strolled across to the next bungalow.

'Have some coffee, have a bath, have some toast!' Yeats, still a human version of a large friendly St Bernard pup, knocked over his chair and grabbed Keith's hand. 'I mean it's awfully good to see you again, sir! The old skipper was frightfully upset when he heard about your close call.'

'Who wouldn't be?' Garrard growled and grinned. 'I've got enough on my hands without having to box you and bury you and tell your sorrowing relatives what a good boy you've always been.'

Keith took a chair and coffee, glancing contentedly around him.

Yeats seemed to do himself bloody well for a subaltern, with eggs, sausages and even kippers laid invitingly on his table.

'I'd bury you gladly, and wouldn't grudge the time, bearing in mind my duty to humanity,' Keith returned insult for insult. 'But reform may still be possible. Suitably fortified by Yeats' sausage and eggs, it is my intention to offer to take you for a walk round our charming countryside, combining instruction with exercise, which you all too obviously need. Does the word "Kulere" suggest anything to your unreceptive mind?'

'At last! I mean . . . Kulere! Try some marmalade, it hides the rancid taste of the butter.' Yeats pushed over the pot, eager to express his gratitude.

'I'm out of luck again. It's Yeats' turn to go on picnic. Oh my God, I've just remembered!' Garrard set his cup down with a clatter. 'Neither of us can go. Somebody on the Gold Coast has discovered the long lost Golden Stool of Ashanti, and they're expecting trouble. Hence our "stand-by" orders in case the Gold Coast W.A.A.F. need reinforcements. Sorry, old man, but there isn't a hope of letting you have two hundred rifles.'

'We won't need anything like that number.' Keith outlined his plan for a small very mobile force which, with luck, would avoid serious fighting. 'And what's more the Pettibone invasion plan is to be officially rescinded. I had a talk with my Resident the day before yesterday at Ron.'

'Must have been something damned important to bring him all the way from Bauchi. It's not much short of two hundred miles by road, and he's supposed to be a very sick man.'

'He is. It was. Pettibone's coming back.'

'Christ! Suppose we ought to have expected it though. There've been rumours from our blokes at Zaria. One of them wanted to push his face in at the club.' Garrard rose and looked at his watch.

'If you and Yeats get scuppered in Kulere I'll be for it. "Inadequate force provided. Major Garrard relieved of his command." That sort of thing. But I never did like the looks of the Pettibone invasion scheme. Too big and complicated for rough country.' He buckled on his Sam Browne and picked up cane and helmet. 'So I'll stick my neck out. Day after tomorrow soon

171

enough, Keith? I'll drop into your office after parade, and we can work out details.'

Griggs couldn't march, and could barely sit his horse Apparently he had been unlucky in his choice of market-women, and was now suffering the consequences. Tactfully Keith spoke of boils on the behind, and sent the sergeant back to Pankshin, with instructions to soak the affected parts in a scalding bath at least four times a day. It would help either complaint until he could get leave to go down country to see a medical officer.

The wound on Moman Wanti's thigh was only partly healed. But no other Messenger knew the Kulere speech. Unwillingly, but to Moman's delight, Keith took him along. To ease things for him, while it was still possible, Keith sent him ahead, to await the party on the border of the Closed Area.

On the third night, suspicion aroused by Yeats' glassy eyes was confirmed when Keith laid a hand on his burning forehead. Malaria, of course, and the only sensible thing was to send him back to Pankshin after Griggs. And abandon the show.

'Bloody young fool!' Keith hardened his heart and tried to get angry. 'You must have felt this coming on before we left.'

'Only a low fever, sir, and I've been taking double doses of quinine. I didn't think it was going to kick up like this. I swear I'll be all right in a day or two.'

'I'll take you with me on two conditions. You'll parade your detachment tonight, and formally hand them over to my command. After that you'll travel by hammock until I give you permission to get up. I'll see about getting poles, mats and a hunting net to carry you in.'

At the last friendly village Keith had to make a tough decision. He could leave Yeats and the loads under Momadu's care, and pick him up on the way back. Or he could encumber a difficult march through unknown enemy country with a helpless young officer, a hammock as awkward on winding trails as a grand piano, and eight hammock-bearers with whom the scanty rations would have to be divided. Success or failure might depend on the choice.

It was Yeats, his temperature slightly down, and touchingly

grateful, who forced the decision in his own favour. 'You know, Keith, I don't think I could ever have faced the old skipper again, if you had sent me back.'

'How was your soup?' Keith demanded gruffly.

'Wonderful. And that johnnie of yours stood over me to see I finished it. Did you know he understands English?'

Keith didn't. But if an emergency called for it, no doubt Momadu would make a stab at Chinese. So that Yeats and his hammock should not lie on hard ground, Momadu had punched holes in opposite walls of the small hut, and stuck the hammock poles through them. Yeats' own boy would never have thought of that. Nor, in fact, had Keith.

'I hate letting you down like this, Keith old man. I'm eternally grateful.'

'Want to prove it? Then shut up and go to sleep! I'll do the rounds, and see your men are all right. What I'm worried about is Moman. He was supposed to wait here until we came, but he's gone on ahead. I don't want him shot as he comes back into our lines.'

Keith passed the night lying across Yeats' doorway, his rifle beside him. Were the fierce little Kulere tribesmen night-raiders? A helpless white man in a hammock might be a tempting victim for a knife-attack.

Keith's conscience was kicking up again. The plain fact was that he had no right to be here at all. He had no right to allow Garrard to endanger his professional career. He had no right to endanger the helpless Yeats, however much the young idiot wanted to be endangered. He certainly had no right to take over command of the detachment. And that was no mere technicality. Captain Ian Keith no longer held a military commission. He was a civilian. As soon as Yeats became incapable of handling his men, the whole outfit should have been led straight back to Pankshin.

So far nothing had gone right. And now Moman Wanti was missing. Moman, the man whose knowledge of the Kulere speech was indispensable.

The Messenger had duly arrived at this village, according to report, and had ordered food to be in readiness for the last hot meal the detachment would eat before going on tinned rations.

Then he had left horse, robe, turban and even sword, and had walked on into enemy country. Without orders, just as, without orders, he had gone ahead and disposed of the outlaw at Ron. The nervous little Hausa's cold courage might easily get him killed, blast him!

Moman arrived at dawn, while Keith was making a final check of his guards before withdrawing them. Winding his way through the bush—there seemed to be no farm paths or farms on the Kulere side of the village—came a barely recognizable figure. Without his flowing Mohammedan robes, dressed only in a cotton loin-cloth and a knife strapped to his left forearm, the man looked more like a plucked hen than a dignified government Messenger.

Keith went out to meet him, in impatience to hear the news, and also to prevent a trigger-happy soldier taking a pot-shot at him.

'The tale,' Moman stammered, 'is of good-fortune, *Ba-ture*.'

Moman's idea of good news might be that a neat little fight could be had for the asking. Keith signed that the messenger should sit and rest. 'Food is not ready yet. Tell all, so that I may see with your eyes; for the people and the country are unknown to me.'

'First let it be told that Mban have driven Barghesh from their village, and the people of Barghesh are scattered.'

That was certainly good news. The rumoured village feud was the reason for taking this particular route into the Closed Area. Neither village would be tempted to take on the soldiers while it had its traditional enemy to fight.

'Where do these villages lie, and are there paths?' The Closed Area was also the unknown area, unmapped from here to its western boundary, where the escarpment dropped down to the plains in the next division. Twelve years ago Carlyle's big expedition, with machine-guns, provisioned by and co-operating with a similar force in the plains, had swept the top of the escarpment. So far as records went, that was the last time a white man had set foot in the forbidden land.

The Hausas are foot-loose travellers; which accounts for any illiterate trader being able to draw you a rough map in the dust of a road with his spear-point. Moman smoothed out a patch of bare soil with the side of his palm, and as voices and cook-fire smoke began to rise from the village, he drew his sketch. Stones and pebbles stood for hills, paths he incised with his knife-point.

Keith took out his pocket-book and copied on a reduced scale. But what scale? That was important. 'How far is a day's march?' he asked.

'For soldiers without carriers . . .' Moman measured a hand-span.

Eight inches to sixteen miles or so.

'There are now carriers.' Keith brought the Messenger up to date. 'The sergeant has returned to Pankshin. The tall soldier fell sick of fever after you left. He is heavy, but eight good Angas men bear his hammock.'

Moman Wanti frowned and considered. Then his hand made the same measurement. 'The hammock can march as the soldiers do, for the land is not steep as in Dallong or the Angas country around Ampam and Kwallak. For the *Ba-ture* and me alone, a march would be thus . . .' two hands covered about fifteen inches.

Call that thirty miles or so. The scale was confirmed as two miles to the inch. Keith made his notebook sketch proportionate.

'We will return to the village, so that you may eat and briefly rest. All else may be told me as we march. My thanks to Allah that you are still alive!'

No professional adventurer, whether soldier, explorer, big-game hunter or administrator, takes uncalled-for risks. He leaves those to the short-lived amateur. What troubled Keith during the long morning's trek was the complete lack of any data to work from. Moman's summary of the people of Kulere was enlightening but scanty.

'They are as wasps, *Ba-ture*. You disturb them, they fear, they sting, they fly away.'

Did they snipe from long range, or press home a vigorous assault, or favour a conventional dawn raid, or, like the Dallong, specialize in ambushes? Each would require a different disposition of the small defence force.

'Against the Ron they rise from the long grass so that the pony shies at them. They shoot then, or if the horseman is thrown they knife him. Then they hide again, running like guinea-hens

175

through the grass.' The Messenger spoke as though an eye-witness. 'But here there is no long grass. Also we are afoot and have rifles. What they will do is unknown to me.'

The first Kulere man had appeared about an hour after the march started. He was barely visible, but of course the line of soldiers and Yeats' hammock caught his eye. He yodelled, and the sound came faintly down the breeze. After a time other tribesmen joined him, appearing and disappearing among the rocks and scrub like ants. They carried short bows and wore quivers. That was all the binoculars could define.

Their numbers grew. Passing unseen ahead or behind the line of march they began to cover both flanks. Sergeant Usuman asked permission to give them a burst of fire. Keith refused to give the order, as the wasps were still safely beyond bow-shot. He dropped back to the hammock in the middle of the small column.

Yeats lifted the sun-helmet that covered his sweating face. 'Better today.'

'Keep up the sweating, and I'll let you have a slice of bully-beef for supper,' Keith promised. If Yeats sweated again all tomorrow, his trouble would be over, except for the putty-jointed feebleness which would follow.

The lashings of the hammock to the pole were secure. Keith raised the matting screen on both sides now the sun was almost overhead, and dropped back to instruct the spare carriers.

'The *Ba-ture* is in your care. If you hear the "fwew-fwew" of arrows, carry the *Ba-ture* behind a rock, leaving the hammock. For the hammock is as easily seen and easily hit as a cow.'

'We may shoot?' The carriers made a gesture of drawing arrows from their quivers.

'When the soldiers shoot. Not before.'

Camp was made early, as a shade-tree, a stream, and a clear field of fire offered a combination of comfort and safety which might not recur for many miles.

After half an hour of bored watching, as the soldiers cut sticks to support the hammock and kindled a useless but comforting fire, the potential enemy melted away. Well before sunset the countryside looked completely deserted.

176

There followed a meal of water, canned beef, and army hard-tack biscuit. Yeats was permitted to sit up and dangle his legs from the hammock, while Keith squatted at his feet. A discussion arose as to whether Yeats, authorities permitting, would be justified in bringing a bride out to this sickly country. Result inconclusive. Keith wandered off and smoked a pipe with Sergeant Usuman Sokoto, listening to the sergeant's experiences in the hungry East African campaign in the last war.

A further consultation with Moman Wanti yielded little further information. It was, however, agreed that since Barghesh was the nearest village, about half a day's march to the north, and Mban had occupied the place, the day's spectators were likely to be Barghesh men, scattered around and hunting for food.

The Kulere people, according to Moman, were more casual farmers even than the Ron, and chronically short of food. A village which had a bad harvest usually accused a neighbouring village of evil magic, in fact of magically stealing the crops. In revenge, and to make good their own shortage, they raided the neighbour and helped themselves to all they could lay hands on. That was what Mban had done.

There was no real Kulere tribe. Kulere was just a nickname. In fact it was the name of their wooden-tipped arrow, the equivalent to the broad-headed *pasa*, or barbed *kibia* in other parts of the division. They had no tribal organization, or chief with enough authority to check these village wars. The result was depopulation, widely scattered hamlets, and the further discouragement of farming. Which in turn left sufficient bush to permit a marginal existence based on hunting.

It seemed as though the Closed Area, the last to hold out against the white man's administration, was the most in need of the white man's peace and organization.

But not too much of it. Government had a way of becoming too damned efficient and reformative. It should supply what the people wanted in the way of reasonable safety of life and goods, at the lowest cost. And let the people grow their own civilization from their own deep roots.

177

Chapter Eighteen

'By the Grace of Allah, it can be done, and we will do it! We cannot look like the people of Kulere,' Moman made an indecent gesture which Keith was to understand later, 'but if we do not look like white men or soldiers they will not fear.'

Next evening, when the sun had lost some of its power, they set off from camp. Moman in sandals and loin-cloth, Keith in shoes and the remains of a pair of shorts. With Moman's help he was colour-washed with red clay, and a thick plaster of clay protected head and neck against sunstroke. It was rather a comfortable kit, though a trifle unorthodox.

It looked like good game country, with ample water and browsing and enough bush and rock for cover. Yet there were no droppings, and the only track, of a small duiker, had been made during the rainy season. Keith spared a bush-fowl, sitting on an ant-hill, as he wanted more imposing game for his purpose. He let a grass monkey scuttle away, and then regretted his soft-heartedness.

It began to seem as though the Kulere had eaten every living thing. Except themselves. They had given up watching the camp, and were doing a neat job of stalking the two would-be hunters.

Only the beast's head showed. But it had to be a klipspringer. Nothing else but a bird could be perching atop that pinnacle of rock. The extreme elevation made a prone shot impossible. Keith rolled over on his back, steadied his rifle against his drawn-up knees, hoped, and pressed the trigger.

The beast leaped, like a diver off a spring-board, spun in the air, and dropped out of sight. Keith marked the spot and ran towards it.

He and Moman came late. Already several Kulere men seemed about to fight each other for this manna that had fallen from

178

heaven. Little folk, a foot shorter than their Ron enemies to the north, their middles so tightly girded with coils of cord that they seemed almost wasp-waisted. Their most remarkable feature was their ambitious penis-case made of goat's horn or carved calabash, and so long that the tip had to be supported by a string to the strange belt. The little wasps seemed in a mood to sting anybody who contested their claim to the meat. Arrows were on bows, and two bow-strings drawn. Not against Keith, but each other.

Another wasp ran up, no bigger, but fiercer. He snapped the two arrow-heads off short with a twist of his fingers. And sat down on the goat-sized klipspringer.

Moman Wanti walked calmly up to him, lifted him off by one ear, and spoke fiercely and at length.

Keith gathered afterwards that the subject of the lecture was the immutable law that game belongs to the killer. Perhaps the first law of property ever developed, and the oldest by many thousands of years. Even the Kulere obeyed it.

The man Moman had removed from the dead klipspringer picked up some earth and slapped it on his head. He cast another handful at or over his followers. The killer-wasps looked like a dejected bunch of children caught in the act of stealing apples. Keith had no idea what was going on, nor could he make any guess as to the meaning of their shame-faced mutterings.

'They say they starve,' Moman translated into Hausa, 'while the men of Mban sit feasting on the corn and goats in Barghesh village.'

'Can you persuade them to bring the meat into camp and eat it there? That will give us a chance to talk with them.'

Moman didn't make the mistake of persuading. He ordered, sharply.

Only a few of the bolder ones and their leader dared to pass the sentries, light a fire, flay and broil the meat on spits. That left more than enough to go round, and Moman, Keith, Yeats and Sergeant Usuman were generously pressed to join the feast. And did so.

With stomachs beginning to bulge beneath their waist-cords, the Kulere warriors became expansive in other directions. They enlarged on the virtues of klipspringer hide for bow-strings. It was so thin, yet so tough, and the hair could be pulled out—this they demonstrated—without weakening the hide by steeping in water. Unfortunately this quarry was the wiliest of all, keen-sighted as a hawk, and always found on the most unclimbable rock far beyond bow-shot.

The man who had claimed the klipspringer had a penis-case so long and upturned that it prodded his navel when he squatted. Clearly a person of consequence. He had a bright idea, and consulted his new friend Moman Wanti.

'He says that he knows a hill where many klipspringer live,' Moman translated. 'He asks that we go with him and shoot another.'

The purpose of risking a shoot beyond the protection of the soldiers' rifles had been to make friendly contact, or anyway contact of some sort, with the elusive Kulere. It had been successful. Now a new idea was dawning in Keith's mind. Was it too dangerous?

He lifted a lump of clay from the back of his neck—it was starting to itch as it dried—and decided to take the gamble.

'Let him come early, at dawn. We will be ready. But let him tell none of this plan, or the meat may not be enough for all.'

If the Kulere were like other people, that warning would ensure that each of the ten Kulere around the fire would tell another friend or two of the good tidings, and they of course would tell others. Probably every man of Barghesh could be relied upon to tag along.

It worked out that way. Stumbling through what to European eyes was still pitch-darkness, but to Africans was already half-light, Keith became aware that the surrounding countryside rustled as though with the march of driver-ants. A soft order, and the sound of bayonets clicking on to their lugs, told that Sergeant Usuman was taking no chances. By Keith's luminous compass the march was heading roughly in the right direction, if his sketch of Moman's dust-and-pebble map could be relied on.

The sky grew a little lighter than the ground. The rustlings ceased as all but the privileged ten who had eaten with the soldiers and white men drew off to a safer distance. Hills and trees began to show. Bayonets went back into scabbards as Keith called a halt.

'One klipspringer, two or even three, would not be enough for all these . . .' Keith waved a hand over the unauthorized followers lurking around. 'Therefore we do not go to your hill, but to another which I know. It lies between Mban and Barghesh.' Or did on Moman's scratch-map.

The little chief sounded surprised. 'But that hill is empty! It lies close to Mban, so that children lay snares there to catch grasshoppers to eat. For there is nothing else.'

'If I find no food for your men, we will then go to your hill.'

That was enough to keep the hungry Kulere vaguely hopeful. Remembering the time one of Sarikin Yergam's men had warned the Funyelang villagers, Keith preferred to say no more.

The march was resumed. As casually as he could, Keith led the talk around to Mban. It appeared that the village was impregnable, being on a slight rise and surrounded by no less than three rings of poison-thorned cactus. Once, when Barghesh had a bad harvest, they had thought themselves strong enough to storm the place, but had been repulsed with heavy loss. In fact that was the beginning of the rise of Mban, and the decline of Barghesh. Mban were noted fighters but it was their cactus defence hedges which counted most. No arrow could penetrate the dense succulent leaves.

Then why did not Barghesh grow a similar protection?

They had, but only a single ring, because once their warriors were so many that they had no fear of Mban, their nearest neighbour. Also the Mban men had taken Barghesh by surprise this year. When the Barghesh warriors had gathered from the fields where they had been collecting the last of their harvest, they had tried to recapture their village. But failed, losing more men.

'So the men of Mban now sit in Barghesh, eating Barghesh corn and goats, and drinking Barghesh harvest beer?' Keith summed up.

Despondently the chief of Barghesh admitted the loss and the shame.

The hill was now visible in front and a little to the right. Mban must now be near. An undefended Mban, in all probability, since every able-bodied man would now be carousing in Barghesh.

Keith pulled his surprise. 'Then we will eat the Mban goats and corn, and drink their beer. We will enter Mban.'

It took a moment or two for the idea to penetrate. Then the Barghesh leader opened his mouth to shout. Keith clamped a hand over it. 'Tell no one!' He ordered fiercely. 'Walk close to me, or you walk into Mban alone.'

By way of subterfuge the column continued to head for the hill. At the foot the Barghesh leader asked permission to call in his scattered men and turn off down the stream-bed from which Mban drew its water. Keith told off Sergeant Usuman to take fifteen men and stay with Yeats at all costs.

Then things happened quickly. A herd-boy of perhaps seven years old saw the strangers and ran to give warning. To save his life from Barghesh bowmen, Keith raced after him, hot on his heels, followed by Moman, the yelling Barghesh and ten excited soldiers.

They made almost a dead heat of it to the opening in the cactus perimeter, and poured through it. The herd-boy screamed his way into the arms of a surprised woman, possibly his mother, whom he knocked flat on the ground. Thus, without casualties or dignity, was captured the strongly fortified village of Mban.

Keith posted the soldiers on guard at the entrance, and raced round the inside of the perimeter, dropping off clumps of Barghesh men at intervals. Back at the entrance he was privileged to view the arrival of Yeats. The convalescent slid to the ground, and tried to demonstrate that the hammock must be tilted sideways to get through. The eight Angas carriers, each with an arrow ready drawn and clasped to his bow, were too excited to understand. They, Yeats, the hammock and the soldiers all jammed in the narrow way. A score or more of goats and kids, deserted by their small herd-boy and bleating shrilly, sought refuge in their town by the same and only way, and at the same time. Barghesh stragglers added themselves to the pile-up on the goal line. It was Yeats' boy and Momadu, accustomed to tidying up after their masters, who did most to sort out the tangle.

A Mban counter-attack should be anticipated. Hastily Keith led Yeats and his small bodyguard to the threshing floor in the centre of the village, told them to stay there as a 'tactical reserve', went back to dispose his other ten soldiers where their fire would be most effective, lost touch with Moman and the Barghesh leader, and found the Barghesh men starting to loot.

With the help of Yeats' bodyguard he caught four and tied them to trees around the threshing-floor. With no Moman available to interpret, he had the material evidence of their crimes exhibited in front of each. That for the time being disposed of that trouble, and sent the other Barghesh men back to their posts.

Next for a show of quiet confidence during the period of waiting. A return trip round the defences, at leisure, mainly to impress on each group that the Mban warriors might bring trees to batter a way through the cactus, so they must stay where they were placed, in readiness. They were puzzled when Moman translated. No one had ever used battering rams, so no one ever would.

Then back to Yeats, to chat and smoke a pipe.

Women came out of their huts and went about their daily tasks, winnowing and pounding a local type of cereal small as grass seed. They showed no fear of the strange khaki-clad soldiers, but open curiosity. Clearly Kulere had the same rule as the more advanced tribes, that women were too valuable to be killed in war. Killing them reduced the present and future population of the enemy, but capturing them increased yours by the same amount. A most practical form of chivalry.

These professional neutrals, naked even to their shaven heads, produced food, for which Keith paid, and sent to his hungry soldiers. The women knew the value of coins, so it looked as though this isolated Closed Area had more contact with the outside world than was known.

It was Yeats, resting with his back against a hut, who first noted the woman with the wooden yoke. In one hand she supported the end of a nine-foot sapling, the other end of which forked round her neck and was pegged and tied behind her ears.

With her spare hand she balanced a basket on her shaven head.

'Why on earth does she wear that thing?' he asked. 'I mean, it can't be comfortable. I know women do extraordinary things to themselves because they think it makes them prettier. But I mean to say!'

Keith thought he knew, but asked Moman Wanti.

'It is a woman-don't-stray, and she is from Barghesh. When she is first captured, a woman is like a dog, always trying to run home.'

'Like one of those things in England that they fasten round a cow's neck when she's a hedge-buster! I mean to say!' Yeats' chivalry was shocked.

The Barghesh woman knelt, a little awkwardly, let the end of her yoke rest on the ground, poured some corn from her basket into a hollow stone, picked up another stone and began to grind.

Keith wished he could photograph the scene, including the perplexed frown on Yeats' innocently handsome face and the far from innocent glances of the bare native captive. A print sent to the idealized Helga might make her more approachable when Yeats took his next leave.

Keith caught Moman's stir of interest, and jumped up.

'They come!' announced the Messenger.

Sooner than Keith had expected. But so much the better, since if a fight developed rifles were more effective by daylight and bows, which gave no betraying flash, after dark. Screams and yells suggested that a fierce battle had already been joined; but when Keith reached the guard on the gateway he discovered that the clamour was only a long-range vocal barrage, intended to encourage your own brave lads and strike terror into the craven hearts of the enemy.

It took time and threats to still the vociferous Barghesh allies. In the end it was curiosity which silenced them. Why were the white man and the stranger who spoke their speech going out to be killed? Or—an equally pleasant hope—were the two about to slay the hated Mban by the same means which had killed the klipspringer?

To pique curiosity Keith did the stiff ceremonial 'slow march'.

184

Half way between the opposing bowmen he halted, raised the rifle high overhead, laid it on the ground, stepped over it, and made the opening move.

'Which village do you want, men of Mban?' Keith shouted. 'Your own Mban, or little Barghesh?'

Silence fell, and Moman had no difficulty in making himself heard. From the enemy ranks—if you could apply that term to their mob formation—a man stepped out and came slowly forward. Keith took a few strides to meet him, and the man walked with greater confidence. He might have been a Barghesh man, with the strange Kulere wasp-waist and exaggerated penis-case; but Moman reported 'Their priest-chief. Mban has no other leader.'

Dignity depends less upon clothing than on a consciousness of inner power. The priest-chief paced steadily up, and confidently delivered his answer to the challenge.

'We men of Mban are stronger than those lizards of Barghesh!'

'But the defences of Mban are also stronger than the defences of Barghesh.' Keith made the situation clear. 'Barghesh you captured only by surprise, when the warriors of Barghesh were scattered over their farms, and out hunting. You cannot take Mban by surprise, for the warriors of Barghesh are inside, and await you.'

The priest-chief was a youngish man, and apparently open to new ideas. He got the point, and waited.

Keith developed his argument. 'If you attack Mban you will lose so many warriors that for years the Barghesh men will outnumber yours. If you do not attack, at nightfall the men of Barghesh will fit 'woman-don't strays' around the necks of your wives, as you have done to the women of Barghesh. Also by day they will eat your goats, and the corn you have harvested, and the beer your women have made for you. And these are more than you have left in Barghesh.'

The priest-chief was troubled. One could not say positively that his penis-case drooped, but it gave that impression. He tried to bluster.

'The gods of Mban are more powerful than the gods of Barghesh! They will not permit!'

There was a trick answer to that. 'The gods of Mban are in Mban. I will tell the men of Barghesh to pour much beer and blood before those gods. Then the gods will say "Where are the people of Mban, and why do they neglect us? The men of Barghesh are better, for they give us more offerings. Never have we eaten so much. Let us aid the men of Barghesh." Such is the way of gods and great ones, to be forgetful of past services, and grateful for the new.'

As Moman translated, probably improving on the text, the priest-chief lost his truculence. He knew the fickleness of gods and guardian ancestors in the giving and withholding of rain and crops and due increase in livestock and humans. Who should know better than the unfortunate priest who stands between these great ones and the common laity who demand good fortune and only good fortune? His life may pay for his failure to perform impossible miracles. And here was just such an impossibility which his people would expect of him—the recapture of Mban! With a jerk of his head he summoned others to share his responsibility and the inevitable blame for an inevitable decision.

The larger audience listened while Keith patiently repeated his arguments. The audience looked at the westering sun, and at the almost impregnable defences which they and their fathers had planted and tended. The cactus said nothing, but its argument was irrefutable. Tomorrow Mban and Barghesh must make peace terms.

With a few half-hearted parting insults, Mban warriors headed reluctantly back towards Barghesh, while Barghesh warriors, soldiers and two *Tura-wa* proceeded to make themselves at home in Mban. More food was produced. Momadu and Yeats' servant poured water over their masters by way of a bath, and served a quite edible meal in rough wooden bowls. The remarkable sight of two *Tura-wa* sitting on the ground and eating just like humans drew a number of fascinated old men and children out of hiding.

To salve his conscience, sadly disturbed by Keith's most unprofessional way of making war, Sergeant Usuman Sokoto posted mixed guards of soldiers and Barghesh men, taking elaborate precautions against surprise. According to Momadu they were

186

superfluous, no Kulere man, woman or child venturing beyond his village after dark among the evil spirits.

As what Yeats called 'Town Commandant', Keith set apart five huts close to the nucleus of soldiers on the threshing-floor, and went round with Momadu and Sarikin Barghesh proclaiming that any woman who wished might take refuge in them and be safe for the night. Perhaps a dozen, mostly with very small children, took advantage of the offer. The others seemed willing to take their chances with the occupation forces.

More than willing in some cases. The woman in the yoke hung around the impressively tall and youthful Yeats, and at last, with blunt gestures forced him to understand her purpose. Not to be outdone, an emaciated old woman tied a cord around her own neck and put the other end in Keith's hands. By request Moman told them that *Tura-wa* had hungry souls which ate the souls of any women they slept with. The old woman found an amenable Barghesh man, and was led off happily protesting.

The night passed without alarms, and dawn broke on the first of several days of hard bargaining. As a preliminary Sarikin Barghesh and a handful of his men set off for their own village to assess the damage there, confident that the hostages in Mban secured their safety. A few Mban men were allowed into Mban for a similar purpose. Then followed several exasperating and richly interesting sessions of what amounted to a primitive court of arbitration and war indemnity.

The opposing villagers sat outside the cactus defences in two groups, with Keith and Moman between them. Heaps of pebbles in front of each group represented bundles of corn on the stalk, or measures of thrashed corn, or roots, or goats, or kids, or cook-pots, or tobacco, or pinches of salt, or any other articles which had been eaten or looted. Long and heated arguments contested each claim, on occasion threatening a fresh outbreak of hostilities.

To apply pressure and force compromise, Keith held up the exchange of women until the last. Slowly the piles of pebbles were set off against each other, pebble by pebble. A balance of compensation, here owed by Mban and there by Barghesh, was met by handing over protesting goats, enormous pots of sourish beer, handfuls of arrows and scores of other articles. Now that a balance of claims between the villages had been struck, it remained for each village to compensate individuals, or to divide the loss between them. Which was just as well, as it would have taken weeks or even months, and Keith still had a division to run, and papers no doubt piling up at Pankshin.

The swapping of women, which Keith had dreaded, was simple by comparison. Barghesh women were led up, indignant at being made to travel so far from their homes. Most wore some improvised 'woman-don't-stray' and a few were led by a cord, or hobbled against escape. Why, Keith wondered, were the Barghesh women so refractory, compared with the easy-going women of Mban?

As the Mban women were led out and lined up opposite their sisters in misfortune, Keith began to understand. Where time had not allowed a forked sapling to be cut, an ordinary roofing stick had been tied to a woman's neck and wrists. Keith's aged inamorata was tugged along by a rope around her neck, the same rope she had offered to Keith. She screamed what sounded like curses, though earlier this morning she had been pounding corn in a mortar, unbound and smugly content.

It looked very much as though the trammels and elaborate precautions against flight were so much eye-wash, intended to convey 'You see I'm not responsible. I was helpless.' Which might save a lot of husbandly reproaches and some beatings.

Barghesh warriors evacuated Mban, and Mban warriors re-entered their village. Keith and his small escort marched with the Barghesh men and women to see them safely home. Once behind their respective cactus hedges, each side could enjoy a precarious and rather hungry peace until next harvest. If either side wanted peace.

That seemed doubtful. Having been wined and dined—or the local equivalent of beered and chickened—by Sarikin Barghesh, Keith was approached with an amiable proposition that he and his soldiers help Barghesh exterminate Mban.

A few miles outside Barghesh next morning a deputation from the priest-chief of Mban met him with food and a counter-proposition. Barghesh women and goats were offered by Mban, thus improving on their rivals' offer.

'We do not attack, we defend,' Keith told them both. 'For a yearly payment of threepence by each warrior, which we call tax, we will place our peace upon your village, and punish any who come in force to rob or kill you.'

Keith's suggestion sounded to the Kulere leaders like a good bargain. Threepence was only the price of a bundle of corn, and if a man did not have to be on guard all the time, and could take better land further from his village, he and his women and children could grow many more bundles of corn. They asked when the *Ba-ture* would return, and promised to have the money ready. They might, or they might not. But it was a start, the first seed of administration ever sown on this unpromising soil.

Marching proudly at the head of his detachment, his empty hammock borne behind him, Yeats cast a backward glance of regret, as the low blue hills of the Closed Area receded into the distance.

'It sounds silly, you know, but I like those johnnies. But they're jumpy as cats, every one of them. D'you suppose it's because the johnnies have never felt safe for a single day since they were born?'

Keith made a mental note to include that pearl of wisdom in his official report.

Chapter Nineteen

THE conical grass roofs of Panyam village came into sight on the east, not bunched for defence as in more backward tribes, but straggling serenely about the peaceful countryside.

'Looks as though they've got most of their harvest in.' Keith turned to Yeats, riding alongside. 'I'll get hold of the chief as soon as we arrive, and try to extract the balance of tax before they turn their surplus grain into beer and drink it all up.'

Mounted or afoot, even after his malaria and in wrinkled, sweat-stained uniform, Lieutenant Yeats seemed to be modelling a picture of military valour, even with a touch of gallant chivalry. A romantic youth whose innocent enthusiasms were hard to live up to.

'Y'know, Keith, I'd give a lot to be in your boots. I mean going round and giving people justice and roads and other things they want, and stopping them murdering each other.'

'I'm less and less sure they want what we give them,' Keith tried another line. 'If the world had enough patience to let the poor devils grow their own African civilization from their own African roots, that would be different. But we're so damned conceited that because we wear pants and vote, we think everyone else ought to do the same.'

'Fwee . . . fifi, fwee . . . fifi.' The whistle of the distant carriers, picked up again at the advanced base, announced that the end of the day's march was near at hand. And here was the turn-off which detoured Panyam market place, leading direct to the rest-house.

A dejected figure, in the ragged robes assumed by a suppliant to arouse pity, rose from the wayside and prostrated itself in deep obeisance.

Keith reined up. It was the rest-house keeper, and with a tale of woe.

'By permission of the *Ba-ture*! He came in anger, and it chanced that there were no ripe pawpaws in the garden. He gave me evil words and dismissed me. Also he was angered with the Sarikin Sura who had not ridden out to meet him, and took from him a month's pay for lack of respect. Though, indeed, we had no word that he would come.'

'Who did these things, and when?' Keith cut short the string of complaints.

'The other judge, Mister Petbo. Three days ago.'

So Pettibone had arrived already. But he had no authority to do these things. Until Pettibone resumed charge of the division the man had no more official standing than a mining prospector or a missionary. Keith's anger flared up.

'Would you mind tucking our mob into bed tonight, Yeats? Tell the carriers I'll pay them off tomorrow at Pankshin. I've got to ride straight through. Pettibone's arrived.'

Instead of a Pettibone chastened by his Zaria experience, and willing to let bygones be bygones, it looked as though one would have to cope with a Pettibone furious to reassert himself, avid to humiliate a tribal chief or even a helpless rest-house keeper. To proclaim his authority.

It was at the foot of Pankshin hill that the next blow fell.

Nyenyam dropped goat-like down the hillside from some lookout where he had been watching for Keith's arrival. Keith had to rein up sharply to avoid him.

'Welcome!' said Nyenyam simply. 'Our house is now here. But there is no food.'

'Welcome, Nyenyam! But why no food? Is the money finished?'

'Sam is in the House of Chains.'

'Sam?' Incredible. But the young Tal ruffian was an earnest child, not given to joking. 'What has Sam done?'

'Petbo was angered with him.'

Keith dismounted, and handed over Orion. An uphill walk might cool his temper. He acknowledged the cheerful salute of the gunners' quarter-guard, avoided the office, and swung over the hill and down to the prison.

A head warder, not the one he had left in charge, but the one he had dismissed, gave him anxious and elaborate greetings.

Keith cut him short. 'Salutations! But who placed you here?'

'Mister Petbo.'

Without a vestige of authority to do so.

'Bring the prisoner book. And open the door.'

'Mister Petbo took the book.' A sly triumph showed in the man's pock-marked face, but he unlocked the door.

In the rectangular mud-walled, mud-floored room thirteen prisoners sat around, bored and morose. All except Sam were chained. He was privileged to wear his stained shirt, shorts and battered but jaunty remains of a felt hat. Six of the prisoners were new, not committed with Keith's knowledge, and hence without legal warrant or authority.

'Come, Sam!' Keith considered the head warder, wondering whether to have him arrested on the same charges which had caused his dismissal. But Pettibone could strike through underlings, Keith could not. 'Bring the prisoners before me tomorrow morning, it is too late today.'

Sam's story was simple, and probably true. He had been eating outside his own cook-house in the divisional officer's compound when Pettibone had arrived unexpectedly and told him 'Take up everything and go!' Off its accustomed tracks, Sam's mind worked slowly. He said something about 'asking Mister Keeta,' but obediently took up the frying pan and waited to be told where he was to go. Pettibone went off angrily in the direction of the office. Sam sat down again and finished his meal.

Then Mister Petbo's carriers arrived with his loads, and by order of red-robes and Messengers started taking away Mister Keeta's things. Sam told them to stop. The red-robes took Sam to the office before Mister Petbo, and thence to prison. He had been there two days.

Sam enjoyed being in the centre of things, even when it was the middle of a stream between Dallong and Yergam bowmen. He was willing, with the slightest encouragement, to pose as a martyr.

The tendency had to be checked. 'For two days you have done

no work and eaten free food,' Keith pointed out. 'But now you must work again.'

Sam's filed teeth showed in a grin. Mailafia's idea had changed the picture. Sam was no longer the victim of injustice. Instead he was a cunning fellow who had defrauded the head warder, and could boast about it.

'Return now to the rest-house, and see that tonight's dinner is good, for I shall be hungry, having taken no food at midday.'

Handling the cook's small problem brought back Keith's sense of balance. When the Messengers, Gofwan leading, came out to meet him at some distance from the office, and gave prolonged and earnest greetings, he inwardly sympathized with their difficult position.

Pettibone sat at the divisional officer's table, Keith's table, dealing with official correspondence—Keith's correspondence. The same immaculate Pettibone, complete with jacket and tie and neat suède shoes. One graceful hand inscribed an elaborate signature, and laid down the pen with careful precision as Keith shadowed the arched mud doorway.

'So you've arrived at last?'

Keith pushed back some papers, cleared a corner of the table and perched on it. 'You know, Pettibone, I think we ought to come to a working agreement. Combined, we could do a slap-up job with this division. And opening the Closed Area is a chance of a lifetime.'

'You won't be here, Captain Keith, when Kulere is opened.' The beringed left hand made its habitual and irritating gesture, smoothing down the over-long auburn hair.

'Meanwhile I am here. I am also divisional officer.' Keith made the position clear. 'Will you remove yourself from my chair, or shall I call the Messengers and have you removed?'

Pettibone hesitated.

Keith called 'Gofwan! Two Messengers, please.'

Pettibone rose as they entered.

Keith gave his instructions. 'Mister Pettibone will work at the little table. Place these papers on it. And let two of you bring the writing machine from the other room.' He changed back to

English. 'Sorry to disturb you, Pettibone, but the light's better here than in Mr McTavish's office. I've got to pound out my Kulere report.'

On his way home, Keith dropped in on Garrard, to relieve his mind in case he had heard some rumour about a sick white man in a hammock.

O.C. Troops was yellow and deaf and shaking with quinine, and needed cheering up. Griggs had been sent off for medical treatment, and the invaluable Fletcher might have to go down country for a course on a new kind of mortar. In dressing-gown over his shirt and shorts, Garrard paced his sitting-room, lamenting the day he had ever applied for service in West Africa, catching his toe in a worn mat, cursing the mat, cursing his unlucky fate to be running a battery practically single-handed.

'All the same, Garrard, you're damned lucky,' Keith consoled him. 'Things could be worse. You haven't got Pettibone to cope with.'

'Who hasn't?' Garrard turned sharply, caught his foot in the torn mat once more, picked up the mat and hurled it through the door. 'First thing he did was to have the flag taken down from the hill-top, and send it to me without so much as a note of explanation. Then he wrote demanding why my quarter-guard had saluted him instead of turning out to present arms. Seems to think he's a bloody general at least. Man's off his rocker.'

'But not insane by legal definition,' Keith amended. To change the subject he reported Yeats' work on the trip.

It was a good move. Garrard sat down, began to beam, and wanted more detail. Leviticus brought in drinks and herring roes on toast. The matter of Yeats' wanting to join the political and administrative department came up.

'All your damned fault,' Garrard insisted. 'The dolt sees you pooping about the countryside, administering the high, the low, and the middle justice with a lordly air, while his poor bloody commanding officer does the company accounts and polishes his soldiers' toe-nails. Now if you were just another gunner . . .'

Keith let the good-natured storm blow itself out, finished his drink and remembered his sun-helmet.

'Come slumming when you have time. I've still got some
drinkables down at the rest-house, unless Pettibone's pinched
them. I'd better go and see.'

Nothing seemed to be missing, but Pettibone's carriers, tired
and careless at the end of a long march, had broken several hastily
packed plates and dishes. Keith hurried through dinner. Nyenyam
said nothing about Hafsatu-Hatasu, and it was improper to
enquire. If any harm had come to them, Nyenyam would have
said so. He had reported that Pettibone had taken back the
Empress.

All the same, it was an enormous relief when they entered.

They were unharmed, unchanged. Gloriously unchanged. Formally, in outdoor wraps, they exchanged salutations and enquiries.
Then, laying formality aside, shed their tent-like coverings, and
cast themselves into his arms. As though to assure themselves by
actual touch that all legs and arms were still attached, and no
Kulere arrow-heads were sticking in him.

'When the loads were taken, Messengers and red-robes made no
trouble for you?' Keith, too, needed reassurance.

'None. We said to Nyenyam "Lay aside the spear! This matter
does not concern you. Place things in boxes!" Since Sam had been
taken away, we gave orders. "Take this load first . . . with that
load be careful!" as Sam would have done.'

'But Petbo?' Pettibone could scarcely have resisted the opportunity to be unpleasant.

They exchanged glances above their veils. 'Petbo came to our
house and spoke foolishly. We did not hear. We were sewing.
We did not rise or answer. He went. That was before the carriers
and the red-robes and the Messengers came. Petbo did not return.
Nor did the others trouble us.'

Whether Pettibone had cursed the twins, or made improper
advances to them, was uncertain. And they considered it beneath
their dignity to say. But Pettibone could be forced to. Gently
Keith tried to release himself from the slender braceleted arms.

'No harm was done, Mailafia.' *Kohl*-shadowed eyes considered
him anxiously. 'Have patience, as an Emir forbears when his
sleeve is empty of coin and a beggar calls curses after his horse.

195

Such a graceless beggar is Petbo, meriting neither blame nor blows.'

'What talk is this that you give me? Why do you attempt to hold me?' Keith's anger, kindled by Pettibone, flared up at their attempt to restrain him. 'Since when has the Prophet granted authority to women? Since when has he put power in their weak arms to hold a man from his purpose?'

With a sigh, and a tinkle of silver bracelets, the arms fell away from him. 'By permission! A woman has no strength save in her love. But because of that love she will beg "Do not spur your horse over the cliff!" And because of that love she will cling to the rein, or cast herself under the hooves of the horse to turn it.'

'This you would dare. But this I would not wish you to do.' Keith spoke more mildly.

'Often has Mailafia said "Let us take counsel together, for three minds have more wisdom than one alone."' There was a note of sadness, perhaps of disillusionment in their voices. 'This is all we sought to do. But let Mailafia's will be made known, and we will accept it. That is his right.'

That wasn't what he wanted either. Great-Lord-and-Master stuff! Yet somehow he must make them understand that he intended to be master of his own actions. Pettibone must wait until that had been cleared up. Wasn't there some Hausa proverb which would sum it up? All he could recall that seemed at all apropos was something he had read in an old manuscript he had bought at Bauchi.

It was too long a tale to tell standing up. But there would be no chair or camp-bed until the carriers arrived tomorrow. 'With permission!' he kicked off his shoes and sat down on the twins' sleeping mat. A little uncertainly they seated themselves beside him, not quite touching.

'There is a story of one, a woman, who came to Abubakr the Wise seeking mastery over her husband.' Yes it was certainly to the point. 'Is it unknown to Hafsatu-Hatasu? Then I will tell it.'

One of the twins rose and blew out the hurricane lamp. There was a faint waft of perfume as the other spread their outdoor garments over all three. They drew a little closer, in the darkness.

'So great was the wisdom of Abubakr of Katsina that people came to him from near and far to ask his counsel and seek his help. Thus it was that a woman asked him "Give me mastery over my husband, who is rich, and I will make you rich."

'Said Abubakr, "I give wisdom, not power, being myself without power." The woman then said "Give me this wisdom. Then I may know how to gain mastery over my husband." Abubakr laughed, and said "Such wisdom cannot be given. It must be sought." The woman asked "Where shall I seek it?" and continued to ask. So Abubakr, to be freed of her importuning, said, "Seek and bring to me the milk of a bush-cow."'

The fable was going over well. One of the twins gave a wriggle of excitement. The other set something soft for Keith's head to rest on. Somehow this wasn't the ill-written screed which he only dimly remembered. It had taken on some of the point and timing of the twins' own method of narration.

'The woman sought bush-cow milk in the markets, offering double the price of pure honey, and yet more. But people laughed and said "Whoever heard of bush-cow milk? It would be safer to milk a lioness!"

'The woman sought the hunters, offering them riches to bring her the milk. But they answered "Allah separate us from bush-cows! Evil beasts that kill even the bravest hunters."

'For long none in Katsina heard or saw the woman. Her husband took other wives. But she returned again to Abubakr the Wise, bearing a calabash bottle, and asking "Do I drink it, or rub it on my husband? This is what you bade me bring. For one year I sought a bush-cow. For another year I drew near to her. At the end of the third year I milked her."

'People marvelled, saying "This cannot be, yet it is! For her words are the words of truth. Praise be to Allah!"

'Then said Abubakr the Wise "Pour it on the dust of the market place." The woman asked "All?" but obeyed. She asked "Now give me the magic which you call wisdom, that I may have mastery over my husband."

'Then answered Abubakr the Wise—and many remembered his words—"There is no magic other than the wisdom which was taught to you by the bush-cow. That you could not have mastery over the bush-cow. But only by patience, and by permission of the bush-cow, could you gain your desire. Seek what you wish of your husband—as you sought it of the bush-cow."

'This is the tale of Abubakr the Wise. And the tale is ended.'

'And the lesson is learned!' Arms hugged him in the darkness. 'We seek no power over Mailafia, only Mailafia himself.'

Keith chuckled. 'Not the milk of the bush-cow, but the whole beast! Yet there is yet another moral, and that Mailafia must learn—not from Abubakr the Wise, but from two women foolish enough to seek counsel of Mailafia. And that is . . . patience!'

Next morning Keith went early to office, but found Pettibone already installed in the divisional officer's chair at the divisional officer's table. And clearly intending to stay there. He gave no answer to Keith's cheerful 'Good morning, sir!'

'Funny business,' said Keith conversationally; 'while I was out on tour a number of people have been getting free rations and lodging at the government's expense. I've told the head warder to bring them up here so I can look into it.' He laid his hat down on the table.

'The curious thing is that the head warder has got it into his head that it was Mr Pettibone who sent the men to prison. Of course this would be quite illegal, and can't be true. The head warder can't show any warrants for these extra men, and pretends that you have the prison register.'

The ruse worked. Without a word Pettibone rose and stalked into the clerk's office. Keith slid into the vacated chair of authority. He called a Messenger. Loshi was incautious enough to enter.

'The other *Ba-ture* will work at the small table,' Keith informed him suavely. 'Clear this table of papers, and lay them there.'

Pettibone returned with the prison register. 'It may interest you to know that I committed the men myself. You will find their names here.' Unthinkingly, and quite naturally, he laid the heavy volume on the table, so that Keith might read and be convinced.

The situation was just as Keith had planned it. Aware that there was some contest between the rival *Tura-wa*, the Messengers had filtered in. Gofwan was at the smaller table, moving Pettibone's ink-well half an inch to one side, and opening the lid so that it might be in readiness. Anta gaped. Tibn waited, as yet uncommitted to either the Pettibone or the Keith faction.

Keith could guess Tibn's mental workings. Had not Petbo come early to seize the table of authority, and held it for a time though Keeta had laid his helmet on it as though to claim it? But had not Keeta seized both table and chair, sending Petbo to fetch papers as once Petbo had sent Keeta? And was not Petbo standing and bowing before Keeta, as he pointed to something in the book?

The head warder came with prisoners and a blacksmith. It was seen that Keeta's will still prevailed, for those whom Petbo had placed in chains Keeta released. While Petbo, sitting apart at the small table, stroked the hair of his head more, and yet more.

Keeta gave orders that those who were left, chained and unchained alike, return to their work. And only the head warder remained. The head warder bowed his head, as before the sword of an Emir's executioner. Keeta said to him one word only,

'Run!'

It was Keeta's way that any thief, murderer, or honest man might come before him freely and depart freely. When all words had been heard Keeta said one of two things. Either 'No harm!' or 'Run!' Those to whom he said 'Run!' had a day and a night to escape, none hindering. Then Keeta laid nose to trail, and Keeta's nose was long.

When the head warder heard the word 'Run!' he turned his face to Petbo. But Petbo was as one deaf and unseeing.

With remarkable self-control Pettibone watched the gaol-delivery. When the head warder, already starting to shed his robes of office, had left, Pettibone made his expected threat.

'You're wasting your time, Captain Keith. As soon as I'm in command of my division, back they all go to prison. Including your cook.'

'What's Sam's crime? Other than his cooking, I mean.'

'He threatened to attack me with a hot frying-pan. I'll try him myself, of course, in the provincial court, so that I can give him a full two years with hard labour in a down-country prison away from your interference.'

Keith had to be patient once more. 'If you had taken all the exams we war-birds were given before appointment, you would know that you were disqualified from trying the case, being an interested party.'

No reaction.

'By the way, Pettibone, may I congratulate you on the wonderful memory which allowed you to fill in all the men's names, and their villages, in the short time it took you to bring the prison register from the clerk's office. Unfortunately you had to leave blanks in the columns for "Name of Native Court", "Nature of Offence" and "Number of Warrant".'

Keith took up a pen. 'Know what I'm doing now? I'm signing my name across all those blanks, so you can't fill them in later. Thus leaving on record, in your own writing, that you have detained people in prison without warrant or conviction. And here's a little precaution ,which may interest you. . . . Gofwan, bring the oil which is used for the writing machine.'

Keith worked an oily finger carefully over his signatures, added more oil, and worked that in too. 'Any attempt to erase my writing, or to write anything else over the top will now be complete waste of time. Don't try any tricks on Sam, or this prison register will be used in evidence against you. And, by the way, if you molest any others in my household you will also face charges in connection with your parades of Angas virgins. The girls I once saw were below the age of consent, and, being herded by a Messenger with a stick, constructively under duress.'

The mild manner masked the challenge from the interested Messengers. To their obvious amazement Pettibone jerked to his feet and began to shout.

'That's blackmail, blackmail! I'll have you arrested . . . arrested . . . do you hear!'

'You're absolutely right!' Keith laughed as though Pettibone's antics were intended as a joke. 'The price of my silence is cheap, though. Let's drop our bickerings, get on with the job, and open Kulere.'

The entrance of Yeats, meticulously saluting first Pettibone then Keith in order of seniority, stopped further argument. Keith opened the safe, paid the carriers outside, and gave Yeats a note to his O.C. asking if the gunners could hold the usual cash board next day.

Pettibone sat up most of that night, checking and re-checking, torn between the desire to be in the saddle again and the suspicion that Keith was tricking him out of another hundred pounds or more. But the handing over went disappointingly smoothly.

The only outward changes were that Timmy could no longer come to office and snore beneath the divisional officer's table, and that Keith, removed to the side-table, was no longer permitted to smoke. Since Mr Ferguson McTavish was fighting his intestinal battle mainly in his quarters, Keith was privileged to do the man's typing and filing. Pettibone was almost courteous, with the punctilio of the duellist who looks forward to the happy moment when he will eviscerate his opponent.

The lull lasted for two weeks. During that time most of Keith's work was undone. Native Courts were again discouraged from sitting. Checking prisoners and the inspection of their food were discontinued. Keith's laborious and far-reaching census work was ignored, and tax totals were changed back to what they had been before—here too much and there too little.

Keith offered no protest. He had no doubt that the divisional officer had applied to have him removed, and he had no intention of providing him with any valid cause.

The end of the armistice arrived with a Bauchi mailbag. Pettibone read and re-read one short note, called a Messenger and had it taken across to Keith's table.

CONFIDENTIAL.
To D.O. Pankshin.
With two officers in the division I expect more than half their combined time to be spent away from headquarters. Unless sick, Capt. Keith must tour for three weeks out of four. In future all references to Capt. Keith must be shown to him, and be initialled by him. Kindly acknowledge, and ensure that your acknowledgment bears his initials.

A. J. Sharpe. Resident.

Since confidential correspondence does not pass through a clerk's hands, the note was in the Resident's craggy scrawl. Its meaning was clear enough. He was tired of Pettibone's complaints about his junior. Also he wanted to have Kulere opened.

It wasn't worth calling a Messenger in to carry the note back. Keith got up and laid it on Pettibone's table. And stood, puzzled by the man's hands. One was bandaged, the other only badly scratched. Angas virgins or other reluctant females wouldn't scratch hands, they would aim for the face. It was just a glimpse, then the hands disappeared into Pettibone's pockets.

'Grand!' said Keith. 'When do you want me to push off?'

'Tomorrow, of course.'

'Where would you like me to go?'

'Wherever you please. One Messenger will be enough for you, as I won't allow any census work, or tax collecting, or interference with my native administration. That includes public works of any kind.'

'Any objection to my asking O.C. Troops if he can spare me an escort?' The Closed Area had no public works or native administration, and census and tax-collection would be out of the question.

'No escort!'

Therefore no Kulere picnic. That was a blow.

Forced, by the Resident's note, to send Keith out on tour, Pettibone intended to allow him no scope. Pettibone's orders were verbal, so needed no initialling, and could later be denied. Keith was to be sent out to do nothing, so that Pettibone could later report on his idleness and uselessness. That's what it looked like.

It seemed a sound idea to drop in on Garrard to say good-bye; and at the same time ask if he could spare space in his battery store-room for such things as Keith could not take on tour. In his present mood Pettibone wouldn't be above withdrawing any watchman Keith placed on the rest-house, leaving his stuff to be pillaged.

'Anyone home?' No answer. Keith called again.

Garrard was there, anyway his voice was. Keith went on in.

To be met with apology. 'Sorry, old man. Didn't hear you.

Voices raised in anger. Ever heard of a man called Pettibone? We were just discussing him.'

Yeats loomed up out of a chair. 'I've been trying to tell the old skipper it doesn't matter.'

'Damn it, you cub, shut up!' Garrard turned down the decibels again, and tried to explain. 'Pettibone doesn't approve of your report on the Mban-Barghesh show, and has written his own comments "copy to O.C. Troops, with request to forward to higher military authority". Here . . . read the tripe!'

Unfortunately it was anything but tripe. It was an ingenious mixture of truth and distortion. It asserted that Keith had "jeopardized the steady progress made by me in my division by a reckless attempt at self-advertisement" and more to the same effect. It hit at Garrard for allowing his men to be used. It summed up:

Captain Keith has wisely glossed over the dangers inherent in his provocative and foolhardy use of a quite inadequate force. Had the villages of Mban and Barghesh chosen to combine against him, the disaster would have been one from which Administration would have taken years to recover.

And ended with as dirty a piece of innuendo as Keith had ever met:

The weakness of Captain Keith's position was aggravated by Lieutenant Yeats taking to his hammock, and remaining there during most of the time this 'expedition' was in danger. He has since made a rapid recovery.

'Give me a pen!'

Yeats found one and passed it over. Keith grabbed it, dipped it, and hand shaking with indignation wrote:

The above remarks are made by one who has never, during his long charge of Pankshin Division, seen fit to put foot within the unruly Closed Area.

His long delay in complying with official instructions to commence the opening of Kulere was the main reason why the

203

attempt could no longer be delayed. The limited force used was on account of the 'Stand-by' order due to trouble on the Gold Coast. The expedition accomplished more than its original purpose, and withdrew on good terms with the inhabitants, and without casualties on either side. The force used may therefore be accounted adequate.

That ought to leave Garrard in the clear.

Mr Pettibone's tendentious comments on Lieutenant T. S. Yeats are as deplorable in taste as they are unbased on truth.

Mr Pettibone has no experience of military operations, or he would have realized that Lieutenant Yeats' hammock would have been the first and most obvious mark for a flight of poison arrows, had hostilities developed. Lieutenant Yeats was willing to take this risk, and I concurred, as I considered him indispensable. In this I was not mistaken, as my original report clearly shows.

Ian Keith.

O.C. Troops read and chuckled. 'That comment, added to Pettibone's, I shall have much pleasure in forwarding to my commandant. After taking several copies! The commandant, by the way, thinks he knew you, in Egypt. Probably borrowed money from you in a Port Said brothel. Have a drink! Have two!'

Long before daylight Yeats appeared at the rest-house with a fatigue party, and took Keith's spare loads to the battery store. He returned again as Keith was sending off his carriers. This time he was mounted, and in full field uniform, including a sword, to do Keith additional honour. He dismounted to deliver a message.

'The old skipper says you're quite right that he shouldn't annoy Pettibone by taking sides. But he says there's no harm in my riding out with you a few miles. That is, if you don't mind?'

The last carrier had disappeared into the dim morning light. Garuba Kano led up Orion. The twins had already gone off on their Hill ponies. Keith had a foot in the stirrup when a red-robe came running down the hill, a chop-box bouncing on his turban.

The folded note that was handed to him suggested that Keith had left something behind in the office. It read 'You may like to take this with you.'

The red-robe set down the box and folded back the lid.

Keith said 'Empress, this is a most unexpected pleasure!' and lifted her out. Yeats put out a hand to stroke her. Keith said hastily 'She's dead!'

Dead, and with a wire tight round her neck.

The first feeling was shock. Then fury with the red-robe. Then came a recollection of Pettibone's scratched hands. So Pettibone had reserved the murder for his own hands and his own personal satisfaction. Because Keith and the cat had been friends.

Keith laid the Empress gently back in her box. Then leaped into the saddle.

But Yeats had mounted first, and had a good start.

Keith overhauled him half-way up the hill, and grabbed his rein, shouting 'Don't be a damned fool!'

'I've got to! Can't you see? Or I wouldn't feel there was any decency left in the world. Please, Keith, old man! Please!'

The gunner sentry had called out the guard. Within sight of the startled soldiers the two horses milled around in the narrow road, Yeats trying to tear Keith's hand from his rein. For a moment Keith thought the quarter-guard would attempt to rescue their officer.

Then he was leading Yeats' mount down the road, and could release him.

'The trap was baited for me, not you. If you hadn't tried to ride into it, I'd have done the same. You gave me time to think.'

Yes, that was it. A long string of calculated provocations came to mind. When Keith had refused to be tempted by the bait of personal insults and official indignities, Pettibone had tried another line. He had hit at Keith through other people. The list was a long one. Sarikin Sura, the Panyam rest-house keeper, two carriers, the twins, Sam, Tibn, a red-robe, the native treasury scribe, and at least half a dozen others suspected of being friendly to Keith. They might, by Pettibone's calculation, be the weak spot in Keith's defences.

And finally Yeats yesterday, and the Empress today. Diabolically cunning!

'I don't get it, Captain Keith.' The ridiculous formality of 'Captain' told of shaken ideals.

'Ride back if you want to. You're calm enough now. You may find Pettibone brushing his hair and waiting. You'll find at least two Messengers prepared to swear they know enough English to recite your threats in Court. You won't be able to lay a finger on Pettibone, as there will be several red-robes with their hand-cuffs open and waiting. Waiting, though they may not know it, for me.'

The chop-box, lid open, waited in the road beside the deserted rest-house. Three vultures circled lower.

Yeats was convinced rationally, but not emotionally. He wasn't safe yet.

Keith dismounted, looped the reins over his arm, and stooped again over the box. Gently he detached the wire, of good copper and long enough to garrotte a human instead of a cat. He thrust it into the pocket of his riding breeches, and lifted the Empress.

'I hate to ask you this favour, Yeats. I know you're looking forward to matching your nag against mine on the Panyam road. But I wonder if you could find a corner in your garden for the Empress?'

Yeats gulped. He loosed the cross-belt of his Sam Browne, un-buttoned his perfect tunic, and found room for the pathetic little corpse.

Keith remounted. 'Just one more thing. We're friends, aren't we, and you wouldn't poach my game? Then remember! Petti-bone's mine, and nobody else's! It may take me a month or a year or . . .'

He snapped his teeth down on the end of the threat. All he had intended was a warning, for Yeats' own good, against getting involved with Pettibone. He had gone on to say what he had never allowed himself to think. Lest the consuming desire harden into a deadly purpose.

206

Chapter Twenty

As the Dallong and Angas hills rose above the general plateau, so the Lankan valley sank below it. Some volcanic upheaval had done its best to tear the eastern half of the division from the western. Even in the deep shade of the rest-house it felt as though those ancient fires still smouldered beneath the mud floor.

It was siesta time, but too hot to rest. To lie down was to cover part of one's sweat glands against the mattress; and all were needed, as the throbbing in neck and temples warned. To sit down was to sit in a pool of one's own sweat. Standing one dripped from chin, armpits, crotch and the back of the knees.

In shorts and sandals Keith paced the length of the sitting-room, his fingers smoothing, caressing the length of copper wire, as the devout tell the beads of a rosary. Pacing slowly, like a meditative monk in a cloister, it was possible to balance the cooling effect of motion against the heating effect of exercise, and show a slight profit.

No *Ba-ture* had visited Lankan for several years. It was a peaceful Sura village which paid its taxes on time and practised intensive farming in the pockets of rich volcanic soil between the almost unclimbable cliffs. Orion, and even the twins' sure-footed Sura ponies had been led and almost carried down. Two loads had been dropped and their contents smashed.

Timmy, stretched out in the doorway hoping for a breath of air, choked briefly and resumed his snoring. The thatch crackled softly, as though burning in the afternoon heat. No other sound, except the pulses pounding in Keith's ears.

There was nothing in the village to demand attention. The young village head was efficient, and apparently just. Which made Lankan a good choice for a fugitive from his own conscience. Tafchin and Takkos had been unbearable. Roads had needed repair after the rains, and so had culverts, market-stalls and the rest-houses. Day after day patient folk had come to lay their troubles before the white man. But the white man's orders permitted him to do nothing. He could not even explain why he had to fail them, for that was a matter between Pettibone and himself.

It was as though he had medicine for the sick and food for the starving, yet denied it to them.

The copper wire, burnished like red gold with constant handling, was straight now, straight as a sword. He halted his restless pacing to hold it to his eye, to make sure. Soon he would coil it again, not tightly to fit a pocket, but in wider loops. It would be quicker to use, and less likely to kink.

There was a break in Timmy's snoring, as Hafsatu-Hatasu stepped over him and entered. Keith said 'Welcome!' by habit, and forgot them.

Once only in the last few weeks had they emerged from the mist which seemed to have gathered around him. That was when the wire disappeared. Since it was in his hands or within reach, by day and night, only the twins could have taken it. He asked for it. They brought it, fear in their eyes. But the fear was for him, not for themselves.

They knew of course. No doubt Anta and the whole household knew what had happened back there at Pankshin. But only Hafsatu-Hatasu, sensitive to his thoughts as they were to each other's, knew what had to happen in the future. The near future. Perhaps tonight.

There was still an alternative. He had tried it. He would try it again. He took his portable out of its travelling case, found paper in the office box, wiped his sweating hands on a towel, sat down at the table, and typed.

CONFIDENTIAL.
To Capt. A. J. Sharpe,
Resident Bauchi.
I charge my superior officer, Alexander Pettibone, with the following offences, ranging from contravention of treasury regulations to unlawful imprisonment, abuse of authority,

and having carnal knowledge of girls below the age of consent. The attached sheet cites time, place, nature of offence, and witnesses or material evidence. Since there is no other Justice to receive my deposition upon oath, I am unable to place this in statutory form.

He rose. The satanic rosary of copper wire came to his fingers as though of its own volition. He resumed his restless pacing.

The charge sheet, four full pages of foolscap, had been waiting for days. Now he had only to add his signature to the covering letter, address and seal the envelope, and hand a few shillings to a runner. Then Pettibone's power would be broken, and Pettibone himself would be broken and gone.

Which was why he had left it too late, and could not send the letter. Because Pettibone had become part of Keith, and Keith of Pettibone.

Pettibone's campaign of calculated provocation had succeeded beyond anything which he could have intended. No official investigation, no Court of Law or prison locks could be permitted to come between Keith and his purpose. Only the copper wire, which slid so comfortingly between the fingers, could bring about the final, perfect retribution.

All that remained was to ride from here to Pankshin, keeping ahead of any warning that Anta might send. Once out of the valley Orion could cover the sixty miles faster than any runner.

The distance alone was guarantee of success. Pettibone would have relaxed his precautions anyway, after this lapse of time. With his early morning tea would come something which Pettibone had no possible cause to expect. . . .

' Yes? '

Hafsatu-Hatasu had emerged from the bedroom and stood before him. Usually in such heat, and in the privacy of the rest-house, they wore little or nothing. But now they were fully dressed. They must have something very formal and important to say.

They knelt, with the smooth grace which even now had power to charm. He hoped the interview would not weaken his resolution. The hardest thing of all had been to resign himself to losing them. Fortunately they were well provided for. The codicil to his will, witnessed by Garrard and Fletcher, had seen to that. They could return to their friend Shetu with ample trading capital.

'Well?' He had to ask them again.

'The fault is ours. We repent!'

'The fault must be told to me. For I find you faultless.'

He held out a hand to each, to raise them up in the formal gesture of forgiveness. To do so he had to lay the wire on the table. They did not take his hands. Their eyes followed the wire.

'Mailafia!' They bent their heads, so he could no longer see their faces. 'We have thought long. Is Mailafia willing to hear our thoughts?'

How could he deny them?

'Mailafia should take another woman. That is our thought.' Two soft voices, in unison, offered the shattering suggestion.

Keith took the blow in silence, glad that they could not see his face. If they were interested in another man, that would lessen the pain of parting. For them. His neglect of them had brought this on himself, so he had no right to feel self-pity.

'You are wise, as always. You are young and beautiful. That is the time to marry, so that the children may grow strong and handsome.' His voice was as controlled and calm as though he were in Court. 'In six months time much money will be yours, and if you put it to trade you will become rich. If the Lame One, whom you met at Ron, is at Bauchi, go to him. He will be your friend, and see that all that is due to you is given you. If he has gone to his country, ask aid of Ni-Ne or another of the *Tura-wa* there. Do not stay in Pankshin, lest Petbo trouble you.'

They gave a cry of protest, and their hands reached out towards him. 'Mailafia, it is not . . .'

'The ponies are already yours, and I will give you money for travel, and a gift.' He knew that he must put his good intentions into words to make them irrevocable. 'If the man is here, take him with you so that I may not see or envy him.' It might be the dashing horse-boy, who for once had brought no woman with him. 'As for yourselves, send me word by a letter writer so that

I may know that all is well with you, and may recall the happiness you have given me.'

Yes, he would have to postpone that other plan. The twins must be far away. Otherwise they might be held for the double inquest, as witnesses to Keith's state of mind. Their newfound happiness must not be marred by such grim reminders of what once had been.

Their future happiness seemed far away. Tears welled from their dark eyes. Then suddenly their heads were in his lap, and he was patting their backs, trying to comfort them.

'It is not thus! Indeed it is not thus! It is that for long our Mailafia has been troubled, neither eating nor drinking as he should, and sleeping scarcely at all. And we, woe to us! knew the remedy, but loved ourselves better than we loved him, and did not hold it to his lips!'

He still could not understand. It sounded almost as though they had no other man in mind, and loved him still. But after facing the thought of losing them, he dare not let himself hope again. One thing alone was clear, that he must set their doubts at rest.

'My trouble was not of your making, but far otherwise.'

'The cause is known to us. But it is the duty of a woman to wipe cares from her man's mind, even as it is her duty to wipe dust from his feet. Yet this we did not do!'

'How could you?'

Two tragic faces looked up into his. Tears had made the eye-shadow run in streaks. Keith felt in the pockets of his shorts for a handkerchief. It was sweaty, but they would not mind. He wiped their faces, as though they were beloved children.

They looked less woebegone, and tried to smile in courteous thanks. But the smiles failed.

'Has Mailafia forgotten when we first came to him? It is said that he was then troubled, as he is now.'

'It is said truly. Perhaps I was close to madness. You lifted the burden from me, or I think my days would soon have ended.'

'This we did, praise be to Allah! Not with skill or wisdom, for we had none, but because we had never known man before. It is well said "A virgin may separate a fool from his folly or a

211

wise man from his wisdom." ' They glanced at each other. 'But we are no longer virgins!'

'If that be a fault, whose fault is it but mine?' Keith was increasingly puzzled. 'And how shall that be remedied?'

Their look of satisfaction told him that somehow he was on the right line. But he was damned if he could see where it led.

'Let Mailafia grant us permission! This we will do, we will give him a new woman, a virgin. We ourselves will pay her, for there is enough money for all three.'

Keith gave a grunt of astonishment. That was all he was capable of feeling at the moment.

'We have talked much of this together, saying "We will send to Shetu to find us one, a good one." But we delayed, and there is no longer time. So this we will do, we will take a girl of this village, neither too young nor too old, cover her shaven head and teach her by signs what pleases Mailafia, and . . .'

'And I would give her a gift and send her quickly away! Lest even for a breathing-space she come between me and Hafsatu-Hatasu, whom alone I desire!'

He expected their relief to equal his own, and in a moment would have taken them in his arms. But they glanced sadly at each other, as though to say 'That hope is gone.'

'Never before has Mailafia refused our request!'

'Seldom have you made one,' he pointed out. 'And none so foolish as this one. Ask what is reasonable, and it shall be yours.'

He was conscious now of an expectancy in the twins. There was something in their minds as of a daring hope. Yet their faces showed no sign, and their voices were subdued as they said:

'Mailafia has given us much money to buy what we desire. But never a present of his own choosing, nor a thing which is his which we may cherish because it is his.'

It was true enough. But what had he got which they could want, or find of use? Firearms, binoculars, compass and a pair of much-patched shoes were probably his favourite possessions. Apart from these he owned nothing of value. And beside, whatever they wanted would have to be a pair, so that they could have one each.

His cuff-links? No, they were gold, and the Prophet had prohibited the wearing of gold by the Faithful. This was absurdly like a child's guessing game, and as in a game the twins offered him a clue.

'It is something of value only to Mailafia. But bracelets may be made from it, one for each of us. These we would value above all the gold and pearls of Balkisu, the wife of Suleiman the Great.'

'It is yours, whatever it is. But I cannot guess. You must lead the blind beggar to the mosque.'

A flicker of uncertainty verging on fear narrowed their eyes. But they were of dauntless Fulani stock. They said no word. They rose as one. They stepped to the table. They returned.

Clutched in four small, desperate hands was the copper wire, the Empress' deadly necklace.

Keith was on his feet too. Doubt, shock and fury must have shown in his face. But the twins stood their ground.

Only the wire could complete his vengeance. He was no common murderer. The wire was a symbol.

Hafsatu-Hatasu had put their courage, and their faith in Keith, to the ultimate test. They could do no more.

Timmy stretched, and gave a squeaky yawn. His sensitive whiskers had caught the first faint forerunner of the evening breeze.

Keith was incapable of thought. He had no will-power. He was a silent duelling ground between Hafsatu-Hatasu's love and his unbalanced hatred. It was no new struggle. For weeks it had confronted him. Always before he had only to handle the satanic rosary to reinforce his bitter purpose. But now it was in their hands.

Grave, gentle, slenderly beautiful, they stood before him, and unwittingly summoned an overwhelming ally to their cause. Keith's love. He could no longer bear to abandon them.

'It . . . is . . . yours.' Slowly he pronounced his defeat.

So far they dared only hope. They could not be sure. But his next words confirmed his decision.

'It is yours. But one thing I ask, that you throw it away where none will find it. Then let me give you silver for your bracelets.

213

Or anklets, so heavy that I will no longer fear that you will run away!'

They would have knelt to express their relief and gratitude, but he caught them in time. It was he who should kneel, not they.

'Mailafia, the afternoon is hot. Is it permitted that we remove our garments?'

'By no means yet.' He assumed the stern tone which always amused them. It was long since he had used it. 'Let The Thing first be thrown away.'

'And then?' They were trying to hide their smiles, as once they had tried to smile.

'Ask Momadu to tell Anta to eat and saddle and make ready to take a letter to Railhead.' The direct route to Bauchi was through Pankshin, but Anta might show the letter to Pettibone; and it would not reach its destination.

'And then?'

'First the letter must be sent, lest the sight of your beauty drive all other thoughts from my head.'

'And then?' They mocked him now, eyes crinkling at the corners, but lips demurely straight.

Keith assumed an air of innocence. 'How should I know? Perhaps in the cool of the evening we will sit and tell each other stories.'

Anta had left with the letter, and the village head had only a few words of Hausa. But the rumour was clear enough, and serious.

'Many soldiers' had gone with the Greater Judge into Kulere. 'Many' had been killed, including, it was thought, one *Ba-ture*. But which *Ba-ture* was not known. A *Ba-ture* was a *Ba-ture*, that was all.

Sitting in his pyjamas outside the rest-house to catch what breeze there was, Keith sought further details. How many soldiers? How many white men? Where in Kulere? Had the dead been left or carried back? That last question would give some clue to the seriousness of the repulse. Was the story true, or had a river been made of a horse's staling?

The news was third or fourth hand, and neither numbers, dates nor anything else could be established. If the basic story was true, then Pettibone had bungled badly, and might even be dead.

'Let a man make ready to take another writing, this time to Pankshin. I will give double pay if he runs by night as well as by day.' That was all Keith could decide offhand. The rumour might be no more than a belated and dramatized version of his own expedition, and the dead white man only Yeats being carried in his hammock.

He dismissed his informants and sipped his drink, and tried to persuade himself that all was well.

Yeats was a keen and able young soldier, Garrard as able and more experienced. Even if Pettibone had decided to take a dangerous gamble, to retrieve his reputation, the soldiers should have been able to utilize the greater range of their rifles to keep all but a few bowmen at a safe distance.

Momadu brought the hurricane lamp, and spread a table-cloth as sign that dinner would soon be served. Keith borrowed the lamp and retired to the rest-house. For lack of table he set the portable on a chop-box, and squatted on his heels in front of it.

If it had been as serious a reverse as the rumour made out, and Pettibone had been killed, Keith would be urgently needed in Pankshin. But he would look a damned fool if he went in by forced marches, and found nothing at all had happened.

In the dark bedroom behind him Hafsatu-Hatasu awaited him. He could hear their whispers. They didn't help clear thinking. He got as far as *The Divisional Officer, Pankshin.* before they glided into the lamplight.

Their tantalizing white veils, so seldom worn of late, gave a clue to their intentions. Bare silken skins, adorned only by silver bracelets, anklets and the scantiest of silken skirt-cloths confirmed their purpose—temptation.

'You have eaten?' He tried to be matter-of-fact.

'We could not eat, because of happiness that Mailafia is restored to us.'

They knelt beside him. The perfume of their young bodies

troubled him. Tentatively their fingers reached up to stroke the back of his neck, to explore the curve of his ears.

'I must send this writing to Pankshin at once.' He caught those distracting fingers in his, and tried to explain. 'Tomorrow we must follow it. But this night will be ours.'

'The night is here already. And we have waited so long, so long!' Soft voices entreated. 'Let not Mailafia be angry, but we fear lest Petbo again part us. And we are women, and have no strength save in our love.'

Never before had they come between him and his work. It showed how desperate was their anxiety, for which Keith and his neglect were responsible. To make matters more difficult, eager little hands had unfastened the buttons of his pyjama top and were tugging at it. It was impossible to go on typing.

Abruptly he rose, slipped out of the jacket, hesitated but ripped out a sleeve. It was fragile with sun and washing, so for added strength he folded it lengthwise. Abruptly he spun Hafsatu—or it might be Hatasu, pulled her arms behind her back and bound them. He did the same to her sister. Their eyes above their veils opened wider in surprise, but they made no protest.

Again Keith squatted to the typewriter. How did you say 'If the Kulere news is true, but you happen to be alive' in a more tactful way?

He was being caressed again. But with a difference. Four firm little breasts stroked his shoulders and bare back.

'It is Mailafia who has taught us. We had not thought of this before. Does it please him?'

'Too well!' he admitted.

'Too long have we sipped of love, but not truly supped.' He could hear the happy triumph in their voices. 'Tonight we will make Mailafia's need as great as our own. And ours is such that we cannot part from him, but will go, bound and unclothed, to stand beside his table and hasten his eating.'

'I will tell Momadu that I will not eat.' That would be no sacrifice. 'Permit only that I write this writing, and give it to the runner who is already ordered. Rest only a little while in the bedroom, and I will hasten to you.'

'We will stay with Mailafia, for we have no strength to leave him.' Veiled lips nuzzled his neck. 'Even though he be angry, we cannot help ourselves.'

There was an answer to that! He tore strips from his pyjama jacket, bound their knees, their ankles; carried them, veils fluttering, breasts rising and falling to their quickened breathing, to the bedroom. He laid them head to foot upon the camp-bed and stood over them, triumphant, panting with something more than the slight effort he had made. He lifted a veil, placed a hand firmly over a girl's mouth and with the other hand tickled her. She writhed and snorted, but her bonds held. He did the same to the other.

To show his complete mastery he removed their silken skirtcloths and bound their adjacent legs thigh to knee, thigh to knee. He kissed each on her bare stomach, to show that he was by no means angry.

'Wait for me!' he instructed. 'Do not run away!'

The message he gave Momadu for the runner was a hasty pencil scrawl. It read *Dear Pettibone, Can I help? Ian Keith.*

Chapter Twenty-one

APPARENTLY unwearied, Orion cantered past the empty Pankshin rest-house, and dropped to a trot up the hill. The guard turned out in Keith's honour, but their unsmiling faces confirmed bad news. A soldier posted outside Yeats' bungalow was chilly ominous. Of course Yeats might still be leading back the survivors, taking short stages because of the wounded in their hammocks.

The first day out from Lankan, Keith had kept his anxiety in abeyance. But next morning, feeling an idiot for doing so, he had left his household and carriers and hurried ahead. To do what?

Outside O.C. Troops' bungalow the grass was still green. Pankshin must have had a belated rain which had missed the plain. A call brought a servant round from the back to announce that his master was in, and to take Orion. An unsmiling servant, who offered no welcome.

Garrard made no movement to rise, no gesture towards his tea-table. He said challengingly ' What are you going to do about it? '

' First I'll take two cups of tea.' Keith laid pistol and hat on table, and poured for himself, using his host's empty cup, since Garrard didn't call Leviticus. ' What actually happened? '

' Haven't you heard? ' The broad, red face was paler than usual. It was certainly less friendly. ' He got young Yeats scuppered. Ran away and left him. What are you bastards going to do about it? '

Keith threw teacup and tea out through the doorway. ' I'll take pleasure in teaching you your manners. That first. Then . . . did you say ' bastards ', plural? Is Pettibone still alive? '

' Of course! In fact I have his written orders to place the whole battery, including its new trench-mortars, under what he calls his " direct command " for what he calls " a punitive expedition ".

I'll see him fry in hell first! No commissioned officer left but me, and I'm no damned use with this . . .' Garrard swung his chair to expose a plaster cast from the knee down.

'Looks as though I'll have to postpone punching your uncivil head. What happened to you? Fall off your horse?'

One of those absurd complications which no one could have foreseen. Shortly after Keith had left, Garrard had been exercising his nag in the usual way along the Panyam road, and it had come down and rolled him. Only a broken ankle, but since there was no doctor at Pankshin, Garrard had ridden on, and somehow got as far as Mongu Mine in the next division, where he had received attention. Within three weeks, leg still in a cast, of course, Garrard had hurried back to Pankshin.

His concern for his battery, left with only young Yeats in charge, was justified. Sergeant Fletcher was now in charge. Pettibone had ordered out Yeats and a hundred men. It was too late for Garrard to do anything.

'What went wrong?'

Garrard stumped across to a cupboard and pulled out some papers.

'You'll need a drink before you're through. Leviticus!'

The statements of Sergeant-Major Dan Beki Kano and some half-dozen other ranks gave a clear picture. Trouble started soon after dawn on the second day, when the Kulere came closer, hitting a carrier, who died. Pettibone gave the order to fire. After the first burst the enemy had taken cover, and Yeats ordered 'cease fire'. Pettibone spoke angrily to Yeats. It was not known what was said. In the opinion of the sergeant-major the cease fire was necessary to save ammunition.

At the sergeant-major's suggestion Yeats asked Pettibone for a halt to enable the carriers to close up. Some were driving goats which Pettibone had brought along for food. Yeats wanted to take out a few snipers, to persuade the enemy to keep at a more respectful distance. Keith could almost hear Yeats saying 'Y'know, Mr Pettibone, these johnnies are being very naughty. I think I ought to go out and slap their hands.'

Pettibone had refused to allow the halt. Confident in the white

219

man's prestige and the superiority of his weapons, he insisted on pressing forward.

They came to a pass. Keith remembered the place as he read. Yeats asked for another halt, to give him time to reconnoitre it, as Keith had done before. It was an elementary precaution against ambush, but again Pettibone had refused to halt. That gave Yeats no time to crown the heights overlooking the track. He had to hurry forward with his advance guard into the pass itself. Moman the fearless had gone with him into the trap.

The sergeant-major, whom Pettibone kept at his side, heard the shots echoing among the rocks. Everyone had heard them, including Pettibone. He ordered an about turn. He told the sergeant-major 'We must protect our carriers.'

At this point the sergeant-major admitted that he had disobeyed orders. With twenty soldiers and some Angas carriers who dropped their loads and put arrows to bows, he ran forward. The firing had dwindled and ceased. There were no survivors. The Kulere had finished off the wounded with their knives. Mercifully, considering the arrow-poison.

The bodies were recovered without opposition. Satisfied, and no doubt with a few casualties of their own to make them cautious, the Kulere bowmen hung on the flanks of the party, out of range.

Next day by a forced march the column pulled safely out of the Closed Area. Pettibone was very angry because the goats he had brought for food were all lost, and his loads had been dumped so that the dead men might be carried.

'Have another drink!' Garrard poured one.

'This is a carbon.' Keith tapped the papers. 'The original went off to your commandant?'

'As soon as we had the men in the ground. They wouldn't keep.'

So the commandant might have his copy already. But Pettibone was a civilian, which made the chain of command commandant to governor, and back down through lieutenant governor to Resident Bauchi. Since comments prejudicial to Pettibone would be marked Confidential, they would be further delayed. Keith's informal Criminal Information should reach the Resident almost as soon. Add another week for Sharpe to send a senior officer to take over the division pending full enquiries.

Meantime Pettibone would do nothing about Kulere unless Garrard would let him take the whole battery, and that Garrard had refused.

'Can you have Orion looked after? My loads won't be along until tomorrow or the next day.'

'You'll stay with me, of course. I'll have Yeats' camp-bed moved in here. I haven't packed his things yet.

'I'm feeling rather leprous from association with my superior officer. Not sure I'm suitable company for a pure-minded soldier.'

'I'd take it as a favour if you'd stay. Don't move into the rest-house at all. It hasn't been much fun going through Yeats' private papers and writing to his people. Did you know he was engaged, and hoping to get married next leave?'

'Her name's Helga, and I've heard a lot about her.' Keith downed his whisky, helped himself to two more glasses of plain water and downed them too. He collected a handful of Garrard's biscuits and stuffed them into his breeches' pockets, slid the heavy Luger back into its shoulder holster. 'The office will be closed. It's a nice peaceful place to think in.'

The same red-robe watchman opened for him, just as on the night, so long ago, when Keith had accidentally stumbled on Pettibone's virgin parade. Here was a pistol under his armpit. Only a few hundred yards away was an unsuspecting Pettibone. But it was as though Pettibone had ceased to be a human enemy, and had become an impersonal evil force.

The first job was to hunt up what Pettibone had written about his shameful expedition. The inquest came to light first. Keith carried it to the divisional officer's table, dropped wax on its polished surface to hold the candle, and read with cold care.

The account seemed as impartial, except for a few omissions, as if Keith had conducted the enquiry. He hadn't expected that, but should have done. Pettibone was smart enough to avoid explanations which might imply that he had any need to defend himself.

There must, somewhere, be a carbon copy of the report on the Use of Armed Force. A long search found the original in Pettibone's handwriting in Mr McTavish's closed typewriter. So it had not been sent off.

One of the candles was finished, and Keith could find no more. By the light of the remaining half-candle he read fast.

There was none of Pettibone's usual symbolism and imagery. He seemed to attempt a terse military style. Its restraint was persuasive. It suggested that Pettibone could have said more, but generously chose to be charitable to the dead.

A few sentences justified the attack:

In view of the adverse impression created in Kulere by Capt. Keith's abortive raid, from which he and Lieut. Yeats so barely escaped, I considered it advisable to take an armed force of a hundred rifles and enough carriers and provisions to allow protracted occupation of the villages from which they had been expelled.

Pettibone admitted that he had been unhappy about the way things looked as soon as Kulere was entered.

I therefore retained the sergeant-major and the main body of troops under my direct orders, ready for an immediate counterstroke should one be called for. Later he congratulated himself on his foresight which allowed him *to withdraw without further casualties after Lieutenant Yeats had so needlessly sacrificed himself and his men in an ambush which a more experienced officer might well have anticipated.*

The last half-inch of candle-wick fell over, and the flame died. Keith laid his head on the table.

Moman Wanti, the Hausa Messenger, bowed low in the darkness, and waited courteously to be heard.

'It was no fault of the Long Soldier. He was the first to die. Mailafia knows how these things are. It is the way of these Infidels of the Hills to sting when one walks into their nests. The fault lay further back with one who . . . one who . . .' The little man's stammer halted him.

'This is known to me, Moman. It is known to the Soldier of the Red Face. It shall be made known to others, so that no shame shall fall upon the Long Soldier.' Keith reassured him. 'Due honour shall also be given to a certain Messenger who walked always without fear. A present shall be given to the two wives he has left, and, if Allah grant me days, I will see to their welfare.'

A tall man gave a smashing salute, and said 'Welcome back, sir! If you're not busy . . . I mean if you are I'll clear out and not bother you.'

Ghosts or not, these friendly visitors were welcome.

'Wonder if you could do anything about the old skipper, sir? He's brooding, as though he'd broken his leg on purpose so I should get scuppered instead of him. Of all the tommy-rot! As a matter of fact if he'd been there, or you had, the silly business needn't have happened at all.'

That was true enough. But one could be tactful, even with apparitions. 'Oh, I don't know. We might have got the whole mob wiped out instead of the advance guard. Never can tell about these things.'

'D'you really think so? I mean really? I wonder if you could tell my people so? We're an army family since before the Mutiny, and it would mean a lot to them to know that I hadn't just thrown away my men. And there's Helga . . . I mean we had grown up together, and it was sort of understood that next leave . . .'

'I'll write to her. And try to see your people when I go on leave. I'll tell them about some of the 'picnics' we've been on together.'

'Would you? I'll be eternally grateful!' Yeats plunged forward and held out his hand.

Keith missed its grasp. Yeats' hand passed through, and seemed to scoop something up from Keith's knees.

'What are you doing here, Empress? Keith told me to look after you. Don't you remember? I've been looking everywhere for you. You're one of us, y'know.'

The sun had barely risen when Pettibone set off for the office, shaven, in creaseless linen suit and carefully adjusted club tie; outwardly impressive, but inwardly ill at ease.

His assured position had recently been shaken. He had taken great pains with the Kulere expedition, which should have overshadowed Keith's previous performance and established Pettibone in official eyes as the first to make a constructive attempt to subdue the Closed Area.

But Yeats had proved himself unworthy of his trust. A soldier should know if there is an ambush. If not his superiors should teach him. Unfortunately Yeats was dead, so sympathy would incline his way. Of course Garrard had felt the loss of his officer —he was already short-staffed—but that didn't justify his positive rudeness.

Garrard had sent off his own report. Since he had no personal knowledge of what had happened he had listened to the biased accounts of his soldiers. And they, naturally, had blamed the civilian officer for their officer's mistake. That made it urgent that Pettibone's own report should furnish the governor of Nigeria and others with the truth, before the military report could give them a wrong impression. Unfortunately it had to be typed in sextuplicate, and the clerk's wilful illness was still holding it up.

The divisional officer stooped to smell the blossom on an orange bush. He almost regretted that he had not answered Keith's offer of help by calling him in. He could have been set to type the report. If he refused, it would be an additional reason for getting him kicked out.

Yes, one quite profitable move had been overlooked. A pity.

Messengers hurried down from the office veranda, and Gofwan so far forgot himself as to stand in the way, saying excitedly 'Mister Petbo . . . with permission, Mister Petbo . . . it should be told . . . I could not polish your table because . . . because . . .'

The wide steps underfoot brought back a feeling of assurance. Here in the office one could enforce an absolute rule, with no risk of disobedience, no Kulere villagers to set themselves in opposition, no stupid soldiers to misinterpret. . . .

At Pettibone's own office table sat, or rather sprawled, Captain Keith.

His face was buried in his arms, his arms spread over some papers. He did not look up. He heard nothing. The pistol lying beside his head seemed to account for that.

A heaven-sent solution of all difficulties, or a more dangerous crisis than any which had gone before? Any farewell note he had left must be found and destroyed.

But there was no reek of burned cordite, though the office had only just been opened. No blood, no spattering of brains.

The man lifted his head. He was red-eyed, coated with dust and runnels of sweat. But apparently alive and unharmed.

'You have returned to Pankshin without my orders!'

No result. Something sharper was required to re-establish discipline.

'Get out of my chair! Go and shave and change. And by all means bath yourself, you stink.'

Keith sat back, yawned, and gathered up a handful of papers. 'Not so badly as your report on Yeats. It's putrid.'

'I shall have to add to the long list of adverse comments I have submitted on your conduct.' It was a pity the clash could not have been postponed until the report had been typed and sent off. But one had one's dignity to maintain.

'Talking of adverse comments, here's one.' Keith held the draft at arms length in his left hand, and lifted his pistol.

The man was mad, as Anta had reported to Gofwan! Pettibone jumped aside.

A roar, and the heavy bullet tore through the pages and knocked a piece out of the mud wall behind.

Messengers jammed in the doorway, but hesitated.

'Arrest Mister Keeta! Call red-robes with handcuffs, and hold him . . . hold him till they come!' Pettibone shouted orders 'Go to the soldier *Ba-ture* and ask for armed soldiers . . . armed soldiers at once . . . Run!'

The Messengers obeyed. They ran. Not towards Keith, but on the safer alternative missions.

Keith snapped the Luger into its holster and stood up.

'You have an unhappy knack of overlooking details, Pettibone. How are you going to explain why I missed you, if I intended to kill you? Anyone knows I can kill a guinea-fowl at thirty paces. Or why don't I kill you now, in this empty office? I'm going to breakfast with Garrard. You can find me there if you want me. Don't forget to bring a warrant.'

After Keith's household and carriers arrived, there followed a delightful week of idleness and apparent serenity. He made no attempt to attend office. He wrote the promised letters to Yeats' parents and girl, and sent them up to Garrard to be addressed. Nothing could be done until the commandant or the Resident Bauchi took action, and it was safer to dismiss Pettibone entirely from his mind.

Fletcher dropped in twice, the second time to ask help with some battery accounts. In return he insisted on mending the hinges on one of Keith's uniform cases. A fatigue party brought down a couple of extra tables and some chairs as a loan from the battery.

With time on his hands, Keith made a point of exercising Orion each morning, in the afternoon overhauled his notes on languages and tribal customs, and in the evening shot for the pot.

The twins received a letter from their father, a reply to some earlier letter they had sent. Their mother was in good health, and would, their father thought, soon forgive them for running away. She prized their gift. It was good to hear they had done well in their trading.

Their mother asked who was this Mallam Mailafia, the learned scribe of whom they wrote? Let their father warn them that a *mallam*, a scribe, did not grow rich as a trader could. Let them send word of market prices and roads. Two donkeys had been born, and two more bought. Thus it was.

Furnished with a reed pen, and hand-made paper as difficult to write on as blotting paper, Keith was set down and asked to reply, as a letter writer would.

. . . and after Greetings, know these are the prices. [The twins dictated a whole page of them from memory.] They

226

are high by reason of the lack of roads and bridges, and because of the many traders who are drowned or killed. [Apparently Hafsatu-Hatasu thought that a father in Bauchi was more convenient than one in Pankshin.] Say this to our mother, that Mallam Mailafia is thin as are all whose food is paper and whose drink is ink. Nor is he young, or likely to take a wife. Since we may not marry, we find comfort in his wisdom, and often in the cool of the evening we have gone to him, and he has been willing to talk with us, though we are women. For this, as is fitting, we have offered him some slight services, such as a woman may.

The letter was sent off, over Keith's mild protests. And with it went three prime leopard skins.

'Some slight services' became a saying between the three of them.

Keith, as an apparently carefree family man, received the tacit approval of the whole household. Momadu Dangana no longer stomped heavily around, seemingly on his ankle-bones, but pranced again. Garuba Kano gambled away the money he had saved out on tour, and with it most of his clothes; but flaunted, like a now tail-less peacock, before two quite desirable women, both new. Momadu's pretty little scold stopped scolding. It was only later discovered that she was carrying on an intrigue with a much-married corporal in the battery. Nyenyam celebrated his light-heartedness in characteristic fashion. He tried to kill his friend Sam with a carving knife.

With the males of the household as arbitrators, Keith heard the case. Nyenyam, whose large mouth and small stomach seemed equally insatiable, had been caught stealing meat from the cook-house. Sam had picked up a piece of kindling, and clouted him on his thick skull. Nyenyam had seized the carving knife—which shouldn't have been in the cook-house anyhow—and tried for the tribal stroke between neck and collar bone. He was too short, or Sam too tall, and he had only inflicted a flesh-wound and torn Sam's shirt.

Sam interceded for the young hellion, but Momadu and Garuba

took a stern view. Twenty strokes on his bare bottom with a finger-thick bamboo.

As a brave and courteous man should, Nyenyam returned after punishment to give thanks for correction, and to express repentance. His own kind of repentance.

'The fault was mine, *Ba-ture*. I did wrong to borrow your knife. But they had hidden my spear.'

The strange peace, like the ominous stillness before a storm, seemed likely to last indefinitely. It ended abruptly.

Politely incurious about the plump middle-aged Hausa woman who served as house-boy, Keith and Garrard were taking drinks with Fletcher. Her ample body swathed in iridiscent gold-green, her dark face lightened by a gleaming silver nose-stud the size of a shilling, she beamed encouragingly on the two guests as she poured drinks and passed canapes.

'So rumble rumble rumble zur.' Fletcher always seemed to imitate Constable imitating Fletcher.

The woman went out, and returned with a folded note, which she handed to Keith.

'Make anything of this?' Keith passed the note on to Garrard. 'This can't mean an enquiry, or *I* wouldn't be put in charge.'

Chapter Twenty-two

'Just the headquarters routine. Not even the cash.' Pettibone seemed amused. 'Surely you didn't expect to take over the whole division. What a disappointment this must be to you, poor fellow!'

'Going on tour?' That seemed obvious.

'Dallong have had the effrontery to drive out two of my Messengers whom I sent to collect tax. An insult to my Messengers is an insult to me. I shall take fifty rifles, and intend to teach the tribe a sharp lesson.'

'But Messengers aren't allowed to collect tax, surely?'

'As I have mentioned, they collected none. Officially I shall represent that a spark from the Kulere conflagration happened to light on Dallong and it became urgently necessary to stamp out the new fire before it had time to spread throughout the division. In such a case of emergency Garrard could scarcely refuse my request for troops. It would be most unwise of him. Most unwise.' Pettibone stroked his long locks and exuded satisfaction.

'Why not send me out to have a look-see first?' Keith offered a more practical alternative. 'You know what Messengers are. They may have demanded gifts as well as tax money. We ought to hear both sides before taking any action. Anyway I won't need an escort. Pupchina the chief is rather a pal of mine.'

Majestic in his indignation, Pettibone rose and paced the floor. He came to a halt in front of Keith's table.

'Captain Keith! I am fully aware of your disgracefully biased attitude against my Messengers, but this is going too far! Also I am well aware of your favouritism towards some of the least satisfactory of my chiefs. If Pupchina has the hardihood to oppose me, and it becomes necessary to kill him, it will add to my pleasure to remember that he is a friend of yours.'

By way of counting ten, Keith drafted a brief reply to an enquiry.

Yrs of . . . We regret that there is no such information at present available in this area. Slowly he pinned the buff slip to the jacket. His voice was quite calm as he said:

'Sharpe would chew your balls off if he caught you doing a dirty trick like that. And I would have much pleasure in telling him.'

'Your friend Sharpe has been invalided home. For good, I hope!' Pettibone's triumph erased his recent indignation. 'Anstruther will be unlikely to accept your unsupported testimony. I have already drawn him a clear picture of you.'

Sharpe gone, and Anstruther of all people in charge of the province. Christ Almighty! Anstruther, an ambitious product of the secretariat, being given a province to play with so as to qualify by practical experience for his future steps to lieutenant governor and governor. He had never met a more primitive native than a golf-caddy.

Worse still. The showdown for which Keith had been patiently waiting would be delayed indefinitely. His letter, covering the 'criminal information', had been addressed to Sharpe personally, so would be redirected after him to his English address.

'Dallong isn't going to be an easy nut to crack, Pettibone.' Keith tried again. 'There are only two practicable passes, and both, to my knowledge, can be easily defended.'

'Naturally I have taken all factors into account.'

Keith put out a feeler. 'I wonder what Garrard will think of the scheme?'

'As a matter of fact he approves, highly.' Pettibone waved off Anta who entered to announce some litigants. 'I went to see the fellow after dinner last night. At first he appeared doubtful. But when I told him of the two-pronged attack I planned he slapped his good leg and said "Masterly! Really masterly", and admitted frankly that none but I could have thought of it.'

If Pettibone couldn't see that Garrard had been laughing at him, there was nothing Keith could do.

Over breakfast, Garrard was as elated as Pettibone.

'Pettibone's playing into our hands. His 'second column' as he calls it, won't reach the southern pass in time. The sergeant-major is so sure of this that I suspect he'll tip them the wink not to. And he has my definite orders to stick close to Pettibone, and to retire at the first signs of opposition on the northern pass.'

' You're underestimating Pettibone as much as he overestimates himself. This time he'll refuse to retire, and Dan Beki Kano will feel he has to stay with him and be scuppered.'

' I don't think so. Since the Kulere mess he hates your senior's guts.'

' So do you. But, damn you, Garrard, you can't do this to your men! '

' I can't refuse Pettibone's request, when he cites ' supreme necessity'. Though I've sent off a telegram to Railhead, asking my commandant to confirm or over-rule. That will take at least a week. Meantime, I'd go myself, only I couldn't march or climb. I won't send Fletcher, who's too simple and honest for dirty work like this, and would only get himself knocked off. Our only hope is your Resident turning up in time.'

' Sharpe's left the country, as Pettibone's just told me. The chances are my letter is now in the hold of an Elder Demster steamer following him to England.'

The idea of sending the new Resident a copy of the charges had to be abandoned. Anstruther was a Pettibone type, who would administer from an office chair. He would either dismiss the charges as absurd, and remove Keith from Pankshin, or he would call Keith to Bauchi to substantiate them. Without corroboration —and witnesses would be nearly impossible to obtain so long as Pettibone had charge of Pankshin—Keith's word would not stand against his superior officer's denials and countercharges.

The urgent short-range plan could be stated simply. The Dallong raid, aimed at cold-blooded butchery of harmless Hill-men, but more likely to result in the pointless death of several soldiers, must be prevented.

But how?

Morning ran into afternoon, papers stuck to sweating hands, carbons smudged, ink spread as though on blotting paper. Messengers fidgeted and coughed. Keith looked at his watch, and dismissed them for the day.

Pettibone had made the disastrous attempt on Kulere because Keith had made a successful one. Each step which Keith had taken to develop the native administration and the native Courts had been quashed because Keith had made them. Strangling the Empress had been strangling Keith. The plan to kill Pupchina and his people was a plan to kill Keith. One need only point this out to Pettibone, and suggest the simpler solution.

Keith addressed a final envelope, and called the watchman.

'The office may be locked up.' He added the expected joke 'Sleep well', and the red-robe grinned.

Pettibone's chair and drink table were in lonely state beside the unused tennis court. He looked surprised when Keith squatted down on his heels and spoke.

'I've got an idea. You may be able to improve on it, but basically it's sound.' Keith pulled out his bag of native tobacco.

'I will listen to you in the office.'

'Here's the idea. We've reached the point where either of us would gladly see the other die.'

Pettibone got the point, but got it wrong. Keith had hauled out his pocket-knife to clear the clogged bowl of his pipe. Pettibone's eyes were on the blade. He placed hands on the arms of his chair as though to get up.

'I don't mean here and now. The thing needs proper staging. First we need a public reconciliation. Then we go shooting together. It's too late tonight, but tomorrow evening would suit me. Then we have a shooting accident.'

Good. Pettibone, though restless, was listening closely.

'In other words we send our horse-boys back so they shan't disturb the game, and settle down to stalk each other. If you bag me, you hold the inquest, so it ought to be simple. I promise to leave no incriminating papers behind. But there again you'll be in luck, as you'll have to be local administrator of my estate.'

'A pleasing picture. But I take it you're hoping to shoot me? And then of course you automatically become coroner.'

Keith got his pipe going. He could do with a drink, but in the circumstances to help himself would be a little ill-mannered.

'Perfect, don't you think? Much better than an earlier idea I had of just murdering you. This way you get a sporting chance.'

'Unfortunately for you, I have a still better plan.'

That sounded as though Pettibone agreed in principle. Good!

'As it happens, I don't want to kill you. I'm waiting for a reply from Anstruther. I'll put you under arrest and have you kicked out of the Service. You'll join your friend Sharpe in England. But he'll have a pension, and you won't.' Pettibone had thought long and lovingly of his revenge. 'Ex-officers like you are still looking for jobs, and starving. You never took your Bar finals, and native customs, treasury regulations, native languages won't get you taken on as a plumber's mate or rat catcher.'

Keith had lost his bet. But having goaded Pettibone into giving away his own plans it would pay to listen a little longer. And Pettibone hadn't finished yet.

'Your only hope would be to take your two bitches with you, and set them up as street-walkers to support you. But you won't be allowed even that. The moment you are safely under arrest, I intend to prefer a charge of some sort against them, and take them into custody. If they're sensible I may take them into my house and keep them till I tire of them. I'd like to give you something to remember me by.'

Keith knocked out his pipe and stood up.

'What does it feel like, Pettibone, to sign your own death warrant?'

From the crest of Dallong Hill Keith searched the plain below through his binoculars. As he had searched and hoped all yesterday. Seldom had he pestered the fates with his private hopes and prayers. He didn't ask much of them now. Just an instant when the foresight of his rifle came to rest in the notch of the backsight and lined up on a sun-helmet.

Pettibone knew what to expect, but his insane egotism would lead him on. The real danger was Garrard. He might have countermanded the escort.

Like Garrard's broken ankle, it was one of those unforeseeable incidents which could ruin even the simplest plan. And Keith's purpose had been delightfully uncomplicated.

233

Orion was being saddled. Momadu had fussed over Keith going without stores or carriers or servants, but had been pacified. The twins alone had to be dealt with.

Between rumour, and guesswork based on their knowledge of Mailafia, they knew that at last Mailafia would kill Petbo, though Petbo would take fifty soldiers to kill Mailafia. They showed no sign of alarm. They seemed to think that odds of fifty-one against one, where that one was their Mailafia, were fair and reasonable.

When a man is prepared to allay anxiety and soothe sorrow, it is exasperating to find that neither needs his care.

'But if it be the will of Allah that my days are ended?' he asked bluntly.

They hugged him. 'Return to us soon! Do not cast eyes on the women of Dallong with their shaven heads and dangling breasts!'

'If Petbo returns, let Momadu lead you straight to the soldier *Ba-ture*. He will be your friend.'

'There is a new bed-play we have thought of, to welcome Mailafia on his return. It will give more pleasure in the big house on the hill, where doors may be closed, and the light of the lamp shine upon us.' They wriggled in anticipation of the promised thrill. 'Let Mailafia think of this, and hasten to us!'

It was then that there came the sound of hooves, cantering recklessly down the hill in the dark. And Garrard's voice . . .

'Keith! Keith! I've got to see you. At once!'

It was a breathless night, so Keith carried out the table lamp. Garrard preferred not to dismount. Also he wanted Keith to mount at once and ride with him back up the hill. It took time to get a coherent story out of him.

Rifle in hand Sergeant-Major Dan Beki Kano had come to Garrard, excitedly demanding ammunition with which to shoot a leopard prowling around the lines. Annoyed at being disturbed so late, Garrard asked why the hell he hadn't borrowed a few rounds from the quarter-guard?

Dan Beki became confused. Suspecting there was something more behind the story, Garrard kept him there, and played on his sense of urgency to get the real story. Then, taking his crutch, he hobbled along with his sergeant-major to Pettibone's bungalow.

234

They burst in the door with the rifle-butt, and found the little girl drunk and naked on Pettibone's knees. The father's relief at finding he had arrived in time was swallowed by his wrath as a Mohammedan that his daughter had been debauched with liquor. With remarkable presence of mind, Garrard had ordered the sergeant-major to place the girl on confinement to barracks, as though she were a defaulter, and have her brought up to orderly room in the morning.

The soldier reacted to years of army discipline. He slapped his rifle in salute, turned sharply about, and went. With the weeping, stumbling girl clutching her clothes to her bare breasts.

Left alone with Garrard, Pettibone jeered 'You can't put up much of a fight on one leg. Will you get out, or must I throw you out?'

Garrard had lifted his crutch, then thought better of it. He spoke his mind, at length. Then left.

That was the story. And what, Garrard had demanded, was Keith going to do about it? Issue a warrant for Pettibone? Garrard would be glad to supplement the unarmed red-robes with armed soldiers.

'If you don't muck it up, I've got a better plan.' Keith spoke casually. 'I'm just starting for Dallong.'

Garrard's eyes, hot and red in the lamplight, opened wider. 'I thought I hated the bastard as much as a man could hate. But you!'

Keith laughed. 'I don't hate him at all. I'm long past that. I've got a job of work to do, that's all. But it occurs to me that Pettibone may decide to take hostages for my good behaviour. Would you see that no harm comes to my household while I'm away?'

Last seen, Hafsatu-Hatasu were riding decorously up the hill, one on each side of Garrard. An armed guard was to be put on the rest-house until morning, when everyone and everything would be transferred to Yeats' empty quarters. Garrard could be relied upon. It was a great relief.

But Keith had overlooked an important detail. As the plain below the Dallong hills continued to show no sign of life, his nagging doubts were on the point of becoming certainties. Garrard might have cancelled the escort, on the grounds that the sergeant-major was in no fit state of mind to command the bodyguard of the man who had tried to seduce or rape his daughter. Would Garrard send Fletcher instead, or stop the whole show?

Keith sought cover under one of the boulders ranged along the lip of the pass. Chocked against rolling by only a few small stones, the primitive weapon looked insecure, but gave welcome shade.

And now Pettibone's column was in sight. Nearer in than Keith had expected them to be, which was why he had looked too far out and missed them. Five mounted men, including Petti-bone, three Messengers in flowing robes, and a man in khaki drill and a fez riding at the head of his soldiers. The fez showed he could not be Fletcher. The line of carriers and soldiers was too long to count, but showed that Pettibone hadn't yet divided his forces. Not that it mattered.

Now the only uncertain factor was Pupchina and his people. They had welcomed Keith warmly. Then came a snag. No interpreter. But a boy rather like Nyenyam did the best he could, and sign-language helped more than a little.

The story of the Messengers being chased out at midnight without time to snatch up their clothes, was told with roars of laughter. As a mimic old Pupchina was alone worth the price of admission. The Messengers' offence was uncertain, but had something to do with women—Pupchina's unrestrained miming made that clear.

Keith's news, that Petbo was coming with soldiers to burn houses and punish the driving out of his Messengers, met with a most generous offer. Would Keith care to lead some of the Dallong men? It was assumed that he would not want to miss the fight. Who would?

When Keith made known his plans, his popularity sank to zero. It was hard to convince them that he wanted the villages cleared of all possessions, and women, children, old and sick. And that everyone should take refuge underground until the troops had gone.

There was no practical difficulty. There were dozens of boulder-choked valleys, like the pass itself, or the place where

Pupchina's uncle had laid the ambush on Keith's first visit. But the idea simply wouldn't sell. Humping bundles of unthreshed corn and household goods and old folk couldn't compare with the fun of flipping arrows at an easy target toiling up the pass, and then rolling rocks down on the survivors. A few Dallong men would be killed, perhaps, but that would mean more women, more farmland, and more boasting for the survivors.

Keith was in despair. If soldiers got killed because he had fore-warned the Dallong men, he would be a traitor. If Dallong people got killed it would also be his own fault, because Pettibone's raid was a symbolic attempt to punish Keith himself. He could not fight on both sides. He could not fight on either.

The small interpreter's few words of Hausa would not allow long persuasive argument. Keith grasped at Pupchina's method of making himself understood.

His miming wasn't up to the old chief's standard, but he did his best. He was a soldier, handicapped with rifle and hob-nailed marching sandals, tripping and stumbling over the surface rocks. He was an old woman far underground, pounding corn, stopping to tilt her head back to listen, making a vulgar gesture and going on pounding. He squatted again, and became a warrior, stretched out comfortably in his rocky refuge, lifting a bowl of beer to the footsteps overhead, and then grinning as he drank it himself.

Old Pupchina caught the idea, and added homely details Keith would never have thought of—most of them improper. Together they sold the evacuation plan as one huge primitive jest. The sort of thing that could be told and re-told for a generation. There weren't any aisles to roll the audience in, but they rolled and guffawed anyway, all over the threshing floor, women and men together.

Approval of Keith's scheme was practically unanimous. One old man, the leader of the opposition and most likely Pupchina's uncle who had been 'given shit' for his ambush, rose and made a speech. Undoubtedly about 'death rather than dishonour'. But the oration laid an obvious egg, and he stalked off the threshing-floor alone. A single aged warrior could do little harm.

Pettibone's column now halted at the foothill. As the carriers caught up Keith could see that brush was being cleared, and a camp started. Horses were led off and picketed. Loads were laid out in line. Bow in hand, Angas carriers wandered off to a near-by stream. So the carriers were to be left behind? Pettibone had learned one lesson in Kulere.

Now Pettibone was searching the pass through his binoculars. To anyone else it would have seemed suspiciously empty of life. Yet he appeared satisfied, and gave a hand-signal to advance.

But Dan Beki, or whoever it was in command of troops, knew his business, and was taking no uncalled for risks. He threw out a scouting point and a small advance guard and flank guards. He held up the general advance until they could get into position. Pettibone, rifle in hand, seemed to be protesting.

The flank guards, who had to leave the so-called path, sling rifles and climb with hands as well as feet, had trouble in getting into position, but did so at last, rifles pointing up-hill.

Technically sound in ordinary two-dimensional operations. But this was Dallong.

A whistle blew, and the column started to climb.

Keith packed up his binoculars, and slithered down, lizard fashion, among the rocks.

Chapter Twenty-three

WITHIN the next hour Keith would be destroyed.

Pettibone had no further doubts. Garrard, in one of his mock lectures on what he called 'Strategy, or the Noble Art of Mass Homicide', had averred that any fool could plan a battle, but the essence of generalship was to take the enemy's plan and turn it against him. And Pettibone had done just that with Keith's.

When the sergeant-major had demurred to the original plan of a two-pronged enveloping movement, Pettibone had welcomed the change, which would allow him to keep an eye on the man, who seemed a little glum—perhaps repentant of the scene he had made over his daughter. When he got her back to barracks he must have discovered that she had come to no harm, and that it was all her own fault. No one had asked her to come to the white man's bungalow for sweets, or known who she was.

To fill in time while the column halted again, Pettibone took out his binoculars, leaned his rifle against his stomach, and searched the rugged terrain above him. Keith was up there, of course, alone, or with a handful of his Dallong friends.

He beckoned Gofwan and Anta—it would be just as well to have witnesses—and called 'Sergeant-Major!'

The veteran soldier sloped arms and slapped the small of his rifle in salute. Whatever his personal feelings might be, he could be counted on to carry out orders almost instinctively. Now was the time to pull the first joker.

'Against my wishes the Lesser Judge has gone ahead of us, seeking to make peace with the men of Dallong. That was folly, for by now they will have killed him. It will be our duty to kill his killers.'

Impossible to guess the thoughts behind that blue-black impassive face. But Keith had always been absurdly popular with the

239

soldiers, so Dan Beki was certain to welcome the suggested vengeance. Which added a charming irony to the scheme.

'When the Dallong men drove out these two Messengers whom I sent to collect tax, they took from them their robes and turbans. I did not understand why this was done, but now I see. The chief of Dallong knew that we would come to punish him, and that when we did two of his followers could use the robes and turbans as disguise to come inside the range of our rifles.'

'And a bow at close range is as good as a rifle. Better.' The sergeant-major took the point.

'That is true.' Pettibone nodded to his Messengers to note this expert opinion. 'And a still better disguise would be the clothing of the Lesser Judge. As you know, Mister Keeta wears little, and his skin has become almost as dark as that of a man of Dallong. So, if someone should come leaping down the pass, carrying a rifle, and his head in a white man's helmet, who would suspect him until his eyes were close enough to be seen?'

That touch of detail about the colour of Keith's eyes was effective. Dan Beki's own eyes, so pigmented against the African sun that no white showed, were now fixed intently on the speaker.

Now for the final cautioning, which might be of supreme importance at the inquest, throwing responsibility for the coming 'mistake' upon Keith and the soldiers, and exonerating Pettibone.

'But warn your men that if such a one come openly, it may indeed be the Lesser Judge, fleeing from his enemies.' There was little likelihood of Keith exposing himself so suicidally to Pettibone's rifle. However, the sergeant-major would not realize that. 'But if a white man's helmet is seen hiding among the rocks, you will know that it is not Mister Keeta but his killer. Then all must fire together.' It was difficult to keep the eagerness out of his voice. 'Give this order to your men, so that they may be ready.'

The plan was perfect now, complete in every detail. Why did the fool hesitate? Why didn't he go and repeat the orders to his men?

'If the *Ba-ture* permits . . .' Dan Beki paused.

'Let me have your counsel.' Supposing at this critical moment

240

the man refused to obey, just because of a silly girl? This perfect opportunity might never come again.

'It is this.' Dan Beki still sounded doubtful. 'All soldiers take pleasure in shooting, but not all can hit the mark. If a man of the advance or flank guards sees the hat that was Mister Keeta's, fires at a distance and misses, then our quarry will be warned, and run, and be lost to us. Therefore let me give the Greater Judge's words to my men, even as he has given them to me, but adding "Let none fire till the voice of my own rifle gives the order!"'

Wonderful! Dan Beki had stepped right into the trap, and suspected nothing.

'Do so! Your wisdom is greater than mine. Give your order, then return to my side.'

Excellent as the plan was, an improvement could still be added, without any change of orders. Why deny oneself the supreme satisfaction of killing one's enemy with one's own hands? The sergeant-major would be near by, and few would know or care whose shot had given the signal. A score of rifles would bark in eager chorus, all using the same ·303 ammunition that Pettibone did.

No medical officer, in the improbable event of one being sent to exhume the riddled body and hold an autopsy, would be able to certify whose trigger-finger had first sent death whining up the sun-drenched Dallong hillside.

Dan Beki's whistle ordered a further advance. One step nearer.

It was cool and dim, with no direct sunlight filtering down. Below was blackness, and the faint sound of trickling water. Keith's eyes began to adapt from the glare outside. He wriggled, crawled, and on occasion had to risk a crouching leap across a chasm, between untold tons of rock above, and unknown depths below.

Three times Keith had to surface before he could find the exact spot he had chosen yesterday. A little off the track, masked completely by boulders on each side, it gave about a six-inch loophole facing downhill.

The advance guard had passed over this area, proving it by all tactical presumption free of any lurking enemy. Just as this morning Keith's binoculars had been sighted too far out on the plain to pick up the column, so Pettibone would be scanning above Keith's head, where the troops had not searched.

He was doing it now. The whistle blew. Pettibone let his glasses hang from his neck by their strap and picked up his rifle. Now he was hidden.

At the next halt he was in view again, but Gofwan masked him.

A further wait. Then the carefully planned situation presented itself. As Keith had known it would.

The range was a bare eighty yards. Keith verified that a round was in the chamber and the safety catch off. He found a comfortable setting for his elbows, cuddled the butt, and briefly closed his eyes. As though he had one shot left for a perfect 'possible'.

He opened his eyes lazily. As lazily took a slight pressure on the trigger. Pettibone was looking this way, making it possible to drill a clean hole just above the centre between his eyes. A humane shot. Not that one wanted to be humane. Just make a perfect killing.

The only trouble was that the foresight of Pettibone's rifle was in the way. He was squatting, elbows on knees, and sighting in this direction. But far too high. Now even the muzzle of the barrel was in the way. To put a shot an inch to one side or the other of it would do the trick just as effectively. But a good executioner, like any other honest craftsmen, tends to be a perfectionist.

The muzzle of Pettibone's rifle kicked up, and a shot whined over Keith's head. He rolled over and looked behind him, idly curious to see what Pettibone had mistaken for him.

From the very top of the pass a Hillman leaped into the air. He must have been sheltering under one of the 'artillery' boulders, as Keith had done. With arms outstretched as though they were wings, the man sailed out; then plummeted down like a hawk in a closed-wing dive. No doubt the man was dead. A truly remarkable shot of Pettibone's, considering the range. Now it was his turn.

Back in the firing position, Keith delayed the final act in order to savour his exquisite satisfaction. Pettibone was drinking from a water-bottle. The sights followed the swaying of his head as he handed the bottle back to a Messenger . . . they steadied. . . .

A rifle which bruises the shoulder on a range has no noticeable recoil when it drops a long-sought quarry. Keith heard the report from afar. Several more shots followed it, then a ragged volley. He ejected the cartridge into his hand, and slid it into a pocket as a cherished souvenir.

Pettibone slumped, still standing, against a rock, hands pressed to his stomach. His head had fallen forward and the sun-helmet covered his face.

The firing ceased abruptly, and with good reason. No small-arms fire could halt those booming crashing boulders. The soldiers had taken cover between rocks. The storm ended as abruptly as it had started.

One moment Pettibone had been there. The next there were no more than sawdust legs, and a long smear over the rock against which he had been leaning.

Down over the valley floated hopeful vultures.

Chapter Twenty-four

O N the dusty clay surface of the Dallong threshing floor, shadeless and baking in the afternoon sun, but the only flat space for miles around, fifty soldiers and twice as many tribesmen squatted amicably together, listening while the *Ba-ture* questioned and wrote.

'Yes, this is the body of Lokr, we know him well. . . .' 'Lokr, it is, the brother of Pupchina's father. . . .' 'The body is much broken, but we know it.' Keith wrote with one hand, and with the other verified once more that the round of ammunition in his pocket had not been fired. He needed the assurance.

The body duly identified, the next step was to establish the cause of death. Sergeant-Major Dan Beki Kano, duly affirmed, since he was Mohammedan and could not be sworn, and head Messenger Gofwan, also affirmed since there was no Bible, both testified that the Greater Judge had fired the fatal shot. Other soldiers confirmed that no other shot had been fired then. The inevitable finding was duly announced in Hausa, and translated into Dallong speech. Permission was given for the shattered grey-blue corpse to be removed for burial.

As the squatting onlookers wriggled aside to make way for the bearers, two sun-helmets bobbed into view, and—astonishingly—Garrard hobbled up, accompanied by a stranger, presumably a new subaltern. Anta the Messenger hurried forward with wooden corn mortars, similar to the one Keith sat on. Keith nodded to the visitors, wondering how on earth Garrard had managed the climb. He would certainly need to be carried back down again.

Witnesses identified the contents of three leaf-covered corn-baskets over which flies hovered and buzzed. A bunch of safe and strong-room keys, recovered from the pocket of once cream-coloured riding breeches, was adduced as additional evidence, and laid at the coroner's feet. A gold signet ring, wrist-watch, broken rifle, some rounds of ·303 ammunition, binoculars, penknife and a few other personal possessions were added to the collection.

So far, so good. Now for the critical part. All depended on Gofwan and Dan Beki, the nearest to Pettibone at the moment of death.

Gofwan, called first, had seen the rocks begin to roll after Lokr had fallen. Calling warning to his *Ba-ture*, he had taken cover between two rocks. He heard the *Ba-ture* shoot again. No, he had not seen the rock hit the *Ba-ture*, but he had seen what was left. Later he had talked with Dan Beki as to what should be done next. Then had come Mister Keeta with the Sarikin Dallong, and danger was ended. Re-examined he said there had been much shooting after Mister Petbo had shot the second time, but it could not hold back the boulders already launched. No one else had been hurt, for all had gone behind rocks.

Like most witnesses, Gofwan told what he believed, not what he knew. For Pettibone had not shot a second time, or Keith would have seen him do it. Nor was that second shot Keith's. The unfired round in his pocket and the unfouled bore of his Mauser had at last convinced him of his miserable failure and unwilled innocence.

The shot, in fact, must have been fired by someone so close to Pettibone as to make it sound to Gofwan as though Pettibone had fired it. The wound, which had made Pettibone clasp his hands over his stomach, could be accounted for by someone shooting from the hip, under cover of the surrounding rocks, and near enough to risk an unaimed shot. A soldier, since he had a rifle. A soldier with sufficient motive.

If the sergeant-major kept his head, and did not try to defend himself against an unformulated charge, all might still go well.

Dan Beki was again affirmed, since this was a separate statement and such was Mohammedan usage. Yes, he had been close to Mister Petbo when the rock struck him. Less than three paces, as the bloodstain below the medal-ribbons on his khaki shirt attested. First there was the *Ba-ture*, then only his legs. He could not be certain of the second shot, for the first had been the agreed signal to open fire, so there had been much shooting until the boulders came. He had given the order to cease fire, but shooting had already ceased. Not long afterwards the *Ba-ture* Mister Keeta had come with Sarikin Dallong, enquiring for the *Ba-ture* who had been killed; and when he saw, took charge. Thus it was.

Anta and a few more soldiers corroborated Gofwan and Dan Beki, differing among themselves on the point of whether the rocks had been launched before or after Pettibone had fired the second shot. The crisis was over, and Keith was able to announce his second finding.

'. . . Alexander Pettibone, Divisional Officer Pankshin, came to his death by being crushed by a boulder launched by Lokr of Dallong or by Lokr's friends in revenge for Lokr's death.'

Keith closed his notebook, and stood to stretch his legs. 'Anta, you will take carriers and the three baskets, and start for Pankshin. Gofwan, you will take your horse from the camp in the foothill, and ride ahead of Anta to have relays of carriers ready for him. You will also give orders that the prisoners dig a grave where the clerk will show them. And first tell Sarikin Dallong that if he has the rest of the tax ready before sunset, I will take it. If not he must himself bring it to Pankshin.'

And now he was free to find out what on earth had led Garrard to risk his damaged leg up the pass, and why he had brought his new subaltern along.

'Glad to see you fellows, though I can't offer you much in the way of hospitality, and I've got to start back before nightfall. To be in time to read the service and that sort of thing.' That ought to explain the position. They weren't likely to have understood much of the rapid Hausa, but would guess what the baskets held. 'But why on earth did you come?'

Garrard's wide face was twisting about as though he were trying to check a grin. He had a pleasant sense of humour, but at the moment it seemed a trifle childish.

It was the other man who answered. A plumpish fellow, and with the skin beginning to peel off his nose—both signs that he was a newcomer.

'Don't blame Garrard. I practically ordered him to lend me a horse and camp kit and bring me along. After serving a fifteen

246

years sentence in the Pen-and-Paper chain gang, I felt it was time for me to see things as they really are.'

He lifted his helmet to mop a balding head. Too old to be the long awaited subaltern, more likely one of Garrard's superior officers, perhaps the commandant himself on a surprise tour of inspection.

'This isn't our usual form, sir.' Keith didn't want the stranger to get a wrong impression. He felt much the same irritation that a housewife does when caught by a visitor in the middle of spring-cleaning. 'We're rather a well-behaved division, unless something upsets us.'

'Admittedly you can't roll rocks on divisional officers every day. The supply of divisional officers would soon run out.' The man must have understood the Hausa of the witnesses. 'I am intrigued by Pettibone's need for an escort of fifty rifles, coupled with his willingness to send you on ahead without protection. Which was the intended victim, Pettibone . . . or you?'

Garrard had slipped behind the inquisitive stranger, and was frowning a warning. But this was Garrard's fault for bringing his senior where he wasn't wanted.

'I went ahead by my own wish, sir. With my superior officer's knowledge, but not by his orders.' The man needed choking off, whoever he might be, before he came still nearer to the truth. 'If you have any further questions, will you be so good as to pass them through my Resident by the usual official channels?'

'That will scarcely be necessary.' Amicably the man held out his case and offered a cigarette, which Keith refused. 'I asked Garrard not to mention my name, because I dislike having things —or words—prettied up to impress me. My name's Anstruther.'

One of Pupchina's warriors presented a timely bowl of beer. Keith took two deep swigs before passing it on to his guests. 'It tastes rather like vinegar, sir, but has a lot of food value, if you stir up the lees with your finger.' A ridiculous irrelevancy, but the best he could do.

'I came to Pankshin to perform an unpleasant task. It was clear that you and Pettibone could not work together, so one of you would have to be removed, for the good of the division.' The

247

Resident sipped, made a wry face, but took a deep draught before passing the bowl to Garrard. 'Perhaps I should not say this, but I am much relieved that the decision has already been made for me.'

Keith stoppered his mouth with his pipe, not knowing if he were supposed to answer 'Thanks very much' or 'I don't know what you mean'. He pulled out his pouch. It was empty; and neither a cigarette nor one of Garrard's cheroots would begin to meet his needs at this moment.

An ancient woman, a bundle of unthreshed millet on her head, a baby—presumably a grandchild—in a leather bag on her back, and a pipe like Keith's in her wrinkled mouth, took in the situation, halted, and fumbled at the string which supported her scanty fore-and-aft covering. This tall *Ba-ture* was the one who had been so comical yesterday, when he and Pupchina had persuaded everyone to go to ground. Perhaps he would be funny again. Meantime he lacked tobacco.

She offered Keith a few leaves, not unlike those she was wearing, but a little drier and browner. Keith's eyes were on his Resident, and he did not notice her. She reached up, took the pipe from between his teeth, crumpled some leaf into it, expertly tapped the dottel from her own pipe on top, and drew on the pipe until it caught. With a cackle of delight at the success of her experiment she replaced Keith's pipe in his bemused face, and stood back to watch results.

'Adaptable and imaginative,' the Resident seemed amused, 'but above all the primitive type such as this country seems to need.'

For a man who had spent most of his service pen-pushing, Anstruther showed some sense. Keith approved of him. 'They have the right ideas about life, these people. I don't mean just Dallong. Are you in a hurry to get back to Bauchi, once the funeral's over, or can you visit some other tribes?'

'Not this time, I'm sorry to say.' He glanced at Garrard, and the two appeared to share a silent joke. 'However my comment did not refer to your winsome lady friend, but to a certain Captain Keith.'

A reply seemed to be expected, so Keith said 'Yes, sir.'

The Resident's mood seemed to change. He frowned.

'Unpleasant rumours of Pettibone's high-handed ways have reached me. Do you want me to clear the ground for you by holding an official enquiry?'

'No, sir.' Let bygones be bygones.

'Then I assume you are willing to take over the division, as from today?'

Now he must make the third and most fateful decision. The first was at Ron, when he had sacrificed his own immediate prospects and allowed Pettibone to return. The second was in the pass below, only a few hours ago, when unaccountably he had spared Pettibone's life. And now those basketfuls of fly-infested carrion still had the power to exact a third and final decision. Pettibone had won the rubber.

'No, sir.' Neither today, nor any other day.

The disabling cause was hatred. The maniac, fondling the copper wire, had been able to think of one thing only, his all consuming purpose. He had become unconscious of the world around him, of the people, even of the all-pervading drumming. Cured of his madness by Hafsatu-Hatasu, he had become outwardly normal, but with something lacking. His link with the people had gone, as a man's hearing is killed by quinine. As recently as yesterday, when he had persuaded these Dallong villagers to go underground, their safety had been only a secondary consideration. The real reason was that they should not come between him and the man he had to kill.

Empathy with the Hillmen had vanished, and sympathy was no substitute. Never again would he know from their drumming what they felt, only from their words what they thought. And words could be false.

A man who has lost his hearing should no longer attempt to conduct an orchestra, for he would do more harm than good. An administrator who has lost touch with his people should no longer pretend to lead them. He should apply for transfer to a down-country Secretariat, where he could become a mechanical cog of government, filling his days with innocuous routine.

Soldiers and Dallong men were wandering off together. Pupchina of the dented skull was approaching with two elders, carrying leather hunting bags which presumably held the tax money they had refused to entrust to the Messengers Pettibone had sent. Behind them in the peaceful sunset sky rose the smoke of cooking fires from a village which might have been a smouldering ruin. But for Ian Keith.

The decision was a hard one. But it had been made.

Out of the waiting stillness came the faintest of voices. No, not a voice, but the murmur of exploring fingers on a drumhead. For long the tribal drums had been silent, or he had not heard them. Perhaps if he listened closely he would hear them again, and they would bid him farewell.

Drumming tells only of feelings, but Keith put them into words. In Hausa, that being less alien than English.

'Afraid and lonely. For it was dark beneath those rocks, and he is little. Now fear is going. The sun still shines upon his land. Also there will soon be food for little bellies.'

Keith's hesitant voice made his words like a question. Gofwan, having delayed his departure as long as possible, to collect the latest news of the *Tura-wa*'s intentions, now saw a chance tactfully to bring himself to their attention. He interpreted Keith's words to Pupchina, and relayed back the reply.

'Thus says the Sarikin Dallong, "It is only the son of my daughter, yet he says what is in many hearts. Tonight the big drums will speak over Dallong. And the drums of Angas, of Sura and even the bitter-hearted Yergam will answer them."'

And Ian Keith would hear them, and understand. That was the unintended message of the little drummer. With the aid of Hafsatu-Hatasu he would develop a deeper insight into the widely different needs of widely different tribes. He would not get far, for the life-expectancy of an administrator in West Africa was short. But he would be on the right road.

'I don't think you heard me, Keith. You seem to be wool-gathering.' Anstruther sounded both patient and puzzled. 'I've appointed you Divisional Officer Pankshin, not just acting, but substantive.'

The Resident had? Or a child with a drum?